FROM THE LIBRARY OF

Douglas

ZIGGURAT

ZIGGURAT

by Robert Katz

Houghton Mifflin Company, Boston
1977

Library of Congress Cataloging in Publication Data

Katz, Robert, date
  Ziggurat.

  I. Title.
PZ4.K1966Zi [PS3561.A773]   813'.5'4   77-23200
ISBN 0-395-25352-7

Printed in the United States of America
V 10 9 8 7 6 5 4 3 2 1

To Stephen Katz, on the road

ZIGGURAT

CHAPTER ONE

THE MAN had dark skin and he moved in waves of dark-skinned people, approaching the Qutb Minar. It was a dazzlingly sun-struck day in April, in the clammy fist of a tropical noon, and he wore a loose white shirt hanging over his waist, the sleeves rolled to his elbows. He had a rabid purpose in his squinting, bloodlined eyes and, as he walked in sandals that beat against the ground among mosques, pillars, and tombs dating back to the sultans of Delhi, he thought, again and again, It is wanted; it is wanted by the ziggurat.

At the entrance to the Qutb Minar, a tower of sandstone tapering to marble, was a sign in English and Hindi reading: "No one admitted unless accompanied by at least one other person." This was a suicide prevention measure, but, from time to time, suicides still occurred.

The man, unaccompanied, bought two tickets to the tower and waited outside near a guard, whose skin was darker still than his. The man was a nuclear scientist. There was no hair on his head, and he reflected the light of the zenith sun like the earth itself. The guard's only distinction was that he had a thousand rupees in his pocket, three times his monthly pay. Fingering the wrinkled banknotes in their hidden place, he spoke the man's name with a proper salutation and a question on the thin line of his voice. The man nodded and the guard said that the person for whom he was waiting was already inside, at the top. The man went in, saying, "It is wanted; it is wanted . . ."

He began to climb the 376 steps of a spiral staircase five stories tall, overtaking people less driven than he, some of the hundreds who wound to the top each day just to say that they had done so. It was dark inside the tower, and he found it hard to see the steps that had given up much of their stone to time and human beings. When he reached the top, he went out on a balcony, his eyes shot with a cannonade of light. He breathed deeply, gorging his lungs with air, searching for the figure of the person he wished to see. Two hands charged him from the rear. He was 238 feet from the ground.

The man's eyes and his mouth and his nostrils opened wide in a silent scream. The crowd below drew back in horror. Body and stone collided, clapping. The man lay dead on the ground, face down in a puddle of blood. A white-skinned man and woman stood in the frozen crowd. The woman was carrying a brilliantly painted Nepalese mask, used in mystery plays illustrating the former births of Buddha. The mask was old and imperfect; it was made of wood and had but a few strands of a yaktail wig.

In Rome, on a rainy afternoon in May, Zack Robertts lay on an iron bed with Deborah Colt, and when she asked him what he was thinking of, he said he was watching a man die, so she did not disturb him.

Deborah had been with Zack Robertts since February, traveling and sharing his *appartamentino* off the Piazza Navona. Last Christmas, he had received a UNICEF card from Deborah, who was in New York. On the edges, she had written, "Getting more and more into . . ." And then a word had followed that he had not been able to decipher, but the message continued, ". . . and it is helping me to relax, open up and let myself experience things. It's tremendously liberating. True!" When she had joined him in Rome, Zack Robertts, if anything, was gentleman enough not to ask, so long after Christmas, just into what she had been. She told him anyway, though she said she was no longer into it. Deborah Colt had been in and out of many things in the years that he had known her, while Zack Robertts was mostly out of everything, moving around, writing for a living, claiming that his lance was free, when in fact he rented it out by the day like Hertz.

Zack Robertts lay watching the man die several times. Then he told Deborah Colt that death was a hoax. Deborah said that she hoped he was not going to say that we all turn into flowers, because that was what her mother believed; but Zack Robertts replied that if you eliminate the fear of dying, you eliminate reality and you can find the way home. Deborah Colt asked Zack Robertts if he were afraid to die. Zack Robertts said, "Who me?" and grew snappy, saying that he thought she wanted to make love. Deborah said that Zack Robertts was completely fraudulent, and they laughed. He told her to move up a little. She said, *"Comme ça?"* and he said, "Yeah," and they made love on the iron bed. Hanging above the bed was a Nepalese mask with a few strands of a yaktail wig.

In a screening room in Langley, Virginia, a tall man with a slouch and a balding head was watching the man die, running an eight-millimeter motion picture film through a Madison Moviola. Since April, he had seen the film many times. It was only a few hundred feet long, and its existence was known to but a handful of persons. They called it "the ziggurat film."

The tall man with the slouch set the Moviola in a hold position, displaying one of the final frames of the film. It showed a dark-skinned man lying dead on the ground, face down in a puddle of blood — a dark-skinned crowd around him drawn back in horror. The grainy faces of a man and a woman stood out because they were white, and because the woman was carrying a brilliantly painted Nepalese mask.

The tall man with the slouch picked up a red grease pencil. He circled the face of the white-skinned man on the Moviola screen, then he stood, plunged his hands deep into his pockets, and began to think. There were holes in his pockets, and so immersed were the tips of his fingers that he could feel his thighs.

Deborah Colt was currently into Hatha Yoga, trying to raise her feminine *kundalini* into her masculine lotus with a thousand petals. She romped on the floor in the nude. Zack Robertts, who had been unemployed since April, was sipping four fingers of scotch in a glass full of ice, studying his French. He was reading *Candide* and had just gotten to the part where the king of El Dorado tells Candide and Cacambo in the language that taught men to think clearly, "I know my country is not much, but when we are comfortable anywhere, we ought to stay there . . ." It was his favorite passage, and when he looked up from the page to savor the words one by one, he saw Deborah Colt bottom-up, standing on her head, her nipples pointing over her shoulders, and he asked her if she wanted to *faire l'amour.*

"*Encore?*" she asked with mild surprise, grunting upside down.

"*Pourquoi* not?" he said, and since the idea suddenly appealed to her, they proceeded to do so, while her nipples pointed over her shoulders.

They were interrupted, however, by the thwomp of a machine that answered the telephone and recorded a message. Zack Robertts had engaged the machine so that they would not be interrupted. But Deborah said that the message might be important, and while she knew that playing it back at that moment defeated the purpose of the machine, she asked him to do so anyway.

It was a call from an antique dealer named Silvio. He said that he had acquired several new pieces from Sicily that were very "delicious," and he asked Zack Robertts to visit as soon as he could. Deborah did not understand Italian as well as Zack Robertts, although Silvio had been speaking his own brand of English, and she asked him if the message was important. Zack Robertts shook his head no and caressed her. The machine thwomped again, and they both jumped. Deborah said that the machine scared the shit out of her. Zack Robertts played back the recording without waiting to be asked.

"Okay, motherfucker," the machine said. "Brody speaking. I am having a job for you. Jean-Marie Vert, a Swiss mother, you have met him in my house. He is working on a project to present at the UN in the fall. They want you in Uppsala for some weeks. This is interesting, but there is problematics. Meet me in Harry's Bar. Seven o'clock. This is all, motherfucker."

Deborah said that it was funny how most people cannot relate well to machines. Zack Robertts remarked that there were two antique shops in Uppsala.

"I've never been to Sweden," Deborah said.

"Neither have I," said Zack Robertts.

Miklos Brody was a huge Hungarian. He had a gray weed on his chin, which struggled for its life on an otherwise hairless body. He was fifty. He had fought in the resistance; he had been a member of the Communist party. In 1956, he had fled for his life from the party. He had a French passport. He considered the Soviet Union an anathema, the bane of socialism. He was an ex-this and an ex-that. He bore a curse to be an ex-whatever he embraced, and it was part of the curse that he had to embrace something. He was not at all like Zack Robertts, who loved him.

He was an employee with diplomatic credentials of the United Nations Food and Agriculture Organization, based in Rome. When Zack Robertts met him in Harry's Bar, in the

Via Veneto, he was drinking a negroni. Zack Robertts ordered four fingers of scotch in a glass full of ice.

"This is going to be a bomb," Miklos said, presumably meaning a bombshell. He lit a Muratti. "Jean-Marie has had about fifty people working since months." He pronounced the "th" in "months" perfectly. "Money, they have had plenty of. From the nonaligned motherfuckers, from the Swedish motherfuckers. But they speak English like I speak English. They need someone to produce their report. Jean-Marie will call you."

"They know my price?" Zack Robertts asked.

"Fuck!" Miklos replied. "Your pimp, I'm not."

"You said there were problems."

Miklos hunched conspiratorially. This seemed to be an orthopedic compensation for the repeated expansive postures assumed when explaining how to redress the sorriest ills of mankind. The ends were expounded with square shoulders and a head as big as the black bronze on the Master's Highgate tomb. The means were slung low, speaking under the armpits.

Miklos looked over his shoulder. A barman stood perilously close. Miklos spoke into his armpit.

"This, I am saying only once, baby: CIA."

Zack Robertts understood something that had long eluded him. Miklos Brody spoke eight or nine languages comfortably. Three of them, including English, he had acquired over the past five years. And Zack Robertts, who had had a lifetime of trouble with his own, suddenly knew Miklos's secret. When one learned the usage of the four-letter words and their compounds, the idiom was virtually in hand; mastery of the "th" equivalents, like rolling the "r's" in Spanish, gave access to the pronunciation; conjugation and syntax could be disregarded, and the rest was mere vocabulary. Zack Robertts was slightly excited. He would go back to his French with insight.

"They are expecting about twenty people at the Uppsala conference," Miklos went on. "One of them is the mother."

"Jean-Marie?"

"This is possible. I don't know. This is why this I am telling only you, baby." Miklos lit another Muratti. "You remember Ram Chatterji?"

"I saw him in New Delhi four weeks ago. He sends his regards."

"I saw him in New Delhi three weeks ago. He is dead." Miklos put his hand to his throat. "How do you say this word . . . *garrotté?*"

"Strangled."

"This is the word."

Zack Robertts felt a familiar constriction in his chest. It was a surrogate emotion, which had slowly replaced other feelings as he got older. Oddly, it served now for both outrage and love. Deborah Colt sometimes made him feel that way. Ram, too, could, in life and now in death.

"I was with him the night before they found him in a pile of camel shit in Old Delhi," Miklos related. "He told me about the mother. He said already in April two men have been killed in this ugly business in Delhi. One they called it a suicide, the other an accident. But Ram knew better. This is clear."

"I was with him several times."

"He said nothing?"

Zack Robertts shook no. "You may be next."

"This is not possible. We met only once, by chance, in the Ashoka bar. We were alone like you and me."

Zack Robertts glanced at the barman. He knew him. He shifted his eyes ordering the check.

"You will go to Uppsala?"

"Not a chance."

"You are a horse's ass, Zack Robertts." He smiled and stared into his negroni like a gypsy reading tea leaves. "But . . . you will go to Uppsala."

Zack Robertts asked why.

Miklos, his elbow on the table, propped up his big head with his palm, making a hill of flesh on his face. He said, "Because it's there, baby."

Zack Robertts left him with the check.

The next day, Zack Robertts rose early to fulfill prophesy, though he believed in earnest that he was only repaying the courtesy of Silvio's call. He was, however, unhappy with the dealer's Sicilian acquisitions. They were decorative wood panels from the sides of nineteenth-century oxcarts, of which he had seen and owned better. But when he turned and started out of the shop, his eye fell on a Roman head. He had come across innumerable pieces of this sort — all copies, but this one glowed like the real, first century item.

Its color was live, as if blood flowed in its veins, and the crystalline forms in the marble were large enough to have come from the ancient quarries of Paros or Naxos. He touched it casually, concealing his respect from the seller. The figure, which was broken at the neck, was about two-thirds life size. It was bareheaded, but there were unmistakable traces at the collar line of the familiar plated jerkin — that of a legionnaire, probably a young centurion. This was a piece worth thousands of dollars, and Silvio would not know a centurion from a bowling ball. Zack Robertts was more than a little excited now. His summer was known: He would sit by and research his Roman find, study and master his French, and, from time to time, make love to Deborah Colt.

He turned his back on the head, feigning a move toward the door. Then, as if taken by only passing curiosity, he asked the price. *"E per quella testa fasula?"* His strategy was intimidatory, perfect. *Fasula* was the most unambiguous word in the language for "fake."

Silvio stiffened indignantly. He said it was genuine,

genuine-*issimo*, in fact, and that the price was eight million
lire, which in dollars was close to ten thousand. The piece, he
swore on some of his closest relatives, had been authenticated
by a professor, an *important* professor, as part of a bust in
Parian marble from the Augustan period, depicting a helmet-
less (and thus victorious) centurion from the first campaign of
the legions. He himself, he said with his right hand raised,
had paid eight million, but he was willing to forgo all profit to
please an old and treasured, very treasured, customer.

Zack Robertts, who of necessity had left Miklos with his bar
bill, thought of the $10,000, which was about the same
amount he owed now since the New Delhi job last April had
helped to pay off earlier debts. Silvio pressed for his intentions, as if there were a long line of buyers behind him. His
strategy was intimidatory, perfect. Zack Robertts picked up
the telephone. He dialed Miklos's number, and when he got
him on the line, he told him that he was waiting for Jean-
Marie to call.

"Fuck!" Miklos replied self-indulgently. "Why I am so
good to my friends, this I don't know. There is an English
chick. Jean-Marie's secretary. You will fuck her for sure."

Zack Robertts went outside. He knew why he was a horse's
ass and why he would never die with an old man's gasp
between two sheets.

In the late morning of May 17, Zack Robertts was staring
blankly at Deborah Colt, who had just come out of the
shower. She had beads of water on her skin, and sunlight
made them gleam. He was wondering how one said "chick"
in French. He was bundled in a hooded terrycloth robe. He
held a piece of paper in his hand. Deborah asked him what he
was doing. He said he was reading his mail, and he did.

"Dear Zack Robertts," the letter began. "Further to our
conversation over the phone a moment ago, I am pleased that

we can count on your cooperation in the finalization of the Pär Sjögren Report on Development and International Cooperation . . ."

The letter went on, but Zack Robertts stopped reading. He glanced at the signature, as he had already done several times while Deborah was in the shower. It was illegible, but the name was typed underneath as follows: "Jean-Marie Vert. JMV/vw."

Zack Robertts was trying to imagine what "vw" stood for. But all he saw was the red Volkwagen camper that he had rented in San Diego, California, years ago. He saw himself inside it with a woman whose name he could no longer remember, heading for the Mexican border, trying to find the way home.

He had always been looking for the way home, it seemed, wherever a plane could land or a road could hold his wheels: boozing in both Sohos, whoring in Schwabing, turning on in Katmandu, trying to be overwhelmed with feelings to give his body every chance to compare different states of existence, but feeling nothing and seeing little, leaving a trail of exhausted words behind him like the burnt fuel of the engines that had carried him wrong.

Deborah Colt hammered her ears and blotted and rubbed her body with a long white towel. She was pink. Her hair was matted around her face and fell most of the way down her back.

"Wasn't there some sort of UN commission of inquiry to find out how Pär Sjögren really died?" she asked Zack Robertts.

"Sounds familiar."

"It was probably the CIA."

"Probably."

CHAPTER TWO

THE TALL MAN with the slouch and the balding head was made of cork — veins and stains and pocks and all — but at the moment, in an audio room in Langley, Virginia, his cheeks were florid. He was listening to a tape of Zack Robertts making love to Deborah Colt upside down — information he had been able to piece together by deduction.

His name was Huntz Merriwether. Huntz Merriwether was born in Culver City, California, in 1939. He had a brother, one year his senior, named Leo. His father used to sell Clean-Sweep, which was an electrical appliance of limited use to swimming pool owners. His name was Jack. Jack died several years ago while demonstrating a Clean-Sweep to a prospective buyer. Jack was electrocuted.

Huntz Merriwether's mother was an actress named Beth Merriwether, who, when Huntz was growing up, achieved a certain fame among film directors in Hollywood, if not the public. The film directors called Beth Merriwether "Death Merriwether," and they called her whenever they needed an actress to play the part of a dead woman. Beth had an uncanny ability to photograph dead, not the least part of which was a talent by which she could suspend the rise and fall of her chest for as many takes as required. Beth's chest was used whenever Linda Darnell, Susan Hayward, Jennifer Jones, and Vivian Leigh died. Beth died playing Maureen O'Hara's chest. She died on the set before the film director could cry, "Action!" While they waited for the ambulance to take Beth's body away, the film director shot Beth's dead chest. No one could ever tell the difference, except Huntz Merriwether, who had an eye for such things.

Huntz Merriwether grew up to earn a doctorate in divinity from the Union Theological Seminary of Richmond, Virginia. He grew up to become a full-time employee of the Central Intelligence Agency, with significant responsibilities. A month ago, Huntz Merriwether had commissioned the peremptory dispatch of Ram Chatterji, who had told Miklos Brody about the CIA mother. Earlier he had arranged a similar fate for another Indian national, whose death was reported as suicide, and for still another — a "freak accident" that befell a lowly guard at the Qutb Minar. That made three commissions so far this year. So far.

Huntz Merriwether shut off the tape machine and sent for his secretary. Her name was Mary Clapperton. She was from Richmond, Virginia, where she had once studied in a convent but had never taken her vows. She was a very thin human being.

"Anything from Abraham, sister?" Huntz Merriwether asked her.

Mary Clapperton winced, zipped open her plastic day file, and gave him a piece of paper. Huntz Merriwether read for a few moments.

"Good O," he said, by which he meant "good omen." Huntz Merriwether thought for a few moments. "Very well," he said, "let us run a quick LISP on this . . ." He glanced at the paper, ". . . this Zack Robertts — for the record. Zack Robertts, indeed!"

LISP was the CIA acronym for Lengthy and Intensive Screening Procedure, and if the notion of a "quick LISP" seems self-contradictory, so be it.

"That will be all, sister."

Mary Clapperton winced and got up to leave. Huntz Merriwether watched her skinny ass until she arrived at the door, then he called after her.

"Oh, yes. Bring me the eight-by-ten still photos of the final sequence in the ziggurat film."

Mary Clapperton nodded.

"That will be all, sister."

Mary Clapperton winced and went. She hated to be called "sister," particularly by Huntz Merriwether, whom she considered odious. But a job is a job.

Huntz Merriwether called her "sister" because she winced. He considered her skinny-assed. But he kept her in his employ because a job is a job and because Mary Clapperton gave good paper.

While he waited for the blowups, Huntz Merriwether drafted the following memorandum on a sheet of ruled, yellow foolscap to a special operative, code-named "Abraham":

TO: Abraham
FROM: HM
SUBJECT: Operation Ziggurat
EYES ONLY.   DESTRUCT AFTER READING

1. The list of "preliminary participants" you sent presents no problems for the nonce. We are of course LISPing all parties unknown to us previously, but do not anticipate any difficulty.

2. I was relieved to see your name on the list, as I had been informed that for budgetary reasons the number of participants was to have been reduced. Apparently the friends of the "nonaligned" have come forth with the requested dose of supplementary funds, which saves us the time, trouble, and money in attempting to bring about the same effect. Good O.

3. Over the years, we have noticed a tendency to pay too little attention to the actual text of reports of this nature. Due to the fact that most of the participants are not English mother-tongue speakers, such documents are often clumsily written, drafted in "bureaucratese," and are thoroughly unreadable, and unread.

4. In this connection, I am pleased to note that the Project has hired as the report's editor this Zack Robertts person. This is viewed here as another Good O. It is true that his usefulness rests primarily with the secret phase of the Operation, but remember, *we must speak consistently in One Language if we are to be taken seriously by the Almighty.*

When Mary Clapperton brought Huntz Merriwether the blowups from the ziggurat film, he asked her to dispatch the memorandum to Abraham via the Greenland circuit to the Stockholm Station. He told her to set the lock on the door as she went out. She left him feeling his eyes on her skinny ass and knowing what he would do when alone.

Huntz Merrriwether removed his magnifying glass from its case. It had its own built-in light source. He studied the photographs carefully, and on one of them, he drew a circle with a red grease pencil around the faces of the white man and the white woman who was carrying a Nepalese mask. After a while, he tired of looking at the man and the woman and the bloody corpse in the foreground, and as Mary Clapperton knew he would, he began to think with his hands in his pockets.

Phil E. Stein was a fat man who wore an African hat when he traveled. Wearing the hat, a fezlike embroidery given to him personally by the president of Zaïre, he carried his bags into the Hotell Uplandia on the Dragar Brunns Gatan in Uppsala. He was perspiring and snorting, and he spoke to the stranger standing beside him.

"That's the trouble with a welfare state," he said, "no porters! I had to shlep all this stuff from the airport myself!"

The stranger was Zack Robertts, who said nothing.

Among the items Phil E. Stein had had to shlep were fifty-seven odd-shaped pieces of plastic and metal concealed in his clothing, his suitcases, a handgrip, and a bogus duty-free package. None of the metal parts was substantial enough to be detected by airport screening devices.

"Concierge!" Stein demanded.

A clerk came up to him and said something neutral in Swedish. Stein handed the clerk his card.

"Ah, yes, Dr. Stein." He reached behind him and passed

Stein a large, vinylite folder thick with paper, a separate sealed envelope, a room key, and a registration card.

Zack Robertts shortly went through more or less the same motions. He, too, was given the materials Stein had received. The envelope had his name on it. He opened it. Inside were 2800 Swedish crowns and a note from the director of the Pär Sjögren Foundation. It read: "Per diem, fourteen days. Fee to be paid in U.S. dollars upon completion of services. Welcome to Uppsala!"

Zack Robertts's room was clean and operational but oppressively small in style and dimension. He had observed, however, that no other room in the hotel could possibly be better, or even noticeably different, and as the Uplandia, the very latest in stick-figure architecture, was obviously the finest the town could offer, he thought it unkind to complain.

He sat on the bed and opened the vinylite folder. It contained an "Amended List of Participants," consisting of twenty or so names of persons with addresses scattered over the world. He recognized a few, particularly his own, to which was appended the information that he was to be the report's "editor." He almost constricted.

A man named Phil E. Stein was on the list, and he took him to be the porterless Dr. Stein of the lobby. Stein was identified as "Chairman of the Board, Psychological Services International, Inc., 1280 Avenue of the Americas, New York, N.Y. 10019, U.S.A."

Miklos Brody was also on the list, and below Jean-Marie Vert's entry was that of a certain Miss Victoria Walsh. He almost constricted.

The remainder of the folder contained several hundred mimeographed pages, which was an agglomeration of variously authored papers to be used in the conference. The only unifying touch was that the disheveled mass began with a statement that made Zack Robertts almost constrict for a third time. "Current changes in world relations," it said, "seem to make possible the establishment of a New World Order." An old man with a stick once told Zack Robertts: "Beware of he who spells adjectives and common nouns with capitals."

Unlike Zack Robertts, Phil E. Stein, in a room no different from his, complained vociferously.

"Larger!" he said into the telephone. *"Grösser! Plus grand!"* Stein knew the words for "larger" in Italian, Spanish, Japanese, Yiddish, and Swahili as well.

He was told that all the rooms were exactly alike. He hung up abruptly and placed the do-not-disturb sign outside his door. He snorted hard and noisily unpacked. He was fifty-two years old, at least that number of pounds overweight, and had been breathing in this fashion since early childhood. He occasionally experienced undiagnosed pains in his chest, and it was clear that he had at best but a few years to live, though he functioned as if he were immortal.

He was a friendly man. In the forties he was friendly to the Communist Party, U.S.A. In the fifties, having left the party in clamorous contrition, he was a friendly witness. In the sixties, broke, he was friendly to everyone who was someone, but he had no friends in his own country, which was why Psychological Services went international, claiming opposition to French neocolonialism, Japanese mercantilism, and above all, U.S. imperialism — earning Phil E. Stein his present reputation as a friend of the Third World.

Now, he began to sort out the fifty-seven small pieces of plastic and metal, which no God-fearing man would want part of, and which — like his African hat — had been given to him in high places.

*

At Arlanda Airport, midway between Uppsala and Stockholm, Jean-Marie Vert and his secretary, Victoria Walsh, were passing through Swedish customs under a battery of harsh white light.

Jean-Marie had the stature, physique, and complexion of a consumptive jockey in his late forties. He wore custom-tailored jeans and a jacket to match fashioned from a mere remnant of denim.

He was carrying into Sweden forty-three tiny pieces of plastic and metal concealed on his little person and among his far more extensive belongings. He was also bringing in, quite overtly, half a dozen decorative candles, gift-wrapped in the paper used in the duty-free shop at the Copenhagen airport, where his plane had made a stop. Each of them was about two inches thick and five inches long, and the total weight of all six was somewhat less than three pounds, five ounces, or precisely 1.5 kilograms.

These candles were not made of wax, although this could not be easily discerned by touch or appearance; nor were they purchased in Denmark. They had been molded in New York from a paraffinlike substance, bought from a mining supplies distributor in Reading, Pennsylvania, and known as "C4."

Jean-Marie was quite prepared to open his luggage, feeling no trace of apprehension, but the customs officer merely nodded for him to move on — a gesture which Jean-Marie, sensitive about his height and appearance, interpreted as an assault on his significance. Unlike Jean-Marie, however, the customs man meant no harm. He was simply eager for the relative pleasure of getting a feel and an eyeful of the possessions of the young woman next in line, Victoria Walsh.

She looked like milk. She was dressed in white, wearing a pantsuit of a rubbery synthetic material with properties that tended to build a static electric charge and cling, and where it clung most was her crotch. She smiled frequently. She had good teeth, as shiny and as orderly as bathroom tiles. She smiled at the customs officer. He looked at her crotch and told her to open her suitcase.

She had been home on her way to Sweden and had spent her last month's pay in Marks and Spencer, and it showed in abbreviated bras and panties and more synthetic suits. The customs man probed to his relative pleasure and then asked to see the contents of another bag.

This was a plastic carryall with an advertisement for Marlboro cigarettes on the outside and had what appeared to be two ordinary aluminum salad bowls on the inside. Actually, they had been handmade at considerable cost and difficulty from an even lighter metallic element, beryllium. The metal had been purchased from the Beryllium Division of Kasai Industries, Osaka, Japan, suppliers to manufacturers of solid-state components for audio and video equipment. Jean-Marie, who had already been flying overweight, had asked Victoria Walsh to carry them. They were about twelve inches in diameter, or exactly thirty centimeters. They would be fused together to form a perfect sphere. Exactness and perfection were what they were all about. Victoria Walsh thought they were salad bowls.

So did the customs officer. He pumped his head for her to go. Victoria Walsh smiled a whole bathroom wall. He smiled a yellow slot. Jean-Marie sneered.

CHAPTER THREE

On Monday, May 28 — the first day of the conference — Zack Robertts awoke with a start to find the sun high and hard in his window. He thought he had overslept, but according to the Telefunken digital clock at his bedside, it was only 3:03 A.M. in Sweden.

He had been asleep since midnight, dreaming unpleasant redundancies, and twenty minutes before retiring he had witnessed the break of day, although he had confused it with what he believed was a northland sunset. It was all quite disorienting, and his head ached.

He had had dinner at the only place in town that stayed open late, a "Pizzeria Steakhaus," with Miklos Brody, a French professor, and a Chilean exile, whose names, and the conversation in general, had been washed away in several liters of crude wine. The talk had been entirely in French, and he had learned the equivalent of "chick" and the eminently useful abstract noun *conerie*, which if one did not mind making a vulgar reference to the female genitals could be employed in describing anything of extremely poor quality. But the lessons given, not to speak of the wine, had simply been one too many.

By 4:12 A.M., even with the drapes and blinds tightly drawn, he was still unable to resume any form of sleep, and he bolted from the bed. He put on his white leather sneakers and his red gymsuit, and went jogging along the cobbled banks of the Fyris.

The sun was moving toward what should have been a proper noontime angle, but the unfamiliar streets were as vacant as anyone's dawn. He ran on his shadow. Zack Robertts jogged often and he jogged well. Jogging five miles (and getting away with it) was for a drinking man of forty-two giving death and reality the disrespect he felt they deserved. He taunted, baited, insulted, and glove-slapped them both when he started mile one, and when he had clocked five in forty-five minutes or less, and the hotline in his chest, neck, and eardrums flashed green, he was living free. When on this day, however, he had done well over four under forty, and he knew he had them whipped once again, the following sequence of events took place:

A whistling sting tore past the right side of his neck and jaw; a low-hanging woody branch, as thick as a jogging man's leg, which had been coming up fast in his track and which he had been preparing to circumvent, snapped like a matchstick; it was ripped from the tree, sent whirling through the air, and it fell into the river about fifty feet downstream; and finally, the whole town seemed to convulse in a shattering, thunderlike clap.

But that was no ordinary thunder, and Zack Robertts dove for cover behind the stone wall of a foot bridge.

He lay in a heap, his head on fire. For a moment, he wondered if he had any head at all, whether he was already dead, or living his last on momentum. Someone with a high-powered weapon had taken a shot at him, and he was sure that he had lost a good part at least of the right side of his neck, but when he managed to touch what hurt most, he felt no jutting bones or jugular spouts, nothing even damp or sticky, only a tenderness like that of a bruise.

Unlike the branch going to sea, Zack Robertts was alive. He had been burned by a ballistic wind, and after he had jumped a passing cab and gotten back to his room, he saw in the mirror that the hairlets of his neck had been singed, clearing a path for an inch-long row of what looked like elongated close-parenthesis signs. It was a graphic record of supersonic motion, a kind of thermal photograph of the bullet's trajectory, and it was branded on Zack Robertts's flesh, forever.

It could only have been the CIA mother, he thought, and the only one who knew that Zack Robertts was aware of his existence — the only one who knew that Zack Robertts rose early to jog — was Miklos Brody, whom he loved.

That day, Zack Robertts wore dark glasses. He wore a foulard of soft Indian silk high around his neck and kept water in his mouth. He also prepared an unscheduled and unannounced early departure from Sweden.

Miklos Brody grinned broadly when Zack Robertts walked into the conference room at nine sharp that morning.

"Fuck!" he said. "You are looking like a movie star."

Zack Robertts's lip curled inscrutably. He had already booked on the evening SAS flight to Rome, telephoning from the front desk of the hotel rather than risk an undoubtedly monitored call from his room, though he imagined that only diminished the risk.

The conference room, still awaiting most of the participants, was in a medieval stone manor in Gamla Uppsala, northwest of the town. It had been Pär Sjögren's ancestral home and where he had lived almost all of his life until he had become Secretary-General of the United Nations. After he had been mysteriously killed in the Congo and the Pär Sjögren Foundation had been established "to promote peace among nations as a tribute to his name and ideals," the rambling old house had been taken over, spooks and all, and converted into a kind of academy for the tranquil study of conflict in the world. The aims were pretentious, to be sure, and the insular, castlelike setting grated, too, but Zack Robertts felt a respectable monastic quality in the air — surely the hand of whoever was running this tribute — which was not disagreeable.

Zack Robertts took a seat at the u-shaped table, choosing a position safely away from the windows, with his back to a wall, and his feet near the door. Ignoring the presence of Miklos, who was casually reading a conference paper, he watched the group assemble. They were a handsome, well-nourished, cosmopolitan lot, and it seemed fair to guess, that if they had ever known starvation, degradation, and disease, which were the problems they had come to discuss, they had known them only as spectators. On the other hand, their choice of attire was patently impoverished by either private political slant or the imperatives of domestic economies. There were a few notable anomalies, but the rich countries wore sneakers and jeans, the Third World had been dressed by the dark-suit-and-tie-makers of Eastern Europe, and Phil E. Stein sported Brooks Brothers and his African hat.

Although Zack Robertts had been unable to place Jean-Marie Vert when Miklos had mentioned their earlier meeting in his home, seeing him now, he recalled him and the evening in question quite well. Jean-Marie was wearing what Valentino had shown in Paris last fall, and last fall, at Miklos's apartment in Rome, he had been wearing what Valentino had shown the previous spring. He was squatting beside Victoria Walsh, instructing her on the use of a tape recorder. Zack Robertts remembered how he had left Miklos's party early, hurrying home to drown Jean-Marie in mind slush — a concoction made primarily of scotch. Jean-Marie was a squatter. He had been squatting almost all of that evening, folded like a half-open pen knife, smoking a Cuban cigar, and spouting Rousseauist philosophy. He had made Zack Robertts sick.

Victoria Walsh smiled more than once at Zack Robertts, and he knew she could be no one else but Jean-Marie's vw.

She approached Zack Robertts and smiled.

Her eyes were as bright and blue and about as expressive as a fluorescent lamp. Her father was a greengrocer with a shop on Fulham Road. She believed that she had moved "light years" away from Fulham Road. She could type more than one hundred words per minute. She spoke French fluently, and had worked briefly in Geneva as an interpreter for the United Nations. She had visited the Third World. She had seen children in the Sahel dying of kwashiorkor and peasants at the Aswan dam rotting with schistosomiasis. At Jean-Marie's suggestion, she had read part of Frantz Fannon's *The Wretched of the Earth* in the original and all of Julius K. Nyerere's *Freedom and Socialism*. She wished she could write. She wanted Jean-Marie to change the world. She was twenty-seven years old, and in her own estimation "very orgasmic."

"You're the writer, aren't you?" she asked Zack Robertts.

Zack Robertts smiled.

"Zack Robertts, isn't it?" She smiled.

Zack Robertts smiled.

"I'm Vicky. I wrote you a letter. I mean, I typed you a letter . . . I'm Jean-Marie's secretary. Why the two Ts? In Zack Robertts, I mean."

"Why not?" Zack Robertts asked.

"Shrewd, aren't you?" she said thinking it over for a while. "The way it sticks in your mind, I mean . . . We need you. I mean, Jean-Marie's English is not . . . you know. I help him as much as I can, but I'm no writer." She smiled diffidently. "Not yet, anyway . . . What kind of writer are you?"

"Free lance."

"Oh, I think that's the best kind. You're free and you're . . . you know."

Zack Robertts nodded. He looked around, wondering when the meeting would start.

Vicky took note of his scarf. "Lovely . . . the ascot, I mean. Did you get that in India?"

Zack Robertts nodded. He glanced at Miklos, who winked at him.

"Lovely. I'm going to India in the fall. After the UN thing is over. The boy I'm living with has a Land Rover." She waited for Zack Robertts to respond.

"Oh?" he said.

"We're going overland. Any tips? On what to see in India, I mean."

"The Taj Mahal."

"Lovely. Is that in Delhi?"

"Near." The thermograph on his neck burned.

"What's in Delhi?"

"The Qutb Minar." He saw a man lying dead in a puddle of blood. He heard wood banging against wood.

"Fascinating! Where . . ."

Vicky broke off in mid-sentence. She said that the conference was starting and that she had to get back to her machine. She rushed to the tape deck and switched it on. The reels began to turn, and she smiled with a sense of accomplishment.

But the wood sound continued in his head. He was drenched. He turned and saw Jean-Marie thumping an uncolored gavel. A sickly man in a wheelchair was being rolled into the room by a tall, blond woman with a glaze on her eyes. The Uppsala conference was on.

The sickly man in the wheelchair was Lionel Barrymore, though Zack Robertts knew he was more than twenty years dead. But he could not have been anyone else: the shock of white hair dropping licks on his forehead, the box-kite face with a pound of jowls on the downsides, the jutting, sylvan eyebrows, the rubber-band mouth, which could be stretched around even the most eccentric word for a perfect fit, the rimless FDR ... No, the glasses were different. They were the glasses dispensed by helpless ophthalmology in the last stages of glaucoma — rings of thumb-thick frosted glass forming a barely transparent spiral staircase into the eye. Yet, what else would one prescribe for a man twenty years under the ground?

Indeed, the sickly man looked as if he had been exhumed that very morning. He was damp. He was yellow. He gasped, sputtered, and coughed without end in his pitiful attempts to breathe. He smoked as if he had not had a drag since the Korean War. He pulled cigarette after cigarette out of the drawer-like boxes of Gitanes, of which he had four in his lap. He lit each cigarette in three tremulous fingers that looked like puny, rotten bananas, holding it not like a pencil, but in the vise of his thumb and forefinger. He inhaled as one might suck on a straw held horizontally, and when he was not puffing, he rolled the cigarette on his fingertips, the lit end pointed at the heavens, and he stared hypnotically at the fire and the smoke.

"I should like you to meet our host," Jean-Marie was saying, looking at poor old Lionel, "the director of the Pär Sjögren Foundation, Joachim von Schwarzwald."

There was a round of polite applause, but Zack Robertts was not fooled. He clapped hard. He knew that that was the part he had been dug up to play: an aging Junker who was head of a Swedish peace organization. What dramatic irony, but at the same time, a role so demanding that only a Barrymore could fill it, which showed the extremes that good casting required.

The ninety-nine-year-old actor, as might be expected of someone with soil still clogged in his ears, had not heard a word Jean-Marie had said, and when the tall, blond woman who had wheeled him in nudged him slightly, he shot around to her; his eyes leaped like a cat after prey, and, waving her away with an astonishingly supple flick of his ancient wrist, he all but growled that inimitable, lovable growl. What a display of benign irascibility!

Zack Robertts almost applauded once again. He had forgotten his wounds and his fears. He was delighted.

Joachim whatever-the-name-of-the-character-was cleared a passage through the smoke in which he was enveloped, and unfurling his eyebrows just enough to cast a thoughtful shadow on his lids, he opened his mouth slowly, at a constant but almost imperceptible velocity, as if his lips were some sort of electronic porthole to his mind. Bravo! What an entrance the man had made and he had not yet uttered his opening line!

"Ve vant just to velcome all of you here and ve hope very much zat your work . . ."

Zack Robertts was stunned. He was an imposter, a fake, a phony, a fraud, a ham. He could not even do a German accent. He was doing Bill Cosby doing Adolf Hitler at the Sahara in Las Vegas. And he was doing it in a wheezing falsetto!

Zack Robertts was crestfallen. Lionel Barrymore was dead. This man was no actor, not even a community-center amateur. He was just a two-bit, cantankerous, glaucomic, emphysemic old cripple, a tinhorn director of a recondite foundation, a stereotyped wurst-eating bureaucrat. He was Joachim von Schwarzwald.

". . . and so, to finish," (cough, sputter, gasp) "as ve say in Shveden," (fire, suck, smoke) "although as you may have guessed, I am not myself Shvedish . . ." He smiled through tightly clamped corn-kernel teeth and revolved to the tall blond woman behind him. "My charming vife is ze Shvede in ze family." The tall blond woman nodded humorlessly, unseeingly. "But . . . as even *I* manage to say in Shveden . . ."

Whatever it was he had wanted to say in Swedish was either muttered inaudibly amid sputters and gasps or not said at all, but as the group had broken into applause, mercifully there was no need to try again, and his "charming wife," quite tactfully, seized the moment and wheeled him out, von Schwarzwald waving coyly to the group with a piano player's flourish on his fingers. As they exited, she whispered something in his ear, and Zack Robertts, being closest to the door, saw him leer at her and he distinctly heard him say, "Shot op, bitch!"

CHAPTER FOUR

THE UPPSALA CONFERENCE emerged rapidly as an exercise in self-interest conducted in the name of a higher morality. The first order of debate concerned the credits each of the participants would receive in the printed report. Almost everyone made a self-effacing little speech about how unimportant this was, but the "unimportant" provoked a lively discussion about the type size and face, order, and position of the credits as they would appear on page one, and this seemed destined to go on and on, but it was brought to a sudden halt by the tardy and stunning appearance of a magnificent woman with jewels in her nose.

A ton of silence fell as she sailed across the room toward Jean-Marie behind a screen of colorful, motion-swept silks. Jean-Marie gave her a tidy, quarter-inch bow and seemed about to take her hand in a European kiss, but before he could cramp this woman's style, she pressed her palms together and greeted him, and then the group, in her own fashion. Those hands, like the rest of her, were long and slender, and as black as the universe on a clear night. Her bearing was Brahmin, for sure: South Indian, Zack Robertts guessed, less from her skin color (since South Indian Brahmins are more often light-skinned) than from the cluster of diamonds she wore in a pierced nostril on the right side of her nose. She was swathed in a dark, multihued sari of the kind so fine that all its six meters could pass through a woman's ring without causing the fabric to crease, and from the way she moved, it seemed one could do the same with her. Zack Robertts was slightly enthralled.

"I should like you to meet," Jean-Marie said in his most

ambassadorial manner, "Shiva Subrahmayan . . . our delegate from the forgotten, oppressed majority — women."

His timing was crisp and brought round-mouthed laughter
from the audience, which was all male except for Vicky, but
she laughed, too.

Jean-Marie turned to Shiva Subrahmayan, and looking her
up and down with some sort of mock reproach, he went on
with his talk-show wit. "But Shiva," he said, "I am afraid
you do not look very oppressed."

She smiled submissively, but Zack Robertts could see her
eyes go sharp and he knew she had him in the gunsight of a
belle riposte at the ready. "I am very sorry, Mr. Chairman,"
she said with a million "rs," honed in God knew how many
semesters in British public schools, "I did not quite hear you.
Did you say . . . 'well-dressed'?"

Even Zack Robertts laughed, slightly.

He looked at the list of participants. She was the only
woman in the group: K. I. Shiva Subrahmayan, research
associate, Gupta Institute of Nuclear Studies, B-6 Mahatma
Gandhi Road, New Delhi 110010, India. He had visited the
Gupta Institute in April and had met most of the small staff,
but not her, and he found that odd now, although she might
have been away.

He had been traveling with Deborah Colt preparing a series
of articles for the *Sunday Times* of London on India's use of
nuclear power as an energy source for economic and social
development. Originally it had been planned as a report on
the government's nuclear testing program, but that had
proved impossible, and the *Times*, with twelve columns to
fill, had had to settle for less. The Gupta Institute of Nuclear
Studies, in spite of its imposing name, was much less. As far
as Zack Robertts knew, it had no direct connection with the
government, and certainly not the defense ministry. It was
one of those information-gathering "clearing houses," of

which there are whole cities in the hardly unique Indian bureaucracy, overlapping and duplicating what more times than not was only fractionally done, and the University of Delhi performed the same service, Zack Robertts had learned, to a much higher degree of competency.

He had already written and filed his compromise story when he went to interview the director of the Gupta Institute. He conducted the interview purely as a courtesy to Ram Chatterji, who had taken considerable pains in helping him to set up appointments in advance of his arrival. Ram had apparently overplayed his credentials — a rather tenuous connection as a once-in-a-while correspondent for All-India Radio — and had indicated, without actually saying so, that he might suffer inconvenience were anyone to be slighted. So Zack Robertts had followed Ram's schedule religiously, and the Gupta Institute had been last on a list too long for his deadline.

The director of the institute had been described by Ram as being "a little crazy," but worth speaking to, since he knew "everyt'ing about everyt'ing" in India, which was much. Zack Robertts found him positively insane. He suffered visibly from heart-bleeding distress and hallucinatory episodes that seemed to visit at five or ten minute intervals with dire ultimatums from Satan himself. Still, he was, by the clock, more often lucid than bewitched, and he knew much.

His name was Jagjit Hanumappa. A physicist, who had been graduated from the Imperial College of London, he had been with Gandhi during the Poona period of house arrest by the British, and had held several portfolios in the early Congress party governments, sinking into ever more profound obscurity thereafter, at least as concerned the public eye. He had, in fact, against opposition and inertia, been influential in framing the new country's scientific policies, which had aimed at, and had succeeded in, establishing a relatively independent, sophisticated technological base, and while he had never gained recognition, he was, as much as anyone else, a father of India's fledgling nuclear power.

He was a bony old Maharashtrian, all pate and glasses, who resembled the apostle himself. The interview was mostly autobiographical, promisingly frank for a while, and always coherent, except when rudely interrupted by those repeated visitations from afar, in which his eyes had shot from their sockets to the stars. Wrapped in billowy white muslin, he sat crosslegged on the floor and shook his head throughout in grand negation of everything said, heard, or imagined. The underlying premise of all was that the Preserver had been decisively defeated by the Destroyer and thus the end of the world was at hand, which Zack Robertts took with quiet equanimity. He was feeling rather soothed by the hypnotic effect of that oscillating globe of a head, which seemed to be signaling a great and timeless truth.

But Hanumappa brought the session to an abortive end when he suddenly doubled up in unspeakable anguish and staggered from the room, murmuring that he had been summoned by the Creator. In similar circumstances almost everywhere, when one hears of a beckoning of such import one expects the start of a one-way journey, and Zack Robertts, for his part, was quite willing to drop the entire matter completely, but a few days later Hanumappa returned, or at least as much of him as was required to make a telephone call.

Ringing Zack Robertts's room at the Oberoi, he announced in a bellowing, confident, wildly triumphant voice that he had something to tell him "of interest to your journalistic purposes." Zack Robertts said he was listening with a pencil in his hand, but Hanumappa insisted on a face-to-face encounter. Zack Robertts offered to come to the institute at the caller's convenience. Hanumappa declared that "too dangerous." Zack Robertts could *hear* him glance over his shoulder.

The appointment was set for noon of that day, and for reasons known best to the Indian, the meeting place he chose was at the entrance to the Qutb Minar, which he said they *had to* climb together.

Zack Robertts, who had more than once seen the tower, was of no mind to scale hundreds of vertiginous steps in the heat of an Indian noon, and when he asked him, "Why?" he could not stifle an uncustomary show of annoyance.

"Because it is wanted," Hanumappa replied. "It is wanted by the ziggurat." He hung up. He had managed to transmit one final hint of a savage euphoria.

Now Zack Robertts, who in a lifetime of dealing in words had collected and sold much more than a million, and had a mental warehouse filled with many he had never used, had not once heard, read, or at least remembered the noun "ziggurat" employed in that manner. Thus he assumed it to have another meaning in Hindi or Mahrati, and in the context used by the user, he guessed it referred to gods good or bad, yet he wondered. But when it failed to appear in the Hindi-English dictionary Deborah had bought at the Oberoi newsstand, and as at that moment the Mahrati was totally inaccessible, he was inclined to forget the word, the twelve o'clock date, and the man, and go shopping with Deborah for Nepalese masks.

Of course that was just what they did, and of course, neurons and circumstance, conscience and vanity, and everything else that pushes and pulls (including some prodding from Deborah), brought them to the Qutb site a few minutes past noon, where in the midst of a crowd drawn back in horror they saw Jagjit Hanumappa lying dead in a puddle of blood.

At the time, he believed the three-paragraph suicide story

in the next day's *Times of India*, and any harbored suspicions were faint and quelled quickly by Ram Chatterji. When they spoke of it, Ram simply shrugged in the way Bengalis have learned to live with cyclones and flood. "Yes," he said. "At the Qutb, such t'ings happen five or six times in the year."

That was that, and by the time Miklos Brody in Harry's Bar had mentioned the man killed in April as a murder reported as suicide, Zack Robertts had neatly forgotten the Hanumappa affair, making no conscious connection between the two. It was only now, seeing K. I. Shiva Subrahmayan in person and print, that the memories conveniently stored began to reappear in his brain appealing for a more sensible arrangement.

Shiva Subrahmayan had taken the floor and was advocating more for women, but Zack Robertts was thinking that the shot that nearly severed him in two unequal parts that morning must have originated from his meeting Hanumappa, and so Miklos's Harry's Bar story was undoubtedly true. The CIA mother seemed surely among them, but Miklos was clean, and Zack Robertts loved him again. He knew now that Jagjit Hanumappa was not so crazy. He had apparently been associated with something more mad than himself, which he shared in an arcane way with Ram Chatterji. Poor old Ram. He had minimized Hanumappa's demise to shield Zack Robertts from peril. He loved him. He thought of the *Mahabharata, Bhagavad Gita,* Max Weber on India. He had read enough of these writings — even when Hanumappa had been ranting in Delhi about destroyers defeating preservers — to be aware of the Hindu trinity, in which the Creator was Brahma, the Preserver was Vishnu, and the Destroyer was Siva. Now, however, a new factor had been spectacularly introduced: the delegate from the oppressed, or as the case may be, well-dressed majority — who was presently standing for the good cause — *happened* to be associated with the

Gupta Institute, *happened* to bear the name Shiva, a variant spelling of Siva, and *happened* to have as her first initial the letter K, which, Zack Robertts felt certain, was probably K for Krishna — a name for the Preserver himself, reincarnate. Keep water in your mouth, Zack Robertts, and catch that night flight home.

Shiva Subrahmayan completed her talk with a lame appeal that the conference adopt a strong position in favor of the emancipation of women. Lame, because she was blacker than ever with lip-biting anger on the verge of sundering her composure. The group had listened to her with gratuitous sniggers and nasty eyes that had leaned rudely on her anatomy. In the end, she succeeded in restraining her discomfiture but could do no more than flutter her eyelids and pander to phallic self-interest; in contempt, to be sure, but it was lost on the obscurant crowd.

"Remember," she said in closing, "the *Kama Sutra* teaches that a happy woman makes a happy man."

This brought on an effusion of barroom appreciation, after which she excused herself and left the room temporarily. When she was safely beyond the door, a man twirled his red beard and quipped, *"Now,* we should talk about women," to which Phil E. Stein inquired, "Do you know any dirty jokes?"

Zack Robertts glanced at Vicky. She was capturing it all on tape, exuding a feeling of privilege, and laughing.

He waited a minute or so, and in a throat-clearing, page-turning pause, he stood and stole for the door. But, without help from him, it opened with a wild swing at his jaw, a near miss, allowing thereby the return of Shiva Subrahmayan. She seemed remarkably reconstituted. For one unsteady moment, their eyes more than met, they entwined, and he wished he could tell her that he had understood her ordeal. But as she passed him, backing him off toward his chair, her gaze tightened down; her nut-colored pupils, set deep into velvet, measured him this way and that in the no-nonsense manner of the tailors of Saville Row. Zack Robertts had a constricting feeling that she knew who he was.

He was more eager than ever to depart now, but the meeting was again called to order, and he sat. Jean-Marie announced that they were falling behind in their work, and if all were to kindly endure a sandwich served at the lap, they could go on until the day's business was done. No objections were raised and Vicky was dispatched for the food.

Now that the apparently frivolous subjects had been set aside, the group showed its serious face. They were a gravely indignant lot; each speaker — presumably the CIA mother included — was one-up on the other in loathing to a passion the unrelieved abomination an execrable minority had made of this earth.

The world, as they claimed to see it, was the dreadful dominion of a shamefully small number of the rich, living high on the blood and muscle of the dispossessed masses of the poor. Reasonable men, to be sure, no longer disputed this. What was troublesome about their thesis, however, was that it saw humanity cloven grotesquely into two monoliths of wicked-alienated haves and wretched-adorable have nots, each of which, with only a few exceptions, dwelt in separate camps — the haves in the north, the have nots in the south. But the final arrogance in Uppsala was that this motley crowd felt itself to be alive at the very moment of the Coming Apart of the Old Order, which had been sundered by the Turning Point.

The Turning Point had been reached only recently, when in the October Revolution of 1973 the "have nots" had raised the price of petroleum. Thus for the first time in memory the wretched-adorable (including the shah, the king, and the sheiks) had recovered a significant measure of disenfranchised power from the wicked-alienated (and had survived), and it would take only an extended, unified policy of relentless confrontation, including A Hundred Vietnams, if need be, to bring the camp up north to its knees.

Zack Robertts saw the human pulp of A Hundred Vietnams.

CHAPTER FIVE

AT THIS POINT, ZACK ROBERTTS found it convenient to slip out of the conference room. No one seemed to notice, and though he had been expecting sirens and gunfire, when the door was closed behind him, he leaned back against it for a moment's respite. His hand felt a key in the door and without thought or hesitation he locked them all inside.

He looked down the hall. Vicky was coming toward him, struggling with four full bags but smiling selflessly.

"Hi, Zack," she said.

She was going to need help. He would have to open the door, take half her burden for sure. He was going to end up serving lunch to those crisismongers inside.

"It's all right, isn't it?"

His eyes narrowed, deepening the lines in his face.

"Calling you Zack, I mean."

"Sure." He had already turned back the key.

"Super . . . They still jabbering?"

He nodded. "Let me help."

"Quite all right. I can manage fine. Besides, I'll bet you're on your way to the loo."

He smiled boyishly.

"When you've got to go, you've got to go," she said. Then she opened the door just a crack, and when the flow of voices trickled out, she added, "Fascinating, isn't it?"

"Got to go," he said trying his best to imitate her impenetrable affability. He turned down the corridor and walked straight.

"See you later, Zack," she called after him, and without

38

turning back, his hand shot up and he waved goodbye.

He could feel her eyes on him for a while, and when he finally heard the door close behind him, he did one or two steps of a jig.

The tall blond woman who had been introduced by the sickly man in the wheelchair as his charming wife was waiting for Zack Robertts by the turn at the end of the hall. She looked as if she had been waiting there as long as the walls. She had the same glaze on her eyes that she had had earlier, but now Zack Robertts understood why. She was a witch, and perhaps when he had heard the sickly man whisper to her harshly he had not said, "Shot op, bitch," but "Shot op, witch." But in either case she could not possibly have merited such treatment. She was a good witch, and if her husband had really been Lionel Barrymore, she would have been Billie Burke.

She was middle-aged, but her skin was fine, buttery, almost the same soft color as her hair, and her brow was large and protruding, bursting with the apparatus good witches need for seeing far. And when she asked him if he would mind having a few words with her husband, he simply followed her, spellbound, confident that she was leading him out of harm's way.

Joachim von Schwarzwald was staring at the lit end of a cigarette as she ushered him into an office furnished austerely with sticks and slabs of blond wood that looked like they had been hammered together with a handful or two of nails. He did not look up; he might have been dozing or even dead.

"*Älskling*," she said softly, with genuine affection, "Mr. Robertts is here."

His optically reduced eyes ascended behind the thick glasses like the cherries of a slot machine. He forced the cigarette into lips that fought back.

"So," he said, "you have had enough of ze schidt?"

Zack Robertts looked around. The woman, who had covered herself with a well-worn smock, had closed them inside and had taken a place at a worktable. Using a blocked sheet of sandpaper, she had begun to smooth the surface of an abstract female form that had been sculpted in plaster.

"*Älskling*," she said without interrupting her work, "I'm afraid Mr. Robertts thinks you were speaking to me."

Von Schwarzwald reproached her with his articulate eyebrows, then turned stiffly to Zack Robertts as if his neck were in a cast.

"Ze schidt. That schidt they are talking in there. Schidt. S-H-I-T!"

"*Älskling, do* get to the point. Mr. Robertts *does* have a plane to catch."

How did she know that?

"Shot op, bitch!"

Did he say "witch"?

Von Schwarzwald rolled his whole brow exasperatedly. "Oh, zat voman," he said to Zack Robertts, lighting another cigarette, although two previous ones were still alive in a cluttered ashtray. "*Sprechen Sie Deutsch, Herr Robertts?*"

"Really, *älskling*. Does it matter?"

"Please, darling . . . Vill you let me shpeak?" His falsetto voice had risen to a screech, and he began to cough as if he would never speak again, until out of sheer fury he punched his chest repeatedly, beating the spasms to death. "Now I understand, Herr Robertts, how Vico could write ze *Scienza nuova* vit his children sitting on his lap. Anything to be rid of a vife."

"He merely wrote his funeral orations with the children, *älskling*, not the *Scienza nuova*."

"Gott damn you! If zat voman does not let me shpeak . . ."

He trembled with rage but he was helpless and perfectly

innocuous. He lit another cigarette. She smiled at some private thought; not once had she looked up from her sanding of two little bumps on the Brancusian chest, grinding them down to suggestions, and the glaze on her eyes seemed a fixed, transparent lid over an immense body of water.

Zack Robertts was as overpowered as von Schwarzwald in the presence of this strange woman. How had she divined that he had had "enough of ze schidt" appearing as she had so opportunely? And the plane reservation, and now Vico, *his* Vico, whose *Scienza nuova* he had in many parts committed to memory.

"Herr Robertts," von Schwarzwald said squarely at last, "these people, they are dangerous."

"Slightly," Zack Roberts said.

Von Schwarzwald smiled widely, smoke barreling like a fog through his teeth. All of his face disappeared in the bluish mist, and when he waved it away, he opened a fresh pack and spoke again.

"So, ve agree."

"We read Vico," Zack Robertts replied, choosing something less than agreement.

Von Schwarzwald nodded, lighting up with a stick match. He examined the fire with one eye closed like a jeweler.

"Herr Robertts, I know vat you are thinking."

Zack Robertts was silent. His patience overflowed; they were, after all, aware that he would soon have to leave for the airport.

"You are thinking that these people are nothing more than a nuisance. But you are wrong. They are dangerous."

"You said that, *älskling*," the woman intoned, a mildly cacaphonic note rattling her voice. "The point, the point! My God, is it too much to ask for the point? This gentle man, through no fault of his own, has been scourged by a gun, and now you, like his enemies, scourge him with words!"

She knew everything, even the time he jogged. Her wiry, antennalike fingers worked the bumps on the figure as if they were crystal balls.

"Peasant!" von Schwarzwald cried. "Scratch a Shvede and you find a peasant, Herr Robertts." It was time to light-up-and-stare-at-the-glow again, but when that had passed, he finally got to the point.

"How ve got sucked into this *Schweinerei*, I vill spare you ze details. Enough to say ve were fooled and that now ve want to get out. Ve want to help ze Third World, Herr Robertts, but ve are a foundation for peace, and peace this is not. First, as you know from our mutual friend and only ally, Miklos Brody, there is ze CIA. Second, there is an inner cell among these schidt-talkers. This inner cell — vit this horrible midget Jean-Marie at ze head — is preparing some kind of terroristic *Schweinerei* in order to shock ze entire world vit this foolish policy of confrontation. What exactly they vill do, ve do not know. Who exactly is ze CIA and what he does, ve do not know. Ve only know that either ze CIA or ze inner cell wants something from *you*, Herr Robertts."

Zack Robertts constricted sharply. He turned to the good witch. For the first time those transparent lids opened and she met his stare. Then she looked away, sadly.

Smoke poured from von Schwarzwald's teeth. Zack Robertts knew instinctively that everything he had said was true, though he was not one to exaggerate the validity of instinct. The whole story might just as likely have been a lie, a limb on a body of intrigue of no concern to him. *Someone* had discovered his connection with Hanumappa, and Ram, too, perhaps. *Someone* believed that he knew something considered essential — which he did not, or at least he thought he did not. This much, he had to allow. But it was a matter of a gross misunderstanding, and he had much else to do. He reminded von Schwarzwald that he was leaving.

Von Schwarzwald shook his head ruefully. "You have heard of O.N.A.N.?"

"*Älskling*, you are playing with yourself again! The point!"

"Please, darling . . . Herr Robertts, I am shpeaking of ze Organization of Non-Aligned Nations, which if you have not heard of them, I would not be surprised. They are secret. No Third World government takes any responsibility for them. In fact, many of ze members are not from ze Third World. They are men like that terrible Jean-Marie; there are Japanese, even Shvedes and Americans . . ."

"Swedes, Mr. Robertts," the woman said laconically.

"And yet," von Schwarzwald continued, "they have support. Very much support. I need not remind you of ze many terroristic acts around ze world that are of an international, rather than a sectarian, character. But . . . almost always they have been ze work of O.N.A.N. This inner cell in there is ze work of O.N.A.N. In fact, it *is* O.N.A.N.!"

He seemed to be losing himself, but he stuffed his lips with two fingers and a Gitane, and spoke slowly now.

"Herr Robertts, do you think that if they want something from you, they vill let you catch planes at ze Arlanda Airport?"

Zack Robertts had half an urge to ask him how he knew so much, and above all, who had taken a shot at him. But he was sure that his answers would be as plausible as they would be — like the entire story — unconfirmable. Instead, he made a point of looking at his watch.

Von Schwarzwald wrinkled his brow disappointedly. "You must help us, Herr Robertts."

"Help?"

"I vill be direct . . . Shpy."

"You hired me to write. Spying costs extra." He had no notion why he had said that. Perhaps he had once heard it in a film; perhaps he had written it. But there was no earthly inducement that could convince him to stay.

"Ve are not without means, Herr Robertts. Ve have only limited funds, but ve are not powerless. Ve have . . . there is . . ." He stiffened exultantly, as if he were playing his trump card. "There is ze SS!"

Zack Robertts looked at him incredulously.

"Shevedish Security . . . You vill work vit us?"

"Of course, he will, *älskling*. But Mr. Robertts needs time for reflection. He is a writer not a spy, *älskling*. He needs to be with his thoughts. He needs solitude . . . and . . ." She gasped, drawing back the word she wanted to say before it could fall from her lips. She was silent and seemed as empty as a mannequin.

Von Schwarzwald picked up an English dictionary, which lay all too well placed on his desk. "You know this word, 'ziggurat'?"

For the second time, the sculptress turned to him, as they both searched for some reaction, but he betrayed nothing, shaking no. Von Schwarzwald opened the dictionary. It was a stringy old book tearing away from its binding. He turned to a page that had been marked with a strip of xerox paper, and he read aloud, straining to see the small print.

" 'Ziggurat. Among ze Babylonians and Assyrians a temple of Sumerian origin in ze form of a pyramidal tower consisting of a number of stories, and having about ze outside a broad ascent winding round ze structure and presenting ze appearance of a series of terraces . . .' "

There was more to it than that, Zack Robertts thought, as von Schwarzwald wheezed for want of oxygen. The definition had touched something in the brackish viscosity of his mind. It would come to him.

"Ve think it is ze name of an Italian ship," von Schwarzwald said when he could. "Ze SS have intercepted a document, a cable." He picked up the xerox strip and read from it: " 'ZIGGURAT ITALIANS ARRIVE PORT OF MALMO NINE JUNE' . . . Cryptographic, of course; there is no ship in ze world registered under that name. Ze document is signed, 'AB-RAHAM.' "

That name, too, stirred the same waters. It would come to him.

"Think about it, Herr Robertts. If it is funds you want, ve are prepared to pay you twice your writer's fee. On ze other hand, you may have it in your power to save many lives."

Zack Robertts turned again to the good witch. As before, the glaze lifted momentarily. Her eyes seemed to be receiving him, and when the lids went down it was as if a part of him had been taken away forever. He felt lighter.

Her head wheeled away from him. *"Älskling,"* she said, "Mr. Robertts would like to go to his hotel."

Von Schwarzwald had offered him transportation, but he had declined, preferring to walk. He had gone back to the hotel, packed his bags, and he stood now at the front desk settling his bill. He paid it from the Swedish crowns he had been given for expenses. He left the balance in its original envelope, handing it to the clerk for return, and he stepped outside in search of a cab. In an hour and a half, his SAS flight would depart for Copenhagen and Rome.

A Volvo taxi appeared at once, lurching to a halt that left rubber on the pavement, and the driver, a massive man with trunklike limbs, jumped from the wheel to help him with his bags. The big Swede looked vaguely familiar and he wondered whether it had been him who had picked him up that morning, rescuing him from the barely astigmatic sniper. He would have found some way to thank him if he were, but the Swede showed no sign of recognition and his Volvo was definitely of a later design, so he said nothing. Instead, he watched with pleasure as his luggage sailed into the trunk and the rear door flew open for no one but him to slide in. He announced that he was going to Arlanda. The driver responded with a nod struck a trifle too soon, as if he already knew, and he closed his passenger inside. Zack Robertts heard the door fall solidly into its moorings — and lock. Three times in a simple act of hiring this cab had his suspicions been aroused, but his wishes were cunning and he sank into the leather and felt Uppsala lift like a load.

The Volvo pointed south on the Kungsgatan, headed between river and track for the Stockholm road, and after a brief flyby of linear concrete and steel, it broke for the forested plain, showing a smooth 150 on the kilometer scale. In a few minutes, Kövsta castle rose on an eastern field. He would have liked to have paid it a visit, as he had hoped for some free time to browse when he had seen that one of the two antique shops was in the hotel arcade. But he had no regrets and he was forgetting fast. He would be poorer than ever now, and the old legionnaire in Silvio's would have to wait. He would wait. Zack Robertts would wait. What was it that Strindberg had said, "The human engine waits/ Like a taxi throbbing . . ." Or was it Eliot?

The taxi throbbed. The tires were slapping the seams of the highway to a soporific beat, and the long line of the Uppland sun trounced the roof, thickening the air inside. He was hot. He tried to lower the electric window. Both of them were stuck. There was a panel of glass between him and the front seat, and he began to tap on it to draw the driver's attention. But the man's eyes were fast on the road; *his* window was open. Zack Robertts tapped harder and harder until he knocked and he banged and he attempted to slide the panel open, all to no avail. He tried the doors; they were equipped with a safety device to prevent small children from opening them. Not that he could consider flight. The Volvo had surpassed 180 by the red bar on the padded clock. Yet he struggled with the latches and he slapped the doors and the windows, feeling like a small child. He could see the Swede's eyes watching him mockingly in the rearview mirror, which made everything worse, until someone in a car they overtook looked at him with astonishment, and he simply stopped. Better to go in style.

Suddenly, the Swede unlocked the glass wall between them and dropped something sizzling inside the rear. Zack Robertts dove for the narrow opening almost losing the tips of his fingers as the panel slammed shut. A bluish square pellet lay on the floor issuing sparks and a thin, mushrooming stream of sweet-smelling smoke. The pellet, he saw, had been stamped by a machine with a skull and crossbones. It was made of a combination of hydrogen-cyanide and a thermal volatilizing agent. In its gaseous form it acted on the victim's red blood corpuscles, inhibiting their capacity to convey oxygen. The symptoms were not entirely unpleasant.

He tried to beat it out with his foot. But it was already too late. His leg felt as if it were immersed in mud. He began again to tap weakly on the separating glass. The gas chamber clouded. He smelled the scent of honeysuckle. He was in the state of California. The Swede turned around and smiled at him gapingly. In his mouth lay the remains of an acropolis: gutted holes and blackened stumps of lime strewn at precipitous angles on a purple ridge of an oozing, lost foundation. The mouth opened wide, wide enough for Zack Robertts to crawl inside. He knew he would soon find out if the Swede were SS, CIA, O.N.A.N., or, poor man, the state of California's pensioned executioner. He took hold of a slender, gleaming wire of saliva, and he hoisted himself into the ruin. But the wire broke, and though he seized and swung for a while on what remained hanging, it slipped from his hands, and he fell into the gully of the big Swede's tongue, tumbling, heading for his bowels, singing *Honeysuckle Rose*, looking for the way home.

CHAPTER SIX

HE DREAMED OF THE HUMAN PULP of A Hundred Vietnams.

It is piled in moist hillocks across the three billion acres of the Sahara desert. In a magnanimous gesture of reconciliation, the rotting dead of both camps have been transported in hundreds of thousands of vats, by order of the triumvirate: the shah, the king, and the sheikh of sheikhs. The remains are to be buried in the sand, and according to the decree of the triumvirate, a fitting monument is to be unveiled "that our fallen brethren, north and south together, shall not have died in vain; lasting testimony to our resolve that from this day forward there shall be neither war nor malice on this our planet earth." Half of surviving humanity has turned out for this historic occasion, and the other half is watching on color TV. Zack Robertts is in the demilitarized northern boundary zone, commanding a capital view of the live action from the press box. He is frowning. He has learned that a cartel of north-south interests has secretly acquired the Sahara property at less than a dollar an acre, having been tipped off by a United Nations agronomist who had been among the team of experts that had advised the triumvirate. The report of the experts proves that the death pulp will not only replenish the soil but alter microclimates and eventually the entire local ecosystem, making the desert bloom. Zack Robertts listens on his headset to the English translation of the TV announcer's preceremony remarks: "Folks, the sense of horror and pity that has gripped this crowd is beyond imagination. Enormous heaps of cadavers, extending as far as the eye can see. That much is on your screen, but what you cannot know is the unbelievable smell of rottenness, of rancid and decomposed fat, which permeates one's clothing, penetrates the respiratory tract, even among those of us wearing gauze masks soaked in a strong deodorant . . . Little can be seen of the bodies, but through the mixture of dried blood blackening in the sun and turning to dust and the ever-present, running human fat, here and there one can see a foot, a skull whole or crushed, now another limb, now a bit of tattered clothing, a shoe . . . Insects are swarming over these remains, and multitudes of larvae feed on the putrid flesh, while thousands of rats dart to and from the heaps, tunneling through the hills of death . . ." Suddenly, the announcer interrupts himself. The solemn ceremonies are about to begin. "And now, folks," he declares as everyone present rises to his feet, "our transnational anthem." The folks, removing their hats, begin to sing. Zack Robertts is standing, his hair blowing in the desert wind. He sings, too, but not the transnational anthem. Zack Robertts, unabashedly, is belting out a song that he has written especially for this historic occasion. The voice that emerges from his mouth is Paul Robeson's, and he sings to the tune of *Old Man River*.

> Oh, Revolution
> what crimes have been committed
> what crimes have been committed
> what crimes have been committed
> Oh, Revolution
> what crimes have been committed
> in thy name

The police are rushing toward him. He stands there, undaunted, unwavering, singing, taking it from the top once again. He knows the fate that awaits him. It will not be so bad. The Old Order is gone. The New Times are here. Arrested, yes; tried and convicted, yes; but only for a term of reeducation. They will take him to New Paris by jet, where he will have a room with a view of the Seine, in the lately reconstructed Bastille.

In his dream, Zack Robertts streamed with richly felt sensations. He felt old-fashioned outrage and love, and his body sweated tears.

He awoke in a Louis XVI, four-post bed, its verticals fluted in the neoclassical style. The smell of fagaceous wood and the worm dust of centuries was in his nostrils, and Victoria Walsh, in her nurse-white suit, was in his eyes.

"Oh, you're awake . . . Lovely. Like some tea? It's fresh brewed, you know."

Morning sunlight filtered in from someplace high. The air was damp with mold nearby and he could hear the footsteps of pedestrians clapping the pavement outside with the heavy heel of Swedish clogs. His head churned, but his senses, sharpened perhaps by his dream, told him where he was: back in Uppsala, in the basement of the antique shop in the Hotell Uplandia. He knew this for certain from the unmistakable smells, and the space that enclosed him was like the rooms above.

Victoria Walsh asked if he took milk or lemon. She smiled and told him that he was recuperating. The door opened. He could hear a metallic tapping coming from another room. Jean-Marie walked inside. He was wearing all new Valentinos.

"Ah, good morning," he said. "I thought I heard voices . . . Vicky, fetch Mr. Robertts some coffee."

"But I brewed fresh —— "

"Vicky! . . . *Du café pour monsieur, ça va?*"

She nodded and left, closing off the tapping sound.

"*Alors,*" Jean-Marie said when they were alone, "*ça va,* Zack? . . . May I call you by your Christian name?"

Zack Robertts was about to start shouting.

"Can you walk?" Jean-Marie asked.

Fear shot through his spine. What had he meant, "walk"? He wiggled his toes under the sheets.

Jean-Marie smiled. "Please, there is no reason for alarm. You were given a mild sleep-inducer, but only to bring you among friends, Zack. And I would like you to meet them, in the other room, where we can discuss, *d'accord*?"

He was anxious to try his legs. He kicked off the covers and found himself dressed exactly as he had been when he had left the hotel, except that someone had removed his low boots and socks, Victoria Walsh, no doubt. He got to his feet with no trouble, although his head took a while to adjust to the new equilibrium. Jean-Marie produced his footwear with the socks tucked neatly inside.

"Magli," Jean-Marie remarked glancing at the instep label. "I know the shop well. *Ces sont beaux*, these boots. The next time I am in Rome, I shall buy a pair."

Zack Robertts looked at Jean-Marie's sparrow feet. "They don't make them in your size," he said dropping a small chip of his anger.

Jean-Marie shaped a narrow smile. "Shall we go?" he said, laughing last.

The tapping sound in the other room, Zack Robertts saw now, was being made by a young Japanese dressed in jeans and a turtleneck sweater. He was working meticulously with a micrometer and a cushioned hammerhead, remolding on a spherical form the two beryllium "salad bowls" carried into Sweden by Victoria Walsh. Jean-Marie introduced him as Tommy Kaneoka and he looked up from his work for a moment. He smiled at Zack Robertts pleasantly enough, shook a lick of hair that had fallen on his eyes, and went back to perfecting his sphere.

There were four other men sitting around an unusually large, farmhouse table doing nothing more than reading conference papers or watching Tommy Kaneoka. Zack Robertts recognized all of them, by face if not by name, but Jean-Marie went ahead with his cocktail-party introductions. There was the "comedy team" of Phil E. Stein and the red-bearded man who had joked about women; the latter was an Iranian ecologist named Muhammed Hajid Rahmani. There were also a squat black African in a Polish suit who nodded to the name of Ibrahim K. Nkele and a certain Olle Johansson, the big Swede with the bad teeth who had gassed Zack Robertts in the back of a Volvo. He was cleaning his nails.

The table was cluttered with an array of laboratory-type electronic equipment and was like a junk shop full of common household and hardware items, including a one-burner electric stove, pots and pans, drills and bits, wrenches of every possible diameter, nuts and bolts, a soldering iron, and varying lengths and thicknesses of wire, insulated and not. The six C4 "candles" Jean-Marie had smuggled stood among others, all exactly alike. The wick had been removed from every one of them.

Most striking of all, however, was a towering object assembled of small pieces of plastic and metal. It rose from the center of the table like a miniature space ship, nose cone and all, to a height of five feet or more. It was held in place by a kind of "launch-pad" rig which touched the low ceiling.

The structure, apart from the fused plastic nose cone, was a cylinder of aluminum, displaying innumerable seams where it had been fitted together like a jigsaw puzzle and soldered. Its precise internal measurements, within a shell one centimeter thick, were in a ratio of four to one, being 160 centimeters long with a diameter of 40 centimeters. Its construction was not yet complete. Exposed copper wires poked through the skin. The cone hung over like the top of an open beer stein. The entire center section was unfinished on one side, revealing an interior support platform that would accept the beryllium sphere. Beryllium is extracted from the same minerals that yield emeralds. It is second only to lithium among the lightest metallic elements. It is, piece for piece, one-third the weight of aluminum, and the entire missilelike structure weighed less than forty pounds — a comfortable fit, if divided in half, in a single, oversized suitcase.

Zack Robertts knew a terrorist's bomb when he saw one — though he never actually had until now. But this one, in spite of its elegant design, seemed less than formidable compared with some about which he had read. He had once written a war film in which a column of German troops was attacked by the Roman Resistance using a makeshift bomb placed in a streetcleaner's garbage cart, and he had gone into much detail in showing how the device was made. A steel casing had been packed with about forty pounds of TNT filled in iron tubing, and while the explosive force of a charge of this quantity was devastating — enough to gut a small, one-story building — most of the casualties were caused by flying shrapnel, its lethalness depending on the weight of the metals employed.

His research had not made him an expert on such matters, but he did recognize that the silvery-white container that stood on the table before him like an ambitious kit-modeler's pride was made of aluminum (he thought the like-colored "salad bowls," which he imagined to be the detonator, were of the same material), and he questioned how much damage it could possibly do. No matter how tightly packed, it would be smaller than the bomb used in Rome, and even allowing for technological progress since then, intimidating a Swedish supermarket, a theater, or to think "big," the royal palace in Stockholm, could hardly be expected to gain much leverage to advance the Good Cause. Obviously, if reason had not gone completely astray, these self-appointed shock troops of a self-formulated policy of confronting Great Power rule by the rich had another program in mind. But when Zack Robertts entertained the idea that the bomb might conceivably be some sort of long-range, hit-the-White-House missile, he dismissed the thought as being silly, and he was left at a dumbfounded loss.

By now, Vicky had returned with the coffee, her indomitable good spirits restored to the full. She poured some for all and served with an airline stewardess's flair, fussing with sugar and cream. Her smiles, bland as they were, were warmer at least than the insipid brew, and Zack Robertts was actually growing to like her. Her manner, especially toward Jean-Marie, reminded him of a stray dog he once found with an awful gash in her neck. He had named her Beatrice Cenci, after the decapitated sixteenth-century Roman noblewoman. It was cruel, perhaps, for him to make such an association, but Beatrice Cenci, a gray shepherd of dubious pedigree who later became just plain Titi, was the most loving creature he had ever known, humans, especially, included. He did not quite see Vicky this way, but she certainly was adoring, and while she could be faulted for having extremely bad taste in Jean-Marie, her tender attentions seemed sincere.

Jean-Marie, on the other hand, paid her no mind, sipping coffee with an eye on Zack Robertts. He had made a show of perverse delight in watching him assess the bomb with grim ignorance, and after he had swallowed the grinds at the bottom of his cup, he finally spoke.

"What do you make of all this, Zack?"

Everyone except Ibrahim looked up tensely, as if a correct answer might sour the grand design. Only Vicky, gathering empty coffee cups, seemed unperturbed.

"Grief," Zack Robertts replied.

Jean-Marie laughed one solitary contraction. Zack

Robertts noticed that the Japanese, who could not have been more than in his late twenties, had finished his remodeling and was now attaching a wire suspension framework to the rim inside one of the bowls. It had a cagelike center, which could support a sphere within the sphere, and he worked it with his hands, continually testing it with a tennis ball so as to make it conform to that shape.

"What would you say, Zack," Jean-Marie continued, his eyes piercingly drawn, "if I were to tell you that what we have here is an instrument that will change the world?"

Zack Robertts reddened.

"I would remind you that I am your prisoner; that I was captured secretly and forcibly by an odious thug; that I'm at a further disadvantage in being kept ignorant of what this vile behavior is all about, and I would say, that if these are the indications of the kind of world you expect to create, it won't be much different from the one we already have."

He had not spoken at such length for longer than he could remember. He felt breathless, enervated, and his head pounded with morose anger, which would have erupted again had he not suddenly heard at his back a delicate round of applause.

He turned. Shiva Subrahmayan had somehow entered the room, and barely perceptibly now, she was clapping the ends of her fingers with genteel admiration.

"Bravo, Mr. Robertts," she said, shifting her palms in the *namaskar* Hindu greeting.

She looked toward Jean-Marie, her long hands still busy, nervously rotating one of the several rings on her fingers.

"Jean-Marie, we must be perfectly candid with Mr. Robertts, particularly since so very much depends upon his cooperation . . . And, really, I do think you exaggerate."

She walked the length of the room, or rather glided like a queen moving on a chessboard, and when she arrived at the cylinder, she set the nose cone loosely in place, tidying the table somewhat, though not very purposefully.

"Our little mechanical device, as it is," she said addressing Zack Robertts, "is merely discrete, a shell, an empty promise, you might say. I am reminded of the stones the rural traveler finds piled here and there along the roads of south India, especially in my home-state of Mysore. To the uninitiated, they are simply stones and nothing more, which is true. But when invested with what we call *puja*, or prayer, they inherit the powers of the immanent God."

She took the tennis ball from Kaneoka and cupped it in her hands. It was as if she had always to be in motion when she spoke, or like a pendulum clock she would wind down.

"Mr. Robertts, what we are building — somewhat like the peasants of Mysore, I dare say — must be invested — not with *puja*, though for my part, that, too, but — and here our hopes center on you — with earthly matter, a quantity no larger than, let us say, this tennis ball, consisting of plutonium."

She tossed the ball to Zack Robertts. He caught it out of pure reflex alone. He could feel the heat of her body hovering on the furry surface. It burned.

"You see, sir," she said now, running her black hands along the silvery skin of the missile, "this is an implosion system, the structural component of an atomic bomb."

Atomic bomb. What an old-fashioned sounding expression. That was all Zack Robertts could think of. He lay the ball on the table, gently, as if it were the fissile material itself. It rolled zigzaggedly for a while, but Tommy Kaneoka picked it up, and shaking the hair from his eyes, he returned to his work.

Shiva Subrahmayan appeared eager to continue her exposition, pausing only to allow Zack Robertts's reaction with the same anticipation she might have employed had she served him a glass of fine wine: Eniwetok 1954, an excellent year.

He was calm. This was old stuff. The fear of someone constructing a homemade nuclear weapon had for years been discussed in the press, and the technical problems involved had been worked out long before, though he had never heard of anyone actually making one. The reasons for abstaining were fairly obvious. They were the same ones that kept whole nations in check. It was simply unwise and impractical to go to such extremes. You could get millions from a single hijack well done; you could free your best soldiers with scissors held at the right person's neck, but he who would confront a big power had better have more than one big bomb on his pad. Maybe O.N.A.N., or whoever these people were, had solved this latter dilemma, but Zack Robertts declined to imagine what that answer might be. Instead, he was beginning to thank goodness for the CIA.

He looked around the room, wondering who "Abraham" could be — if he (or she) were present — and whether anyone of O.N.A.N. knew there was a spoiler in their midst. The Iranian introduced as Muhammed was stroking his beard, gathering the hairs to a point, spreading and gathering again. Phil E. Stein was making notes with an eighty-dollar Mont Blanc pen. The block-shaped African, Ibrahim, sat motionless. He had sunk into the empty spaces of his ill-fitting Polish suit and he looked like a tortoise going under his shell. Ibrahim/Abraham? If one thought hard enough, one could find a connection with "Abraham" in each of their names or character; it was a useless exercise. His eyes caught Vicky's. She was sitting legs crossed on a valuable Gothic revival side chair placed off to a far side. She smiled. Fascinating, isn't it? she seemed to be saying.

"You knew Jagjit Hanumappa, Mr. Robertts?" Shiva Subrahmayan inquired.

"Yes."

"He was a brilliant theoretical physicist . . . until his unfortunate illness, which, as you must be aware, ended in suicide."

Zack Robertts was tempted to say, "murder," but he restrained himself. He was in a position requiring the reception, not the transmission, of information, and the rule was to ask little, ideally nothing at all. It was an old journalist's interview trick. Beginners posed questions, sharp or dull, often formulated by sitting up late at night making naive discoveries. But the interviewee, in the usual case, was well ahead of the game; he had his best answers rehearsed, since more times than not, he had been asked the very same questions before. The pros simply stared coldly, with their most inhospitable eyes, chipping away with unnerving silence at the inherent disadvantage. The thoughts buried deepest surfaced quite frequently only to fill an unsavory, conversational pause.

The Indian apparently was not under such pressure; not yet. She took no notice of his failure to comment and moved on.

"Shri Hanumappa designed this highly sophisticated bomb, Mr. Robertts, more than ten years ago. Think of that, sir! Before China exploded her first, crude nuclear weapon, not to speak of India. Pandit Hanumappa was my guru at the time, and I later had the honor to become his first assistant."

Her eyes shone with pride. What manner of woman was this, Zack Robertts thought. There was at least a possibility that she herself had thrown Hanumappa from the tower, and whatever the extent of her betrayal, it was surely big. Yet she spoke of him now with schoolgirlish reverence and devotion. He tried to guess her age, and while he settled arbitrarily on thirty-five, it was impossible to feel reasonably close. She had that immaculate beauty that ripened early and stayed long, a body and a charm that conspire to demolish indifference and leave one torn between two propositions, unable to decide for an old-young or a young-old. She could have been anywhere within the range of a score of years, maybe more, not that he could find reason for it to matter. Unwillingly, he felt himself drawn to her in a clash of mind against genes. Reason stood sentry at the membranes, but somehow she was being called by the acid of his cells; or was he being summoned by hers?

She explained in consuming detail how the Hanumappa bomb would work. It was ghastly in its simplicity — all the more so when, to impress him with cunning organization, she revealed how the components were either purchased openly in this or that local store or brought into Sweden under the eyes and electronic devices of a host of sober inspectors.

She called the weapon a "shaped-charge" design, which could yield an explosive force equal to twenty thousand tons of TNT - more than that of "Little Boy," the Hiroshima bomb, though it was less than 1 percent of its weight. Little Boy had killed one hundred thousand people, she recalled with pious remorse; her bomb was meant to kill no one, she claimed in the same soft breath. But when installed in a "strategic place," it had a potential of "creating multiple Hiroshima effects."

Just as she chose not to elaborate as to where the strategic place might be, she refrained from disclosing, for now, how Zack Robertts figured in their plans. She had a flair for literary construction, and though her comrades must have already known all that she was saying and more, they listened, like Zack Robertts, with the attention gained by laying the bricks of suspense.

Continuing her description of the Hanumappa design, she said that the ball of plutonium sat at the core, "floating" in the center of the beryllium sphere, which she defined as a "reflector." She reviewed the properties of beryllium, speaking in a didactic meter and noting that it was an *excellent* reflector, or "neutron scatterer," because it had an atomic structure more dense than any other element. In fact, one needed only to consult the standard textbooks, Samuel Glasstone's, for example, to learn that the amount of plutonium required was least in a beryllium reflector. She said it was Hanumappa, however, who had discovered an ingenious design technique by which the minimum diameter of a plutonium core in a beryllium reflector ten millimeters thick, such as the one that lay on the table, could be reduced to only sixty-five millimeters and yield, pound for pound, more than one hundred times as much as Little Boy. Such a core would indeed be the size of a tennis ball, weighing 3.3 kilograms, or somewhat over seven pounds. All this, provided one knew Hanumappa's secret, which she promised not to withhold, though she seemed to be saving that, too, for climactic effect.

She lifted one of the wickless "candles," handed it to Zack Robertts, and asked him to smell it. He took it reluctantly and had no intention of going as far as putting it to his nose. It had a pale yellowish color, and though it looked quite ordinary, it felt more readily malleable than a candle, rather like fresh beeswax. Its aromatic quality did not escape his nostrils. Even at a distance it issued the familiar odor that permeated the approaches to airports, more precisely that of toluene, the antiknock constituent of aviation fuel.

As he returned it to her, their hands touched and there was. something that spoke of sensuality in that fleeting contact, which made it fall from both of them, plummeting to the floor. Everyone lurched apprehensively, and Zack Robertts had a fair idea of what it was.

She picked it up, smiling. "This, sir, is C4, a plastic form of trinitrotoluene, better known as TNT. The wicks have been removed as a precaution, though a candle flame — or a short fall to a wooden floor — makes for a very poor detonator." She squeezed it tightly, leaving the imprint of her fingers, before setting it down beside the others. "In fact, we shall have to heat it to a proper temperature, then knead it carefully by hand around the reflector to an absolutely constant thickness." She looked at Kaneoka. "A very painstaking, and I might add, extremely dangerous task."

One of the most problematic aspects of a shaped-charge design, she clarified, was that the high explosives, such as TNT, used to initiate the nuclear chain reaction, were themselves good reflectors, and as the C4 was slowly packed on the sphere, the risk of collision between the atoms in the core and free neutrons steadily increased. Since the plutonium was already only minimally subcritical, that is, of a density slightly less than that needed for the chain reaction, the additional material could cause the nuclear explosion to go off in the bombmaker's hands.

Zack Robertts glanced at Kaneoka, who winked at him like an old friend. Apparently Hanumappa had disposed of this difficulty, too, or Kaneoka thought so.

"As you know, Mr. Robertts," Shiva Subrahmayan went on with her short course, "the implosion method is dependent upon a shock wave to achieve chain reaction. The force of the TNT, when detonated — in this case, by a radio signal — and *shaped* by high explosive lenses, compresses the beryllium reflector, and subsequently the core." As she spoke, her right hand curled slowly into a tight fist. "The diameter of the plutonium ball decreases, and its density increases in inverse proportion, until it reaches critical mass. Then . . ."

Her long fingers flew open, and Zack Robertts could see the negative flash of retina-ripping light, the white hole punched through the universe with a shaft of boiling sunrock — the whole sickening-marvelous reel of the eyes-and-ears-of-the-world newsfilm in scratchy, peeling black and white. Once, when, as often, he was trying to improve his French, he had read a book in that language on Hiroshima. Little Boy, from what he was able to make out, had been dropped on a hot, sunny Monday morning, when people were going to work. Two men had been lingering, one sitting on the granite steps of a building near the Sumitomo Bank — which was at the epicenter of the explosion — the other standing beside him, in idle conversation. They were vaporized in a matter of milliseconds; they simply disappeared like dry ice, leaving no trace, not of flesh or bone, not even a mangled ring or a watch. But their shadows remained. Their bodies had been less reflective than the steps, and had left their silhouettes embedded in the granite, much in the same way as the sniper's bullet had marked Zack Robertts's neck. Years later, he visited that city of Kirin beer and sewing needles, and there they were, chatting on the steps, waiting for duty to call, killing time, and beneath it all, wondering what this day might bring. Just like everyone else, only worse. At the time, he wished that they could be somehow released from their eternal misery; but, he thought, one could tear down those steps, grind the granite into dust, and give the dust to the winds, though these garrulous, fear-harboring shadows were indestructible like the living smoke of the Jews that had spread from a Polish sky and one still breathed in and out every day. There was no rest after death, not unless you knew the way home. Zack Robertts touched his neck. The immortal bullet ached.

She had been speaking for over an hour, but her voice was as upright as a player piano and a great deal more mellifluous. She had promised to reveal Hanumappa's secret, and now she said that she would, but only partially, since it was a God-given gift to be left with something to ponder. Nevertheless, it was a sign that all her other well-husbanded culminations could not be far behind, and that she was coming to the end, which distressed Zack Robertts. The more they told him — and already much had been said, far beyond the salutary threshold — the larger he suspected his ransom would be. With all the secrets given, there would be nothing further to say, and he would be expected to perform. He had noted earlier that there was no one in the room bigger than he, except the Swede, who sat hulkingly by the door, his ears pointed like a Doberman on watch. Zack Robertts preferred jogging, but he had been a high *kyu* in Kodokan judo and he had studied karate in Okinawa, though he had never wished to systematically callous his limbs. Perhaps he should have; yet he was decisively outnumbered, and the first lesson in offensive karate had been to count numbers.

The "revelation" of the Hanumappa secret, partial and cryptic as it was, was strictly of a technical nature, more of interest to bombmakers and other scoundrels than to gentle men, but Zack Robertts paid close attention.

"The bomb I have described to you," Shiva said, "is a marvel of engineering design, but Pandit Hanumappa knew all along that it could never have more than tactical value. It was 'fizzle-yield hardware" to use the jargon of nuclear weaponry. The shock wave in a device of this size was just too feeble to even approach the kind of yield I have been talking about. But, as I said, one cannot increase the neutron-reflecting shaped-charge without escalating the risk of spontaneous chain reaction, and Shri Hanumappa had already gone to the extreme that safety permitted."

She began to walk around the room, her eyes straining for a distant place where experience might be relived.

"One day, however, I found my guru full of jubilation, and when I told him how pleased I was to see him in such a fine spirit, I was rather taken aback by his unfathomable reply ... 'When a prizefighter wishes to knock out his opponent,'

Shri Hanumappa asked me, 'does he put his glove against the other man's head and push?' And this, Mr. Robertts, was well before his unfortunate illness. My voice fluttered as I spoke in abject humility, saying that I had never in my lifetime seen a prizefight, and begging his kindest indulgence, I said I had no notion of what he meant. As he had every right to, Pandit Hanumappa laughed loudly at my patent stupidity, although by now I had supposed he was referring to striking the plutonium core harder. But then he allowed me, as I do you, sir, to exercise the powers of reason."

She sat and breathed deeply, her breasts rising and falling. Was that all? Was she leaving him to twiddle his reason, ruminating by the sight of her undulating, nipple-tightening silks? She filled a glass from a pink-labeled bottle of Evian, but took only a sip.

"Mr. Robertts," she said at last, her voice more mellow wetted down, "Shri Hanumappa, in true guru fashion, never told me his secret, but, as I like to think he knew it would, it entered my consciousness through proper meditation. It was only by his genius, in any event, that what you see here became possible. High yield and portability are *the* essential elements of our plan. A strategic weapon, and ease of transport to that strategic place I alluded to before — in our case ..." She stopped, and now she drank the entire glass of mineral water, while he waited for it to be drained. "In our case, Mr. Robertts, the North Pole."

She smiled almost audibly, as profanely pleased with herself as a Renaissance courtesan counting her cardinals and popes. But Zack Robertts was disinclined to believe what she had said of Hanumappa. What was the man who had been at Poona with, of all people, Gandhi and Kasturbai doing making pocket nuclear bombs? And the boxing analogy seemed cast in the wrong idiom. An apple could fall on Newton's head, but you could not make Hanumappa think with gloves on anymore than you could draw light bulbs over Socrates's brightest ideas.

The North Pole finale, however, reeked of acrid truth. He recalled the telegram von Schwarzwald had read about what was believed to be an Italian ship arriving at the port of Malmö on the ninth of June. They were already close to the Arctic Circle and the old sledge route to the Pole — when getting there first was the noisiest turn-of-the-century sport — lay straight through the Norwegian Sea in the summer. What profligate mischief they would do there, was another matter, and he shrank at the thought.

CHAPTER SEVEN

MUHAMMED RAHMANI, the Iranian ecologist, still flattening and sharpening his red beard with an air of mysterious purpose to it all, spoke in a studied American English that was only subtly foreign. He said that it was incorrect to use the term, "North Pole."

"In the first place, it's not exactly true," he went on, "and second, the precise location is a programmed unknown. I'd rather broaden the parameters and put the site as being somewhere in the permafrost, north of the eightieth parallel, which is an area of about one hundred and seventy-five thousand square miles."

Shiva acceded with a mere shrug, and Rahmani, leaving his beard unattended, leaned forward on one elbow and continued at a quickening pace, his eyes pinned now to Zack Robertts.

"What we're going to do, Robertts, is to plant Menes-II — which is what we call *our* Little Boy, after the first pharoah, who history tells us unified the north and south kingdoms . . . unfortunately it also has another connotation: Menes as in menace, but maybe that's not so bad. Anyway, Menes-II is going *somewhere* into the Arctic permafrost, where a nuclear explosion in the range of twenty kilotons would melt or set adrift enough of the polar ice cap to raise the sea level of the North Atlantic by about twenty-five or thirty feet. I think you can guess what that means."

It was not difficult. But Rahmani left little to amateur speculation.

"When I was at Stanford, a group of us worked out the

geophysics of such an event. You can read our paper in the *American Journal of Ecological Studies*, fall, 'seventy-two, I think it was. I don't want to go into the science of the harmonic constituents of tides — you can find it all in our paper — but since heat rises, the warmer water would be pushed up by the melted and melting ice causing huge tidal waves, in some cases, hundreds of feet high, depending on the local basin. London, and most of the British Isles, would disappear, as well as maybe fifty miles of coast from Amsterdam, or Copenhagen, to Lisbon. Serious flooding would reach as far inland as Paris, Brussels, and so on, but the worst damage would occur on the eastern seaboard of the U.S.A.

"Boston, New York, Washington, everything coastal as far south as Miami, perhaps, would go under. The tops of your skyscrapers would become the monuments of lost cities, though eventually they would sink, too. Of course, the waters would recede as the ice refroze. Nature has her healing ways, but she works slowly, say, in fifty to a hundred years.

"The economic disruption, I barely need mention, would be total. Your societies would grind to a halt, and after a period of savage chaos, you would be thrown back hundreds of years. You would become, like the Third World, hungry, impoverished, diseased, underdeveloped countries . . . The death toll? That's anyone's guess, Robertts. As for those affected by the initial flooding, we're talking about a population on two continents of around one hundred and fifty million. But don't take us as revenge-seeking mass murderers, please. In the first place, we'd allow ample time for evacuations, if we're taken seriously — and we think we will be. Second, we don't even imagine that it would ever come to that. Our demands will be minimal, just, irresistible, and even our worst enemies will be unable to hold back the tide — excuse the expression — of public opinion clamoring for a fair settlement of our grievances.

"We shall ask for a one percent solution — and any child will be able to grasp the simplicity — and the justice — of it all. Each year, until some sort of equilibrium is struck, there will be a one percent transfer of wealth from the rich to the poor ... To start with, one percent of your gross national products; a one percent geographical redistribution of industry and technology; a one percent shift in the control of the world's natural resources. That means the entire lifesupport ecosystem of this planet's land, water, and air; a one percent shift in the control of man-made resources: education, health, science, communications, and so forth; and most important, a one percent turnabout in the so-called balance of power, leading to a true balance in which power is exercised not by chiefs of staffs, boards of directors, and other bigwigs, but by the people, democratically ...

"Robertts, the era of exploitation, of what you Westerners like to call 'man's inhumanity to man,' is over ... The transformation will be long, but relatively painless, requiring the same amount of time, more or less, as it would take for the flood waters to recede. Thus the choice will be clear: fifty to a hundred years of barbarity *or* morality; one could even say, heaven or hell. But in either case, make no mistake, the meek *shall* inherit the earth."

Rahmani eased to one side, as if he were dismounting a horse, and he slipped one thumb into the lizard-skin belt that girded his waist. A religious silence descended on the room. Zack Robertts needed the time to think. These people were organized, to say the least, not of the more prevalent species of mindless terrorists.

"Have you nothing to say?" Jean-Marie asked him.

He looked around the room. Everyone seemed definitely interested. A sign of weakness, he thought. Here they were, changing the world and waiting on an offhand opinion.

"Sure," he replied. "I would say ... inflatable rafts are a good investment."

"So you think the imperialists will opt for the flood, huh?"

It was Dr. Phil E. Stein who had taken the floor, and he spoke the language of last night's televised news. "No way, my friend."

He unfolded an enormous colored handkerchief and blew like a suddenly untied balloon, trying to clear his nose, but he continued to snort fulsomely nonetheless.

"We've worked out all the scenarios, and there aren't too many, I can tell you. Sure there'll be a big hue and cry at the outset. Lots of passive aggression, to the age-old sound of rattling sabers, empty threats about holding the entire Third World responsible, and fancy talk of a *grand alliance* between NATO and the Warsaw Pact countries, with a Moscow-Washington axis. But self-interest will whittle that away quickly. After all, the only ones who really get hurt are the British and the Americans, all the rest not counting for much. Before long, Washington'll be on its own, giving orders to London only.

"First they'll try to find a way to disarm the bomb, but that'll prove impossible. It's the needle-in-the-haystack dilemma a thousand times over, and even if they learned where it was, we would threaten to explode if they came anywhere near. Next, they'd probably come down with a bad case of retaliation psychosis: your city for my city, *ten* cities to one; you name it, friend. The State Department'll try to play one poor country off another, but we'll hand over control of the bomb to the Third World, which will be a great unifying force, and the poor can do the same against the rich; don't forget, China can always take out Japan.

"Sooner or later, this phase is bound to end with some bright-eyed boy wonder in the Pentagon dreaming up the idea of mining the *Ant*arctic. But that won't work either, because before you bomb or flood the Third World, you realize that it can't mean much more than ruining a lot of shantytowns and rice fields, and whatever wealth you destroy, more often than not, it's your own. I mean, think of the fifty billion dollars the transnationals — most of which are basically U.S. corporations — have as direct capital invest-ment in the poor countries, netting them a healthy twenty percent annual return, by the way.

"So, Washington and public opinion, after successive waves of name-calling, hand-wringing, soul-searching, breast-beating, and what have you, are left with putting their best minds to work on a negotiated settlement, and from whatever angle you look at it, it'll be pretty hard to top the one percent solution, where no one really feels the hurt and everyone gains. Of course, you can send your toughest, most hard-hearted bargainers with an offer of a half a percent, or even a quarter, but once the dynamic is set in motion, the victory for the masses will be complete, winning on its own momentum."

He blew a nasal blast into his handkerchief, and silence returned. Zack Robertts was tired of being too long on his feet. He was nauseated and he hoped, to avoid being overly rude, that they would not ask for another opinion. Now he really would have nothing to say, though it was plain enough to him that only death and destruction could come of their extravagant machinations — unless the CIA mother inter-vened. They had worked out in fine detail the configurations and the choreography of an event as fantastic as *Carmen* or *Oklahoma*, neglecting the simplest of life's rules: one does not ask the unaskable. An old man with a stick once told Zack Robertts why wealth, power, and prestige were nonnegoti-able without the letting of blood: the poor have nothing to lose but their chains — which is why they have nothing to offer.

The O.N.A.N. scenarios, like those of *Carmen* and *Oklahoma*, could only take place on a stage or in the theater of the mind. If Menes-II really went into the ice cap, he had no doubt that it would be exploded the moment all the smart money had moved into inflatable rafts. There were, since memory began, fortunes to be made in calamity, even more so in reconstruction, and only the dead and the mourning say war is no fun. In his own scenario, which was at least as possible as theirs, he saw the Statue of Liberty lifting her lamp to welcome the flood. They had forgotten that America was the land of opportunity, and it would never knock harder than with the rebuilding of New York. And these spineless Onanists, by their own admission, were not even mass murderers. Only a few million losers would drown, which was the acceptable standard whenever a fast buck was turned in a war. As for the bloated losers, with the Arctic in their lungs, Zack Robertts felt himself among them, going down the shitstream of the Harlem, the Hudson, and George Washington's Potomac, which was why he was presently thanking goodness for the CIA.

"We are not unaware of your writings, Mr. Robertts," Shiva said now, "and personally, I have found them enlightening and inspiring, a consistent support of the downtrodden — with anger, and may I say, bitterness directed towards the imperialist system . . ."

God! he thought, was he the expectant father of the flood? But he loved the struck-pewter sound of her voice, the audibly breathed pauses that lifted her breasts, the way she vented words like "rrreyettinks" and "enggerr," and he could not say that he was offended by her taste.

"We were hoping," she continued, "that you might join us." Her invitation seemed completely genuine, as if she were asking him to come along on an outing in the countryside.

"You flatter me, madam," he said, "but with your permission I think I'll pass." They smiled, exchanging another quantum of cell-felt energy.

"I am afraid that will not be possible," Jean-Marie intervened. He was suddenly holding three yellowing copies of the London *Sunday Times*. And Zack Robertts knew that they were dated last April.

Drumming his fingers on the newspapers, Jean-Marie put a leg up on a corner of the table and tilted his chair backward, exposing his aquamarine-striped shirt and a naive painted tie almost as wide as his little chest. He puffed a Romeo y Julieta. He looked very un-Swiss, more like a natty French gangster, or someone acting the part in a Paris-made film.

"Shiva has told you that we would like to have your cooperation, *cher* Zack, but she has put it rather mildly. We are lacking the most important bit, but this was foreseen, and it is quite nearby. It needs only to be 'obtained.'" His Havana went out and he relit it, muffling his next few words. "Of course, I am speaking of three point three kilograms of plutonium . . ."

The flames, which he held away from the end of the cigar, flared, lighting his eyes with pinpoints of red, and he settled back again rotating the cigar in his lips.

". . . preferably the isotope known as two-thirty-nine, but two-forty will do almost as well. A single ingot of plutonium, about twice as long as a cigarette packet and less wide, weighs two point five kilos, so we shall have to 'obtain' a pair — worth about fifty thousand American dollars, by the way — which will then be remolded. There is a plutonium recovery plant five or six kilometers southwest of Uppsala, the only one in Sweden, and an ultrasenitive, maximum security installation."

He lifted the copies of the *Sunday Times* and waved them at Zack Robertts.

"As you yourself have written in your well-informed reportage from India, plutonium is a by-product of the uranium fuel used in nuclear reactors. Sweden has several reactors, and the used fuel is brought to the Uppsala plant by rail, mostly via Stockholm. The processing is completely automated, and once the raw material enters the facility, no human being can approach it, without being killed by radiation, until the plutonium ingots are deposited in a sealed storage room at the other end . . .''

Jean-Marie droned on, consuming with fire and water both ends of his cigar, but Zack Robertts listened poorly. He had toured such a plant in Hyderabad, and his mind was cast back into the eerie purple light of dying atoms. The uranium arrived in steel containers that were immersed in deep pools of distilled water. Mechanical claws closed in on them with the same avaricious immediacy as subaqueous carnivores charging their prey. They picked them apart, exposing the burnt-out fuel rods that issued the venom of nuclear decay. It was the beta rays — the vomited electrons of a nucleus breaking down — that caused the purple glow that hovered on the pools, and it was said to be perfectly safe to walk around them since the water absorbed the radiation. On the day he had been there, a frail young man had fallen in. He was fished out almost at once and rushed to an infirmary, but Zack Robertts could still see the terror bulging in his eyes, and he wondered now about the purple marrow in his bones.

''. . . which is where *you* enter the picture, *cher* Zack.''

His wandering was arrested by the sound of his name.

''I'm sorry,'' he said, ''I didn't catch the last part of what you said.''

Jean-Marie grew testy. He flicked a tube of ashes on the floor. He had apparently noticed his listener's distraction.

''Really? I thought I was clear. Perhaps it is my English,'' he said sarcastically. ''*Alors*, I was trying to say, Zack, that we should like to know the security arrangements concerning the plutonium storage room, and that we expect you, pursuing your well-known journalistic interest in nuclear reactor technology" (he held up the newspapers again and let them fall to the table) "to discover this information for us. After all, how can we obtain the required bit, if we do not know how to get in . . . and out? Some of us shall have to do exactly that, a sort of . . . How is it in English? A caper? In any case, we are well prepared . . . Am I clear now?"

"Let's see," he said returning arrow for arrow. "You want me to pose as a writer, conduct a fraudulent interview with some unwitting fellow at the Uppsala plant on the pretext of preparing a nonexistent article."

"Pose? But you *are* a writer, with unquestionable credentials, and how you do it, that is your business. I shall say only that you must begin at once. Shiva will go with you. Not out of mistrust, you understand, but it *is* possible that you may not 'catch' everything that is said."

Zack Robertts felt his heart beating wildly, though he spoke with apparent calm. It was easy to be caustic to Jean-Marie, but he knew they were moving quickly to a sinister obstruction. He went on nevertheless, glancing at Shiva, whose eyes shifted as if she had been staring at him.

"I hate to upset your plans, Jean-Marie, even for the 'good cause,' but as I already told the lady," again, he looked at her; this time she *was* staring, "I'm passing, which sometimes, it seems you don't know, is a more polite, colloquial-English way of saying no."

Jean-Marie pushed out his lower lip. "I suppose, then, we shall have to find someone else. It is said to be unwise to ask a man to compromise his principles, and you seem committed to this . . . 'passing.' Unfortunately, however, we shall have to kill you."

He looked in the direction of the door, and before Zack Robertts could turn his eyes, too, the Swede had withdrawn a

.357 Magnum equipped with a Swedish-made Sven Thorsson silencer.

Vicky drew in a high-pitched gasp that sounded like a hiccup, and Shiva and some of the others seemed startled, but Zack Robertts was no more unnerved than before. He had half-expected this kind of scene, and he could not imagine that they would have gone to such lengths as they had thus far, only to dispose of him so summarily without attempting secondary persuasions.

"I believe you have already met Olle Johansson," Jean-Marie said, "but what you probably do not know is that Olle is a most proficient marksman. That early morning shot you may have heard yesterday while you were doing your gymnastics was not an unintended miss, Zack, I can assure you. It was simply a demonstration of Olle's talents. He can hit, or miss, more or less as told."

Zack Robertts stared at the Swede, who beamed back at him with swagger on his junkyard mouth. Why was he telling him all this, he thought. It was certainly of interest to him to learn before dying who the sniper had been, but one did not need to advertise the qualities of sharpshooting to a target ten feet across the room eye-to-muzzle with a Magnum, which could make a window through a steel door. It was only secondary persuasion number one, at least he profoundly hoped so.

He peered down the barrel of the gun. "Go ahead and shoot, Olle." He had used his best Bogart voice, its steady timber rendering his doubts opaque to the outside.

The Swede's eyes moved a fraction. He seemed quite ready, needing only minimum instruction from Jean-Marie — a contracted facial muscle, even an involuntary twitch.

Zack Robertts held his body and gazed remarkably straight. Jean-Marie was directly behind him, but from the corners of his eyes he could see everyone else in the room. All of them, with the exception of Ibrahim, who was as immovable as ever, displayed various signs of tension, not at all in command of the hardier nerve their program demanded, but there was something in Shiva, in her eyes, on her lips, or in the air that flowed through her pores, that stood witness to a more complex phenomenon. Exactly what it was, he had no time whatsoever to reflect on, but in that small part of a second in which all this occurred, he could have sworn that she had the look of a woman at prayer.

"You're going to have to do it sooner or later, Olle," he said. Now he was scared. Had he gone too far? There was no point in pressing the matter, even if he were calling Jean-Marie's hand.

"Quite the contrary," Jean-Marie said, relieving him immensely. "The longer you consent to remain alive, the more valuable your life becomes to us. You enhance our credibility immeasurably, which is why we wish you to know every detail of our activities. When the time comes, you shall publicize them to all the world, as well as how you were driven at gunpoint to cooperate. There may be those who tend to doubt us, but *your* objectivity in this situation would be beyond question. Quite a journalistic scoop, wouldn't you say so, Zack?

"Your only chance of survival is to cover our story, *completely*. Make notes. Record every conversation. Above all, observe. We shall be your frankest informants ... and the sincerest guardians of your health. Naturally, our offer precludes any premature communication with our adversaries, or escape, in which case our guardianship would come to an end, with most untoward consequences for yourself."

All this was what he had hoped to hear. He remained silent for a while, then he spoke softly.

"Do you mind if I sit down?"

Jean-Marie smiled, crushing the stub of his cigar under his

CHAPTER EIGHT

JOACHIM VON SCHWARZWALD was probably *the* richest private individual in the world in terms of liquid assets. His annual salary at the Pär Sjögren Foundation was forty-four thousand Swedish crowns, or approximately eleven thousand dollars. He had no property. His account at the Handelsbanken in Uppsala, which he shared jointly with his wife, represented their entire life's savings and amounted to about half of his year's pay. However, his late father's holdings in several banks in Switzerland, to which he had uncontested access as his sole survivor, consisted of many hundreds of millions of Swiss francs — perhaps billions. Von Schwarzwald the younger had not the least idea of the figure, nor was he aware that his bankers and a few officials in the Ministry of Finance lived with a nagging fear that he might one day demand all of his funds, which, depending on his intentions, could cause a financial tempest of international proportions.

Von Schwarzwald the elder, Albrecht-Christian, opened these accounts in 1944, and they had not been touched since, though the money had multiplied staggerlingly. Albrecht-Christian, for many years prior to his suicide in 1945, was a director of the I. G. Farben corporation, the huge German chemical firm. During the Second World War, in a joint venture with the government, I. G. Farben was involved in the building of such installations as Auschwitz, initially to secure a source of labor, and later on, to recover and recycle the chemical and physical by-products of the laborers themselves, as well as their families, when, as often, they died. The life span of a laborer at Auschwitz was three to six months; the life span of the families was about an hour.

As a result of these investments, Albrecht-Christian did exceedingly well financially, and when it appeared that his vastly increased estate — not to speak of his personal safety — might be jeopardized by the government's failure to win the war, he transferred part of his assets to Switzerland, absorbing a 90 percent loss in converting reichsmarks into francs — 95, if one counted the fees and the blackmail of his agents. Nevertheless, he was left with over a hundred untouchable millions in five interest-bearing Swiss accounts. After the war ended, to thwart enemy arrest, he shattered his skull with the aid of a pearl-handled Lüger that had been a gift from Heinrich Himmler.

All this — including the activities and the true fate of his father — did not become known to young Joachim until years later. He had spent the war as a student of political science at the University of Uppsala, avoiding military service through the influence of his father, who assured his ingenuous son that he was exempt because he was engaged in an "essential endeavor." It was at the University of Uppsala that he met and befriended Pär Sjögren, and when the vile revelations came, Pär Sjögren and Joachim's future wife, Kerstin Luns, nursed him through a protracted and nearly fatal crisis of mind, body, and soul.

This period ended in a solemn resolve, undertaken by von Schwarzwald the younger, never to touch or inquire about one centime of his father's nefarious booty. That was in 1950, and while he had never wavered since, there had been times when he was unsure whether he would not one day succumb to unforeseen temptation. Not that he ever craved material gains, but there were friends, for example, who counseled that he give his misfortune to charity or the otherwise needy; but as a student of political science (and a reader of Giambattista Vico), he had come to conclude that choosing one or more causes over another required divine wisdom, of which he knew he had none.

Now, almost sixty, crippled and dying of emphysema, he felt secure that his oath would accompany him to his grave; and thereafter, he believed, with the money continuing to accrue beyond measure, let he who would spend or invest it either come to terms with its eternal, abominable curse or choke on it. His wife, who was his only potential heir, agreed, and for this, their last wills provided. Damnations, however, have a way of being less than eternal.

In his overcast quarters on the second floor of the Pär Sjögren Foundation, Joachim von Schwarzwald sat with Miklos Brody. His wife, Kerstin (pronounced Sherstin), was working on her Brancusian bumps.

"Ze SS have rung me up to say that he was definitely not on that flight to Rome last night, neither on any other," he was saying to Miklos, who showed no sign of surprise.

Miklos had already been told quite straightfacedly by Jean-Marie, who was in the same building conducting the second afternoon session of the conference, that Zack Robertts had not reported to work, had checked out of his hotel, and that they would have to hire a new editor. Even then, Miklos had shown no sign of surprise.

"They have no news of him, Miklosh."

"This is not good."

Von Schwarzwald shook his head in agreement. "If he is not already dead, ve must assume that he is either in ze hands of ze O.N.A.N. or ze CIA."

"Or both, *älskling*," Kerstin injected without looking up.

"Quiet, voman, and let me finish shpeaking, please!"

Von Schwarzwald reddened under the force of arterial pressure. He tried one of Miklos's Murattis but ground it out immediately in disgust, substituting his own Gitane.

"I must tell you, Miklosh, that ze SS have no interest in our friend if he cannot shpy, and if he cannot shpy, they cannot touch ze O.N.A.N. They are more concerned vit ze Italian ship they are expecting in Shvedish waters. Ve must therefore find and make contact vit Herr Robertts on our own . . . and our funds are limited."

"This is not good."

"There is a way," Kerstin said, and they both turned to her. She was looking into an empty space beyond the window and pressing her fingertips on her globular brow as if her head ached. "Infiltration!" she cried, her fingers rolling on her forehead.

"You are insane, voman! Shot op! It is impossible!"

"Miklos knows the way," she replied, as if he had not uttered a word.

Von Schwarzwald turned to Miklos, who seemed completely dumbfounded.

The telephone rang, and von Schwarzwald lifted the receiver with evident annoyance.

"Ja? . . ." He listened for a moment and his eyes brightened behind his thick glasses, as he tried to light a cigarette with one shaky hand.

Miklos leaned forward with a struck match, and von Schwarzwald, drawing on the flame, covered the mouthpiece.

"They are putting through Shtockholm. . . Ze SS . . . *Hej!*" he said into the phone, over-aspirating the Swedish greeting in a spray of smoke. *"Ja . . . ja . . . ja . . . ja?"* He jolted disconcertedly. *"Är du säker på det? . . . Ja . . . ja . . . ja . . . Jo visst! . . . Hej på!"*

He hung up. Miklos looked at him expectantly.

"They have learned who is this 'Abraham,'" he said with a note of sorrow, addressing Miklos only. "They have an agent working in ze CIA Shtockholm Station, which is how they got this ziggurat telegram . . . I am very, how to say, shocked. You know this 'Abraham,' Miklosh — one of our best Third World people, who sits in there right now vit ze schidt-talkers. It is Nkele . . . Ibrahim Nkele!"

"Motherfucker," Miklos said quietly.

Kerstin continued to gaze out the window. Suddenly, she shouted in an exhausting, rending wail.

"Lies!"

Her head dropped violently, as if the stem of her brain had snapped, and she began to weep.

On M Street, where it angles off New Hampshire Avenue, in Washington, D.C., there is a gray concrete building with smooth walls that accommodates the offices of Ratio Medicus, Incorporated. RMI, established in the 1930s, is a private firm that abstracts, indexes, and cross-references all of the scientific papers in the medical disciplines published in the United States, Canada, and the United Kingdom. It thereby performs an invaluable service, since, by the 1970s, tens of thousands of such original works were appearing each year in hundreds of medical journals, far more than any researcher could ever read or even skim.

What began with handwritten notes on little green cards, later typed, later transferred to microfilm rolls, was now a rich store of millions of random-access memory cores on an IBM Mark-IV computer. One needed only to touch primary-colored sensors, with an experienced hand, to be sure, for the easy and swift retrieval of all the known English-language sources on any given medical theme. And all this for a reasonable fee.

RMI was still using the green three-by-fives when it registered a then recent reference in the *British Journal of Gynecology*, volume CXXIV, number IV, to what remains to this day — according to RMI's IBM — the only recorded case in English of a living "diaphrodite."

This is a condition so rare that its name had to be composed by its discoverer, the late clinician and member of the Royal Society of Medicine, Sir Ian Hughes-Moncrief. Indeed, history, with customary cruelty, would have undoubtedly remembered Sir Ian less for a lifetime as a distinguished physician than for his chance finding, were it not for the fact that the surviving copies of his publication are barely more extant than the diaphrodite herself.

For reasons that can only be explained by the predilections of some human beings to privately collect and horde curiosities, volume CXXIV, number IV, cannot be publicly consulted today outside the British Museum, the New York Public Library, and a very few specialized libraries. There appears to be no copies in Washington, D.C. RMI, due to limited space, periodically discards after use the material it reads, and the copy in the Library of Congress was poached years ago. But there was one in nearby Langley, Virginia, in the rather less accessible files of the CIA.

Nevertheless, whether acquired from RMI's trash bin, the Library of Congress collection, or elsewhere, this copy had the dogears of frequent readings, and its most frequent reader was reverend-agent Huntz Merriwether.

Huntz Merriwether had an abiding interest in the Hughes-Moncrief syndrome, and while the language of medicine is often stiff and esoteric (though always charming in Sir Ian's case), the passage that uplifted his hackles and titillated most fills almost all of page 1417:

Patient X [Sir Ian wrote] sought medical advice initially in early adolescence, when it was realised by her parents that since the menarche, which seems to have been established by the age of eleven, her menstrual cycle was only a fortnight, the average duration of menses being forty-eight hours. At the time, she was assured by a physician 'not to worry' (this, in mid-twentieth century England!).

Upon referral to our service, at the age of eighteen, she expressed not as much concern for her abbreviated menstrual cycle, which caused her no discomfort, as for what she variously described as an obtrusive sensation of being 'oversexed', 'obsessed with sex', etc. These symptoms, she confided with poignant difficulty, could only be temporarily relieved by 'frequent' masturbation, since, while professing to be heterosexually 'libertine' in outlook, she encountered morbid anxiety at the prospect of coital relations, which must needs, she believed, result in a 'dreadful embarrassment' (*Regina Victoria regnum etiam nunc*).

Clinical observations revealed that Patient X was a true, congenital diaphrodite, in contradistinction to the known instances of pseudo-diaphroditism. Two fully functional reproductive systems were recognized and examined gynecologically.

The internal organs consisted of four distinct, albeit diminutive, ovaries and oviducts (each pair communicating with separate posterior vaginal orifices), and a didelphic, as opposed to a bicornuate, uterus with an overall volume of a normal uterus of a celibate female of her age, weight, and stature.

The vestibular surface presented a single urethra, but manifested two anterior vaginal orifices, upper and lower. Two vaginas, not to be confused with the more prevalent septate vagina, were found to be slightly narrower than normal, and each of them led to its individual cervical canal, terminating in the corpus uteri. The entrance to the lower vagina possessed an intact hymen, and, according to the patient, this was the condition of the upper vagina until a recent, virginal coital experience, which ended in the anticipated 'dreadful embarrassment' referred to above.

The pubic symphysis, covered with a normal display of pubic hair, showed no outwardly visible indications of diaphroditism, but the external genitalia were characterised by a superficial bifurcation of the labia majora, and an equally bifurcated labia minora, becoming more pronounced in the clitoris, which was virtually two integral organs. These lavishly innervated clitori were the twin ramifications of a parent stem. However, the patient declared that she had convinced herself empirically that each clitoris was capable of independent, multiple orgasms, and when, only rarely, they occurred in both organs simultaneously, the intensity was such as to produce a state of ecstasy of unusual duration, leading invariably to cerebral ischemia, or, to use the patient's own words, 'a heavenly swoon'.

Patient X was advised that diaphroditism, apart from being a rather extraordinary phenomenon, appeared perfectly consistent with sound health, as well as a relatively normal reproductive and sexual life.* It was further suggested that in the event of preg-

---

* Cf. McCombe, Selwyn Bor, Walmsley, and Schlägel, all of whom reported various forms of pseudo and true diaphroditism in the nineteenth century.

nancy she should be placed under specialised observation.

In respect of her 'embarrassments', it was pointed out that relatively minor surgery could remove the wall between the upper and lower vaginas, creating the purely cosmetic effect of a single anterior vaginal orifice. The same was said in respect of her clitori, that is, the surgical excision of one of them. In this connexion, however, she was duly cautioned that in the former case the resulting vaginal volume would be larger than normal, which might interfere with satisfactory intercourse, and that in the latter case, a partial clitoridectomy might engender a loss of intensity of the unusual, and presumably desirable, sensations she had described.

Expressing immense relief on learning the true nature of her condition, Patient X chose not to undergo either surgical intervention. Upon reflection, she stated that she would prefer to attempt to overcome her psychogenic morbidities, psychotherapeutically, if necessary, and that now she felt fortunate, rather than handicapped.

To better understand her state of mind, perhaps it is fitting to quote her, as best as can be recalled: 'I am a woman twice over', she remarked in a spirited manner, 'and what more could a woman desire than double the joy of any other, while remaining a virgin until Mr Right comes along'.

Interpreting her reference to virginity purely in the figurative sense, or concerning only the lower vagina, an aging scientist and practitioner long in Hippocrates' service could do no better than to take the petal-like hand of this blossoming feminine flower and wish her a rip-roaring, headmaster's Godspeed!

Huntz Merriwether, with dictionary assistance, including *Blackstone's* illustrated medical, had long ago learned the meanings of all of Sir Ian's words, and now they read like *Playboy*. Sometimes he pretended that he had a pair of peni.

It was coming to him now. But he needed the word of God.

He was alone. They had given him a windowless room, which was otherwise the same as the one he had had on the fifth floor above him, and he lay in the same kind of bed, the same kind of digital clock-radio at his side. It was 23:04 and he imagined the horizon sun coming up or going down — he could not remember which.

Von Schwarzwald's definition, or it may have been Menes-II, had made him think of T. E. Lawrence digging among the Hittite ruins at Carchemish, and Lawrence had worked under Woolley, who had found the clay banked by the Flood. Years ago he had read Leonard Woolley on his excavations at Ur of the Chaldees, where the Euphrates tires, laboring southeast through its marshes to unite as it must with the Tigris, and where Abraham son of Terah was born.

There, forty centuries back, when Abraham lived and kept sheep, ziggurats were built. Woolley had described the Sumerian ziggurat at Ur, a gently sloping tower, as having been shaped in the image of a mountain, a temple dressed in living foliage to please and deceive the approaching eye. This much, he had learned from Woolley, but the ziggurat Zack Robertts was trying to seize in his mind, he knew, rose to the north, on the Babylonian plain of Shinar. He lacked the word of God.

He lay under a sheet naked, carried by thoughts that shifted like cumulous clouds, stirring now and then to an interior call that warned against falling asleep. He had undressed to feel loose, but he had decided to sleep with his clothes on; there was no way to prepare for the unexpected, but one could always be readier to run.

He was about to get up and dress before sleeping (the idea amused him), when someone knocked at his door. He had kicked himself free of the sheet and now he wound it around him wildly, inviting the knocker to enter.

It was Vicky, unclung, in a gold polyester robe, which was tied at the waist with a braided cord. She carried a tray.

"Oh," she said seeing him in a white tangle.

"It's a toga."

"Super!"

She closed the door with an ample hip and set her tray on the digital clock.

"Brought you some tea, Zack. There's no coffee this time, I promise you, but I did manage this."

She held up a frosted green flask of Remy Martin, the pint-size sold on airplanes. He saw no cup for the tea, two glasses for the cognac, and Vicky's silhouette was hinting.

"That's very kind of you, Vicky."

He said nothing about the cups, and gave her a fair chance to leave, but she just stared at the changing numbers of the clock, her face going capillary by capillary from fair, to pink, to red. She had that Anglo-Saxon skin that betrayed emotion, he thought, and the feeling revealed now, there appeared to be no cause to doubt it, was that Vicky wished to be friendly — even if, as he suspected, it were some kind of order from Jean-Marie's high command of her devotions.

"Why don't we open the bottle," he said setting her at ease.

"Fantastic!"

She tried before he could, but the flask had a scored, breakaway cap, which was fine when it worked, but in this instance it did not, and she was left turning it in an endless circle. He took the bottle from her, his "toga" falling to his waist. Suffering a slight cut on his finger, he managed to open it, and he poured into the glasses held in her hands.

"You're bleeding."

He sucked away the drop of blood.

"Does it hurt?"

"Only when I laugh."

Vicky laughed, throwing back her head, her hair hanging free of her shoulders. She sat on the floor crossleggedly, tucking her robe around her, and looked up at him with Beatrice Cenci's eyes. It unsettled him.

"Well," he said chiming her glass with his, "power to the people."

"Mmmmm."

They drank.

"You were super today, Zack."

"You should have seen me yesterday."

She laughed again, giggled. The cognac was arriving. He could see it gilding her capillaries.

"You're funny . . ."

He drank slowly, wishing he were dressed, readier.

". . . but shy," she added.

"I didn't think it showed."

She nodded several times. He poured for both of them.

"I used to be shy m'self. But it's just self-conscious rubbish, you know, something to be put out for the sweeper. That's what I did, Zack. It wasn't easy, I promise you. Had to have my head shrunk and all that. But it worked . . . I mean, I can walk right up to a man, if I've a mind to, and ask him to . . . y'know, sleep with me."

"Hm . . . I'll bet you don't get many turndowns."

She laughed a short one. "Oh, I'm not all that promiscuous. Just liberated. I'm bloody well not going to pass up the right boy because of something as silly as shyness."

"I'll admit it decreases one's chances."

Silence. She began to scratch ovals on his ankle.

"We're alone, y'know. I've got the room next to yours."

"Alone?" He was dubious, but interested.

"Oh, there's Olle. But he's no bother. Actually, he's quite nice when you get to know him."

"I'm sure."

"He's at the outside door. Sort of guarding, you know . . . We could fuck."

Zack Robertts cleared his throat more than once. Could he take on Olle, Magnum and all? He stroked the chopping edge of his right hand. And what had she meant by the "outside" door? He had no notion of how he had been brought into this place.

She rose, undoing the braided bow of her robe in a long, sweeping motion, and in a moment, she was as naked as he was, only more handsomely exposed. Her breasts and her hips both phrased and exclaimed far mightier than a four-letter invitation. But why did she have to have those adoring Beatrice Cenci eyes?

She sat beside him. His time was running out.

"What do you think of all this, Vicky?" he asked, feeling ten warm fingers on his back. "That bomb in there. The whole . . . 'approach.' "

She lifted her hands, sat erectly, and thought for a moment. Then she spoke measuredly.

"I think . . . I think Jean-Marie is just . . . amazing. He's everything, y'know . . . which bothers me sometimes . . . I mean, the Mercedes and the big flat in Geneva, and all that. But yet, he's so . . . dedicated! To helping the poor, I mean. He's just . . . amazing! Do you know what I mean, Zack?"

"Sure."

Zack Robertts poured a long one and drained it. Vicky crawled along the bed and puffed up the pillows.

"Fun time."

He looked at her once more. She was on all fours, her paws on the pillows, and she turned to him, adoringly.

"I've got a pretty bad headache, Vicky."

"Oh." She came up behind him and began to massage his shoulders separating his muscles in strands with a comforting touch. "You did look quite smashed when they brought you in last night."

"I guess I overdid it."

"I'm good, y'know. I know I am. Been told I'm very . . . orgasmic. Let's try it, Zack. They say it's therapeutic."

"We will, Vicky, Another time."

"Oh . . . Is there *anything* I can do?"

Zack Robertts considered the offer for a while. There was *something*, but it seemed inappropriate to present circumstance.

"Well . . ." he said hesitantly.

"*Anything*, Zack. I mean, I used to have qualms about fellatio, but now it zaps me out . . . We all have our hangups. Believe me, I know . . . Once, I worked for this chap. Right and proper, he was. Queen's List, and all that. Well, it took him long enough to own up — stammer and stutter, hem and haw, just like a bloody schoolboy; you should've seen him, Zack — but in the end all he wanted was a bit of S-M — specially M. Chains and ropes and all that. Well, I felt sorry for the old titfart at the time, and in a funny way, Zack, *honored*, if you know what I mean. Imagine: little old Vicky, greengrocer Walsh's daughter, whipping an O.B.E.! Anyway, I asked my shrink what to do. And y'know what he says, Zack?"

She looked at him intently, and for the first time he saw a seething vitality in her eyes and in the way her speech reverted to a neighborhood sound, dropping all pretension. He was thoroughly enchanted with her story, and Beatrice Cenci, paws and all, was gone.

"What did he say, Vicky?"

She sat stiffly, her breasts lurching forward. Then she lowered her head as if she were peering over the rims of eyeglasses, and her voice fell two whole octaves.

"He says, 'Vict*aw*ria' — he used to call me Vict*aw*ria — 'do as you please, my deah. But when the blighter's been properly tarred and feathered he's going to demand you make love.' Well, I was shocked beyond words, I promise you. I was just a kid at the time."

She became silent as if that were where the story ended.

"What happened then?" he could not resist asking.

"Oh," she said somewhat diffidently, "we did it once or

twice." She shrugged. "I enjoyed the whipping part. But I didn't hurt him or anything like that."

She seemed to regret what she had told him, but he was amused to the quick and he showed it, relieving her immensely.

"But let's talk about you, Zack," she said with new excitement. "You've got super eyes." She brushed them faintly with the back of her hand. "Lovely."

Her skin was breathlike and kind. He had viewed her invidiously, and all things were suddenly possible.

"C'mon, Zack, out with it."

"Huh? . . . Oh." He had almost forgotten what he had wanted to ask her, and now he was sorry it had gone this far. "Well, what I would like is going to sound odd now."

"Odder than old fuckwit?" She was flabbergasted.

"It depends on how you look at it. What I happen to need, what I could use, Vicky, is a Bible."

She looked at him strangely, backing off. "What are you going to do with it?"

"Read it."

Her suspicions were hardly abated. "While doing what?"

He assured her that he had no perversion in mind. He pretended otherwise, but it was more than a simple request; he did not want the others to know. At least one of them, he thought, would understand. He said something vague about reading the Bible being a remedy since his childhood whenever he had a headache — foolish, he knew, but effective. She reacted disappointedly and seemed only weakly convinced, which worried him.

"Well, where am I going to find a bloody Bible?" she asked when she had redone her robe.

He shrugged trying to appear as if he could do almost as well without it.

She picked up the tray and went to the door lost in thought, and when she opened it, she called to him softly.

"Zack?"

"Huh?"

"You're not . . . uh . . . impotent, are you?"

"Only when I have a headache."

She smiled. "Then it's not . . . uh . . . me?"

"Vicky," he said looking deeply into her eyes, "I think you're just . . . super!"

She grinned now with all the parts of her mouth. "One Old Testament, with a New on the side, coming up!"

She backed out standing tall, and if one hand had been free, she would have blown Zack Robertts a kiss.

He lay awake in the dark listening to the Telefunken purr and the minute numbers fall at least a hundred times. Now and then he heard Vicky moving beyond the wall and he slept for a while. When he awoke the sheets were wrapped around his ankles and it was 5:03. There was a note on the clock. He read by the glow of the dials:

4:17. Dear Zack. You forgot, silly: this is a hotel. Ever hear of the Gideon Society? Yours (anytime), Vicky. P. S.: I think *you're* just super! You look fantastic when you sleep! Can't wait till your headache heals! V.

He opened the drawer by his bed. There was a Bible inside. He turned on the light, and knowing precisely where to look, he saw God.

"Behold," God said, "the people is one, and they have all one language; and this they begin to do: and now nothing will be restrained from them, which they have imagined to do. Go to, let us go down, and there confound their language, that they may not understand one another's speech."

He had read that passage many times, but he had never

seen it, as he did now, with the ground still damp with the Flood. He *saw* the Day of Rendering, the Primal Slash of the One and the Infinite, cutting one man loose against another in a universal, unique, and for all that was known, permanent enfeeblement of an entire species of living things, compelling them by the wound inflicted to repeat, to repeat, to repeat until that which was repeated became nothingness and emptiness and blinding . . . and welcome.

The common plainsmen of Shinar, speaking one language with mud on their shoes, had found how to do whatever they had a mind to, and for a start, they were building the ziggurat of Etemenanki — the Tower of Babel — challenging *God's* sky. And when He, the God of Abraham, caught on to what they were up to, He *made* history. But there was no allegory in history repeated, nor could there ever be, and the history being repeated in Uppsala gave reason to welcome the CIA.

Ziggurat, Zack Robertts knew now, was not the name of an Italian ship on a course for the Pole. There was much he did not know, and his head rattled like the cubes in a dice man's fist, but he understood that ziggurat was the CIA scheme to intervene, the sacrilegious byword of men in the employ of the unholy gods against the vulgar neo-Babylonians. The repeated, Uppsala version was only a tawdry imitation in which all things had become their opposites. The not-so-common Uppsala plainsmen were not one people with a single language, and the sky they threatened was not the Almighty's but the sky that belonged by right of conquest to the merely Mighty, who, guns drawn, would sooner or later declare, "Go to, let us go down . . ."

Zack Robertts felt himself to be in the muck of barbarians, yet reasonably secure. In spite of everything, he still had the human failing to believe that someone was looking after him in Washington, D.C.

*

The name of the Italian ship was the *Colomba Bianca*, and it rocked in the harbor at Porto Ercole, flying, to gain a taxation advantage, the Nicaraguan flag. Once called *Il Falcone*, it had been rechristened by its newest owner, Fabrizio Bentivoglio, who in recent years had made millions selling BMWs in Italy, had bought the ninety-six-foot yacht and a castle, and to protect his investments, had joined the Italian Communist Party. Unknown to the Communists, Fabrizio Bentivoglio was also a closet supporter of almost all the other parties, including the Fascists, and when he voted, he invariably cast a blank ballot, an anonymous, no-confidence vote for all.

As might be surmised, Bentivoglio was a prudent man, though not one in whom great trust ought to be placed, particularly since he had a record of several convictions, mainly for thievery and trickery. But this dated back more than two decades, when life in Rome, where he was born and raised in a Trastevere slum, was more severe. Yet while the Italian Communist Party will accept anyone who agrees to obey the rules printed on the back of its membership card, one would think that Jean-Marie would have been more discriminating. Such is the mystique of left-wing ideology, however, and in any case, Bentivoglio's "contract" called only for transportation to the permafrost and back.

They had met two or three years ago at Valentino's in Via Condotti, and the Italian had extended various invitations to the castle and the yacht, which when accepted and passed in good, right-thinking company, had convinced Jean-Marie that Bentivoglio was the man for the volunteer job. Obviously, money alone was not the biggest attraction in Bentivoglio's life. Indeed, having read Marx, Lenin, and Gramsci's *Letters from Prison* (while in prison), he considered himself an intellectual by self-education (he could recite the *Communist Manifesto* by heart, or at least: *"Uno spettro si aggira per l'Europa — lo spettro del comunismo . . .")* and a sailor and sportsman by natural inclination.

His favorite sport was yachting, of course, and Fabrizio Bentivoglio knew no finer pleasure than to breathe the salt of the sea, sipping a sambuca by the side of his shipboard pool. So much the better, if the pool were filled with his friends, and better still, if the friends were the beautiful women with whom he was often seen on the pages of *Oggi, Gente,* and all the other magazines that cover the "good life" of Rome.

A gregarious, generous man still in his forties, he had recently separated from his second wife, and it was said by those in the good life of Rome that Fabrizio was "making up for lost time." But everyone at the Bolognese, Rosati's, Mastino's, and the other right places in town knew — and it burned him — that his wife, an actress seen less in films than on the beaches of Fregene, was an unfaithful wench and an ingrate besides. He had given her a castle, or had bought it in her name (to gain a taxation advantage), and she had given him the horns.

Fabrizio, it was said in his favor, was not prone to vendetta, but were it not for the new divorce laws, for which the Communists had fought with valor, he would have considered entrusting the fate of his wife and a man he knew only as "Peppe" to his several Palermo connections. It must be added in all fairness, however, that such thoughts were never articulated — thanks to *comunismo!*

Now, at Porto Ercole, he was more concerned with his imminent voyage than with anything else, planning from his suite in the Hotel Eden the tiniest of details — not the least of which had been the unusual and costly equipment needed. A small, specialized craft, which would be lowered from the yacht when the floes became too dense for safe passage, had had to be purchased, not to mention the cranelike apparatus that went with it and the Arctic weather supplies and clothing

— all of which had been impossible to secure in a Mediterranean country.

But Fabrizio Bentivoglio was ready. From his window looking over the crescent harbor he could watch the *Colomba Bianca* taking on provisions and fuel. He would sail for Malmö at sunup with a trustworthy crew of twelve (recruited with the aid of his Palermo connections) and a quite recent acquaintance, a beautiful foreign woman with long legs and hair that reached down a span below her waist. He had wanted at least one female companion on board. The journey to Malmö and the eightieth parallel and back would mean twenty-nine abstinent days. But the women he knew in Rome were incorrigible gossips. The party, among others, would surely disapprove of his mission, he knew, and though the women available through his Palermo connections were bound by *omertà*, all of them wore black. The foreigner, an American he had met on the docks near his boat, wore a tight bikini by day and Mexican lace dresses at night. She was unlikely ever to breathe a word to the party, and he would leave her at Malmö, or if she turned out to be any kind of inconvenience, later at Palermo. Her name was Deborah Colt.

The good witch had provided, and Miklos Brody had, after all, known the way.

CHAPTER NINE

THE DIRECTOR OF SVENSKA NUKLEAR AB, Sven Gustafsson, told Zack Robertts by telephone, while Jean-Marie and Shiva listened in, that he was "deeply interested" in public relations, which was good for security, and that he would be happy to explain the plant's safeguard system, characterized by him as "impenetrable."

He said, however, that he rarely visited the Uppsala installation, since he was considered a potential hostage, "Class A." If this had been meant to impress him as a sign of efficiency or otherwise, it was lost on Zack Robertts, who instead sympathized with whoever might be in "Class B" or below. He failed to understand why Gustafsson could not just as easily, if not more so, be seized elsewhere, but perhaps there were reasons nonetheless. In any event, he was certain that O.N.A.N.'s prospective attempt to break in precluded the taking of hostages, if only to preserve secrecy, so he thought no more of the issue.

Gustafsson, who had the try-hard-to-please telephone voice of an encyclopedia salesman, said that he was prepared to meet Zack Robertts and Shiva Subrahmayan at his office in Stockholm, where he had a three-dimensional scale model of the entire facility, security system and all. The earliest possible time, he said apologetically, was Sunday, June 3, at four in the afternoon, which was days off, but Jean-Marie nodded for Zack Robertts to accept.

Zack Robertts waited for Sunday. He was left in virtual solitary confinement from mid-week on. Olle stood guard and brought him food, and Tommy Kaneoka came around now and then to putter with the nuclear bomb. But the others vanished completely, and even Vicky no longer returned to the room next to his, which he was beginning to find disappointing. He imagined that they were working on the conference report, having a difficult time without his editorial guidance. He felt sure that he had guessed correctly, yet he dismissed such thoughts as vanity and vexation of spirit.

He wanted *something* immediate to be vanity and vexation of spirit. He had been abandoned with nothing to read but the Bible, which was fine with him, though he had stopped reading the King James Version, except for comparative purpose, when the more scholarly and more sensibly written New English translation appeared. He made a hopeless attempt to recall how the latter had rendered the Tower of Babel episode; the King James would have to do. He read it hour after hour, particularly his favorite Old Testament book, *Ecclesiastes*. He empathized to the full with the Preacher, who after a lifetime of having seen *all* "the works done under the sun," had concluded that *all* was vanity and vexation of spirit.

Zack Robertts thought again of escape, but not very seriously now. For the first time in a long time he was *involved*. As Deborah had expressed it, "getting more and more into —— and it is helping me to relax, open up and let myself experience things. It's tremendously liberating. True!" Olle had to sleep sometime, and Zack Robertts kept an eye on his movements to establish his pattern. But when a man equal his size and demeanor showed up the first night to relieve him, Zack Robertts willingly discarded the idea. He could no longer leave in the middle; the end was the blank he was "into." It had to come sooner than O.N.A.N. expected, but he felt himself drawn by the magnets at the Pole. He wondered if his watch would stop there.

He missed daylight, even the nagging northern sun, but that was all. He ran in place for half an hour in the morning and did pushups in the late afternoon. He no longer constricted. He felt an unblunted excitement that had left him years ago. When he was not reading the Bible, he tried to project how he would write of his adventures with O.N.A.N., but the attempts were useless. For him, this was an adventure as unpredictable as every wave in the sea had been to Columbus, and while that was a cause of uneasiness, he was anything but bored. He explored the meager spaces allotted to him, which he magnified by care in observation, examining, for example, the antiques stored in the room inch by inch. The only ones of personal interest to him were the few pieces of eighteenth-century country furniture, and even among those only the fastenings that held them together intrigued him. He had learned to recognize the handmade nails of earlier centuries by the heads in fashion with the blacksmiths of different times, and while they could not always be relied on alone for dating, it was fun to know.

When Tommy Kaneoka came to putter, they talked about the bomb, breaking into the plutonium vault, and later on, about life in general. Tommy chuckled when Zack Robertts told him that Gustafsson had claimed that his plant was impenetrable. "If one guy can get in, so can another," he said without boasting, speaking flawless American English. When he was eighteen, he recounted, he and two other "good men" had robbed a Tokyo bank that had also been pompously advertised as "impenetrable." Its vault had been watched by a radarlike, ultrasonic sensor that could detect any movement in the field of its transmitted waves and trigger an alarm. "They don't use that one anymore," said Tommy with a punctuating wink of his eye.

Observation, study, and preparation were the keys that could open any lock, which was a method Zack Robertts understood. Security systems, or parts of it, Tommy said, had to be shut down sometime or other so that people could work. But when people were around, a job could get "messy," and it was a much more rewarding experience to whip a machine at its own game, outwitting it in the stillness of night.

Safecracking was the easiest part; alarms were the thing to beat. He knew of few vaults in the world that could resist an electric arc whose electrodes were fed by pure oxygen, and fewer still that could stand up to a 3.5-inch bazooka. In the Tokyo robbery they had used the arc, but he had also had occasion to use the bazooka. As for the ultrasonic sensor, he said that all alarms, no matter how sophisticated they might be, always had their own specific "neutralizers," which were usually far simpler in design. In Tokyo, inside the bank, they had built an ordinary wooden platform, a bridge above the acoustic beams, from which they worked with impunity to the steady hum of the wave transmitter. With superior knowledge of how a safeguard had been made and a brain at least the equal to the maker's, you could beat any system.

He spoke in a way that conveyed the sense of pleasure he felt at hurdling obstructions by a leap of the mind. Small, personal satisfaction, to be sure, which Zack Robertts imagined to be like the feeling of dating a sideboard by its nails.

You needed luck, too, Tommy admitted, shaking his head in reflection. When after seven or eight hours of grueling labor they had finally entered the "impenetrable" vault they expected millions, of course, but had found it as empty as a dead fish's stare. Only a single foreign coin lay waiting inside to receive them. They had cased the bank for months but could never figure why there was no money in the vault; the embarrassing failure of the vaunted ultrasonic system would not be publicly revealed. An unforeseeable quirk in the perennial routine had repaid all their trouble with a thin

American dime. Tommy Kaneoka grinned: ". . . and we had a helluva time splitting it three ways!"

Tommy became a sort of friend. Zack Robertts assumed he was a hired expert, a free lance like himself. But when he gathered enough audaciousness to ask him, "How much are they paying you, Tommy?" Tommy looked at him offendedly and said, "You don't do things like this for money, Zack. You do it for your kids."

Zack Robertts shut up, and their friendship, such as it was, did not suffer much. Zack Robertts had rudely overstepped its boundaries. At least Tommy had not said Good Cause or Higher Morality, and fortunately, he had no kids.

He was born in 1946. His mother was from an old landed family near Osaka, where their peasants grew flowers even during the war. She left after the bombs, profaning sacred tradition by announcing that she was going to live in Tokyo alone and had every intention of marrying outside her "tribe." Instead, she lived in Tokyo with an American GI named Tommy from Passaic (Tommy-what, she never knew) and did not marry at all. Big Tommy went home to New Jersey before Tommy-*chan* came along and Big Tommy was not heard of again, although Tommy-*chan* knew many GIs in his childhood. His mother died in occupied Tokyo, ramming the PX Bakery in a stolen car, and his grandparents proved unable to reconcile broken sacred tradition with Tommy's presence in their home, but they found him other homes as required.

Tommy was rich at eighteen (not all his luck in crime was bad). He was poorer at twenty, but with sufficient will and resources to start fresh in the U.S.A. He studied engineering at the University of Michigan, where, standing consistently at the top of his class, he was considered by his fellow students as the "yellow peril." While still at Ann Arbor, in graduate school, he paid his way as a research assistant in computer technology, working under Pentagon contracts. But this was the sixties and Tommy was getting "political." The Pentagon was not pleased, and very soon afterwards, neither were the FBI and Immigration; the latter inviting the "yellow peril" to leave, the former transferring his file to the CIA.

He hated Tokyo, which had suddenly become a "center of capitalist exploitation." He enrolled at Tokyo University. He worked, when he had to, for various electronics companies in the Marunouchi district, for Hitachi, Sony, and J.T. and T. — a spectacular feat in a country where job-hopping went against the rule. In his own land the "yellow peril" was known as the "American" and the "boy genius." His fields were quantum mechanics and the more marketable microwave circuitry. But he spent less time in Marunouchi (or at the university) than in the tiny upstairs and downstairs bars of Juku, where students lived well on Japanese "scotch," sashumi with seaweed and the petals of chrysanthemum, and the heady, after-midnight air of the coming revolution.

Here they called him Tommy-*san*, the honorable, a reputation earned by his avocational expertise in the weaponry and burglar's tools needed for the coming revolution. But the Honshu revolution began to appear long in coming and Tommy-*san* made impatient trips abroad, lingering in Amsterdam and in Beirut, which was when terror imported from Japan first became a plausible idea. Tommy's reputation grew. One day, he heard from Jean-Marie.

On Sunday, everyone came back. It was like a class reunion. Vicky, beaming, kissed Zack Robertts on both cheeks. Shiva shook his hand, which he regarded as being more familiar than the simple *namaskar*. Jean-Marie apologized to him for not having provided newspapers and some "serious wine." Tommy slapped his back. Zack Robertts felt good, and while he did not care much for Muhammed Rahmani and Phil E. Stein, he was beginning to take to the silent stolidity of Ibrahim.

They held a brief meeting, during which Jean-Marie reviewed the latest developments. The conference report was slowly but unquestionably progressing. The *Colomba Bianca* was on its way to Malmö. "Friends" had made a sizable contribution for whatever expenses the group might incur. All that remained to be done in Uppsala — the hardest part, he granted — was securing the plutonium "bit" and assembling the core of the bomb. After that, the Arctic. There was not a shadow of aroused suspicion and, thus, nothing to fear but catching cold. The mood was bracing, and Zack Robertts thought he saw even Ibrahim move his lips in a fleeting smile.

In the afternoon, with Olle close behind him and Shiva at his side, Zack Robertts felt the sun and unconditioned air sweeten his skin. He was ushered from a service door to the Volvo, which stood in a courtyard exhausting gray smoke from the rear, and he knew that this must have been the way he had been carried in days ago, probably on Olle's clifflike back.

They sped across the plain on the same airport road as before. The windows worked. He opened his and let the wind wash his face and his hair. He was like a dog let out, and if he had had a tail he would not have been able to sit. Shiva and he were in the back. She had nothing to say. She hugged the side of her door and, right from the start, she had lowered the armrest between them. He made attempts at conversation, closing off Olle's ears with the plate glass divider. Her responses were short, final words. He watched her here and there from the corner of his eye and more than once found her looking at him in a melancholy way. He tried to decipher the hieroglyph of the intrusive armrest, but if it were meant as a *cordon sanitaire*, was it for her or for him?

"What does the K stand for?" he asked her.

She looked at him with a wrinkle around her eyes.

"Your name."

"Krishna."

"The I?"

"Indra."

These were all names of male deities — Krishna, Indra, and Shiva — rarely given to girls, and the spelling of her surname was an oddity too; perhaps there was a streak of snobbishness in her family, but Zack Robertts saw no reason to ask. Instead he said, "You have so many beautiful, significant names. How do you like to be called?"

"It depends on who is calling."

"Shall I call you . . . Abraham?"

She turned to him. "I'm sorry, I don't understand."

Zack Robertts stared at her with his journalist's eyes until she looked away.

"Would you mind closing the window?" she asked peering straight ahead. "I'm cold."

She folded her arms across her breasts and held herself tightly together, rubbing below her shoulders.

Zack Robertts obeyed. To every thing there is a season, said the Preacher, and a time to every purpose.

They passed Arlanda, reaching the new towns of Stockholm within an hour. Then they slowed by Lake Mälar, taken up by the traffic flowing toward the island city center.

Gustafsson's office was in the Hötorgscity in an eighteen-story building rising from a mall, and when they arrived they were a half-hour early and the entrance was locked. The streets were empty and the shops were closed except for a bookstore named PUB. They bought a map of the city and wandered as far as Gamla Staden, the medieval old town. They strolled like sightseers in the echo of their heels on the cobbles. Olle tagged behind, his hands deep in the pockets of his trench coat, undoubtedly clutching his unerring Magnum.

It was cold, more like a day in a January thaw than the third of June, but the sun helped to harmonize the difference. By the water they got a look at the seventeenth-century imperial warship *Vasa*, which stood across the bay. It had gone down on its maiden voyage in Gustavus II's time and it was dredged and restored as good as new three centuries later. Zack Robertts had little details like that at his fingertips and more about Swedish history and architecture. Shiva listened.

On the way back, they walked up and down steps, detouring slightly to see the Italianate Royal Palace, and when the woman sentry wearing combat dress stiffened to attention (for no one but them, it seemed), she raised her automatic rifle to the ready, which made Olle jump and hustle them away. They laughed. Shiva appeared to be loosening, and on crossing a narrow street, barely wider than a suddenly oncoming tram, he instinctively took her hand, and they ran as she gathered her sari, leaving Olle standing as thin as he could against the stone buildings behind them. Her hand remained in his, unconsciously perhaps, until Olle caught up. She withdrew it. It might have meant nothing; but they both knew that they both knew that it did. Her hand had felt cold and moist.

Gustafsson was as genial as he was cooperative, and his confidence in the inviolability of Svenska Nuklear's security proved to be not without foundation. He protruded like potatoes in a sack from a tan, high collared sweater, which Zack Robertts was sure he wore only on weekends, and he served chocolates and small bottles of effervescent water. He was straightforward and precise, and he had a peculiarity of speech: he made an audible gasp when he drew breath between words, and this disconcerted Zack Robertts, who imagined each time that their deception had been suddenly uncovered.

He swiveled in a black chair upholstered in plastic, and when as often he got up to illustrate fine points on the three-dimensional scale model of the plant, the chair sprung forward and rolled free on its wheels, only to groan loudly on the pain of his weighty return.

His favorite word was "impenetrable," of course, and "in principle" was a phrase he used more than once, notably when asked if one could obtain a blueprint of the nonclassified features of the security system.

He kept them two hours, leaving nothing to guess at. Olle studied his fingernails. Shiva took copious notes, and Zack Robertts cringed at the lies he was forced to invent. He adjourned them promptly at six, saying quite matter-of-factly that they were already late for a "little supper" his wife was preparing at his home near suburban Farsta. Zack Robertts was a willing would-be guest, if not very hungry at so early an hour, but Olle's face expressed rude disapproval, prompting Shiva to make polite, collective excuses. Gustafsson insisted. He said that they simply had to get a glimpse of the nuclear plant at Ågesta, which heated all Farsta and could be seen on the way, and when that brought only further hesitation, he added, grinning coyly, that the copy of the blueprint they wanted could only be acquired after engaging the defense ministry bureaucracy — that, too, "impenetrable" — or from a desk drawer at his home. The choice was irresistible.

They drove in separate cars, Olle following Gustafsson, who saved them from an embarrassment by suggesting that he go alone so that Shiva and Zack Robertts could discuss their meeting in privacy. In the Volvo, Shiva went over her notes, which she had made on hotel stationery folded neatly in half. She raised her eyebrows often and finally put her papers aside.

"What do you think?" she asked him.

" 'Impenetrable.' . . . Agree?"

" 'In principle.' "

They exchanged smiles.

"You look almost disappointed," she said with discerning eyes.

"Oh, Jean-Marie'll dream up something else . . . Let's see, there must be a way of getting the plague into mother's milk."

She looked away from him.

It *was* true; he *was* disappointed, if that were a word to describe a feeling of sliding into the absurd, of watching the entire affair end in a "little supper" in suburbia. Gustafsson's system had stood up to his claims, or at least he had been overwhelmingly convincing. Yet Zack Robertts could never accept prosaic justice, which was akin to the justice of getting through life without being flattened by a truck or coming down with pernicious leukemia. A thing, this thing, had to run its course or it would be nothing, and Jean-Marie, or whoever did his dreaming, *would* get the plague into mother's milk. Zack Robertts was rooting for Tommy Kaneoka, but Tommy, he knew, would have to think hard.

The Svenska Nuklear plutonium recovery plant occupied 4000 square meters, or an acre, in a clearing surrounded by woods. There was no other structure in the vicinity, not for a mile in any direction, and unless one walked through the woods, the plant could only be approached by a service road that ran along a one-way railroad siding going into the building and out.

The clearing lay within a double chain-link fence, a perfect square, 100 meters corner to corner. The fence was twice the height of a man, barbed at the top, and wired to trip an alarm if cut. But in fact it served only a superficial purpose, to keep out the merely curious or petty vandals. Anyone attempting a serious incursion could easily find a way to vault or tunnel the fence.

On the principle that guards invited the taking of hostages, there was none. The entire plant was unmanned 90 percent of the time, and when shipments of spent uranium arrived for processing, they were invariably accompanied by a heavily armed escort of the Swedish military.

The area around the plant, 18.5 meters, or about sixty feet, from the building to the fence on any perpendicular line, was patroled by dogs, Doberman pinschers, who were fed by a machine and trained by the army to kill. Inside the compound night never fell; whether the sun was up or down, or obscured by clouds, high-intensity lamps bathed the enclosure in an even stadium light that could sometimes be seen from as far as Stockholm.

The outer walls of the building were made of reinforced concrete 1.5 meters, or five feet, thick. The windows were of an equal thickness, and each consisted of a dozen panels of glass in a sealed frame, weighing ten tons per unit. The doors were made of layers of high-carbon, drill-proof steel, with an outer layer of high-thermal-conduction copper. This latter property acted as a heat dissipator, rendering the doors resistant to acetylene torches and explosives. Walls, windows, and doors contained heat- and pressure-sensitive alarms, and over the front door there was a bronze plaque with a Gustafssonian touch that read: "Wide is the gate, and broad is the way, that leadeth to destruction . . . Security first."

It was theoretically possible to enter the building by means of a labyrinthine ventilation system, whose ducts terminated at various points along the walls and on the roof. The surfaces around these baffled openings, however, were alarm-responsive to touch or weight, and unless one could somehow be shot through the slats covering these holes without brushing their sides, they were fail-safe.

Inside, beyond the lethally radioactive zones, an array of

electronic devices stood sentry. They formed the components of three complete, independently powered systems, and should one or two of them fail, any could do the work of all.

The plutonium strongroom, as might be expected, was protected best. It was equipped with many of the same safeguards installed in the silos containing the U.S. nuclear armed missiles that were ready for firing. Embedded in both sides of the walls and the ceiling, no deeper than the point of a nail, were interlocking networks of sensors that were alarm-responsive to any rupture of the surface, including a scratch. The entire floor reacted to any force in excess of fifteen grams per square centimeter, which meant that a mouse could stand on or run across it with immunity, even a cat, but no human being could do either, not a child, midget, or dwarf. But a mouse or a cat, too, would not go undetected; the strongroom was watched by four-channel, closed-circuit television, each channel, like all of the strongroom systems, energized by separate generators.

The plutonium ingots themselves were stacked on shelves in the strongroom inside a vault. Made of the same materials as the outside doors, the vault could only be opened — without engaging the alarm — by knowing the combination of the lock. The combination was a variable controlled by a computer that altered the eight-digit number every ten seconds. Thus, the combination was literally known to no one, at least for no longer than ten seconds at a time. To get into the vault it was necessary to employ another computer programmed to predict what the number would be in a prespecified ten-second period — say, at 11:17:25 three days hence. The second computer was located in an equally, if differently, protected facility forty miles south of Uppsala, in the Ministry of Defense.

The Svenska Nuklear security system, or complex of systems, was continuously monitored by three police units, none of which was more than seven minutes away from the Uppsala plant. At any given moment, each unit consisted of no less than fifteen men trained in, and equipped with, advanced weaponry, and this response was reinforced by a contingent of the armed forces that could reach the plant within a half hour. Moreover, if the security system were breached, the intruders would have no knowledge of the alert until the police arrived. All of the alarms were silent.

Gustafsson lived in an old wooden house with an enormous oak and a lawn in the back, which was where the "little supper" was given. The chill in the air was pronounced, but tradition was such that in June, as long as the sun was shining, guests were received in the garden. Gustafsson's wife, a gaunt woman with a sallow complexion and wistful eyes, greeted them amiably and handed out bulky knit sweaters. Olle preferred not to part with his trench coat.

Their children were personable adolescents who spoke English well. The girl, a sixteen year old who had an interest in Scandinavian peasant costumes, wore a red and white dress in the fashion of Queen Kristina's era, and the thirteen-year-old boy, Harald, introduced himself as a filmmaker, inviting the company to view his latest production after the meal. It was going to be a long evening.

Others had been invited, too: the neighbors next door (a middle-aged couple, both of them mathematicians), a plump widow who ran a pottery shop in the old town, and two of Gustafsson's staff, a boy and a girl from the mailroom, who were still in their teens and who, Gustafsson declared in good fun, were coming late every day to the office since one had moved in with the other.

Zack Robertts enjoyed Gustafsson's avuncular style. He forgot everyone's name on hearing it, but he immediately liked them all. Years had passed since he had seen so many unfettered happy faces, and his was among them. Shiva was as graciously Indian as a well-played *raga*, and Olle, too, who had somehow been placed at the head of the table, seemed to be getting on splendidly with the widow. She was seated beside him, filling his plate.

Almost everyone took a hand in the serving. They ate smoked reindeer first, then sweet matjes herrings accompanied by steaming, boiled new potatoes, sour cream, and a flat, brown, hard bread that looked like a cracker with craters. They drank various qualities of aquavit all along, and when it seemed everything had been finally consumed, bowls of fresh strawberries were brought to the table, which was de rigueur for the season, as was the delight one was bound to express in the eating.

Earlier, when Zack Robertts had been introduced as a writer, sometimes of books and of films, Harald had been visibly thrilled for a full twenty minutes, and the mathematicians had inquired uneasily about what he thought of Lagerkvist and Sjöberg (one author apiece). But now, after a swift and pleasing transition, the table talk was all strawberries. Zack Robertts preferred it that way, and was as transported as Harald had been on learning that the domestic strawberry crop was not actually in yet and what they were eating with such wolfish joy had been imported from Italy. Obviously, there were spaces for innovation in the native tradition, and he liked that. His leanings were always to the side of a tolerant people, loose to the rituals of an unknowable past.

The drinking of aquavit endured long after supper, increasing, with waning interest in quality, as the evening temperature dropped. By the time the party withdrew for Harald's film, all the bottles were empty, though fresh ones were being opened inside. Shiva had the rare, admirable trait of being a nonpious religious abstainer, who went along with the mood.

Zack Robertts was a consummate drinker, embraced gently by spirits and hardly ever crassly let go. Olle was drunk.

Apparently he was also uncomfortably warm. He removed his trench coat, tossed it carelessly aside, and as the lights went down, he opened his collar and put his Neanderthal arm around the waist of the widow. Zack Robertts and Shiva, who sat side by side, saw all.

Harald's film was precocious, and the boy, operating the projector deftly, glanced around for approval, especially from Zack Robertts, the writer. His parents certified his pride and his yearning and the others were full of praise. Zack Robertts was distracted, however, training one eye on Olle and feeling Shiva's on him. At one point, the trench coat fell to the floor with a thud. Shiva grew rigid. Olle was oblivious. Zack Robertts sipped from a glass that had been refilled many times, but he retained all the presence of mind and physical agility required to seize, if he chose to, and gain control of the Magnum in an instant. Still, the prospect of rising gun in hand, interrupting Harald's evening and the good feelings aroused in the others, was utterly distasteful to him. He knew that he could also take the gun stealthily, hoping to use it later without offending good form, but he thought of himself, too, of rooting for Tommy Kaneoka, of the course that had to be run. The film, which showed children in the roles of women and men, splashed colors and sound all around him. He picked up the coat and piled it on a chair, letting it fall silently by the weight of the gun.

Shiva sighed. She squeezed his arm in the dark and whispered brokenly in his ear, "I will come to your room when I can."

CHAPTER TEN

IT TOOK THREE MEN exerting their utmost to carry Olle to his car. He had passed out during the film and now, around 11 P.M., Zack Robertts, Gustafsson, and the mathematician stretched him out on the back seat, while he grunted in stuporous Swedish. The widow covered him with the trench coat.

Shiva and Zack Robertts apologized for Olle. Everyone laughed heroically as snores issued from the Volvo, and even Harald refused to be slighted. The boy asked Zack Robertts for his autograph. His sister kissed his cheek. Gustafsson, at the last moment, ran into the house to get the blueprint of the Uppsala plant, all thought of which had slipped out of mind. While they waited, Mrs. Gustafsson invited them back whenever they might be nearby. Zack Robertts felt like a cur.

Finally, they took leave, and when Zack Robertts started the engine, the widow came up to his window.

"Please tell him to call me," she said, in a faintly trembling voice lowered so none of her friends could hear.

"I will," he replied.

She smiled. He drove away with waving hands in his rear-view mirror.

"Absolutely charming people," Shiva said, after they had turned onto the northbound road.

"Yeah. If Olle hadn't made such a mess of things we could have stole the kid's projector."

Shiva frowned and they continued in silence until the outskirts of Uppsala, where Zack Robertts stopped the car and got out.

"What are you doing?" she asked worriedly.

"I'm tired of driving."

He helped Olle to his feet. Olle had expelled most of his dissoluteness in turbulent sleep, and after he vomited in a drainage ditch by the side of the road, he seemed reasonably restored. He bolted for his coat, and finding everything in order, he looked at Zack Robertts incredulously.

"She wants you to call her." He made motions with his hands: a telephone; a woman. *"Förstår du?"*

Olle understood.

Olle drove the rest of the way with Shiva up front. Zack Robertts put his feet up in back. Gustafsson, he thought, could lose his job. At least he had salvaged Olle's, and if Olle should ever have to kill him, he had sensed from a passing reflection in his eyes that it would only be done with a measure of regret. He did not for a moment, however, expect an end such as that.

They arrived past midnight. Jean-Marie and Tommy Kaneoka were waiting for them. Jean-Marie looked like a father who had stayed up late for his daughter and he demanded an accounting of their time.

Shiva began to explain, but when Zack Robertts produced the blueprint, Jean-Marie lost interest in her and he rolled it open across the table like a paper hanger. It did not contain many technical details, none that might jeopardize the systems. It was the sort of schematic drawing used in newspaper illustrations, indicating the extent, types, and positions of the alarm network, but not how they functioned.

Jean-Marie looked at it bewilderedly. Tommy stood beside him, unsheathing a Sanyo scientific calculator from a leather case. Shiva summarized what Gustafsson had told them, as Jean-Marie sulked. Zack Robertts found a small pleasure in watching him despair.

Tommy Kaneoka pulled up a chair and began working over

the blueprint with consuming intensity. He tapped numbers on the calculator with the hand movements of a musician and the instrument responded in a soft blue light that expanded and contracted to the virtuoso's touch. The sides of his cheeks pumped rhythmically, and, as was his habit, he continually shook away a falling lock of hair. He shot questions at Shiva and Zack Robertts, most of which they were unable to answer since they had failed to inquire at the source ("You mean you didn't ask if the generators were three-phase?"). He chewed his lips in ripples of frustration; occasionally he smiled at a thought inside his head, and all along he scribbled in kana Japanese, making rows of crooked walls with a green felt pen.

Suddenly, he dropped his tools and pushed himself and his chair from the edge of the table. He wrinkled up his boy-genius face, scratched his head, rubbed his eyes, and yawned.

"I've got to get some sleep," he said, returning his calculator to its case.

Jean-Marie was irked. "We will all sleep better if you can tell us, Kaneoka, whether you have any ideas."

Tommy stood. He radiated an appreciation of his own worth that shielded him from any attempt at intimidation by Jean-Marie. He simply shrugged.

"Only one, so far . . . thanks to Zack Robertts," he said nodding in his direction and smiling.

"Which is?" Jean-Marie asked, unamused.

"Well," Tommy said stretching his words, "we're going to need a *lot* of inflatable rafts."

Everyone stared at him. He said something about seeing them all in the morning and walked out.

"The inscrutable Oriental," Jean-Marie said sourly, gathering some papers together and starting for the door. "Are you coming, Shiva?"

Her eyes fell on Zack Robertts, who trapped them in his like a spider.

"Yes . . . Of course."

They left. Zack Robertts knew no more than they did about what Tommy Kaneoka had meant, but he was pleased at his acuity in having foreseen a good financial investment. He went to his room and waited for Shiva.

He freshened himself with cold water and paced the floor, finishing the few remaining drops of cognac from the bottle Vicky had brought him some nights before. He listened for Vicky. Her room was still and he supposed she was sleeping, or, poor Vicky, working with Jean-Marie. He hoped for everyone's sake that she would not slip into his room, not tonight. There were suddenly too many women in his life, which felt good, like having too much money in the bank.

He forgot about danger, or relegated it to the sack of inevitables all men carried on their back and so grew accustomed to its weight. He thought of his life now as being like that of the obscure fifteenth-century man whom he himself had discovered in his erratic studies of French. His name was Jean d'Orreville, who was from Picardy, and who, for reasons he never cared to divulge, called himself "Cabaret." He was the first free lancer. He traveled around Europe living on "advances," putting words together for this duke or that prince, then going on his way. Zack Robertts wondered if Cabaret had ever found the way home. He thought of the king of El Dorado's advice about when you came across a place where you felt comfortable you ought to remain. Perhaps that was all finding the way home really meant, and when you found it, you stayed there. Zack Robertts was getting comfortable in this kinky El Dorado of his day.

Shiva knocked at his door at two in the morning. She had changed her sari, added highlights to her hair, and she wore old silver around her neck and an emerald on her nose.

"The sun is shining brightly," she said. The white of her

eyes and her teeth against the black of her skin were like distant suns themselves. The emerald was like a planet.

"You are beautiful," he said.

"I feel beautiful . . . And you may touch me."

He did. He brushed her face with the side of his hand, and her head leaned and revolved in pursuit of the sensation.

"Krishna?"

"Yes. Say Krishna when we make love."

He drew her close to him, and she moved as if she were a leaf given by the wind.

"We are making love," she said when they were, which was soon.

"To all intents and purposes."

"I have a feeling . . ."

"Mmmm."

". . . I shall become . . ."

"Mmmm."

". . . very excited."

"That happens sometimes."

"When I do . . ."

"Mmmm."

". . . I shall have a desire . . ."

"Mmmm."

". . . to cry out . . . loudly."

"Don't be inhibited." He hoped it would not be too loud.

"Then . . ."

"Mmmm."

". . . I may do something . . ."

"Mmmm."

". . . which you will surely find . . ."

"Mmmm."

". . . 'unusual.' "

"I look forward to it, Krishna."

"I am happy you said Krishna."

"It was easy."

She began to cry out in a pitch that grew more and more emphatic. It seemed she would burst and he hoped no one would be disturbed, though he imagined she had somehow come to terms with Olle. Then she did something he considered "unusual" indeed, her exclamations rising still. He tried to identify, repeat, and embellish whatever brought on the cries, until, in one final, shattering series of shrieks, she fainted — in a heavenly swoon.

Zack Robertts would have been overwhelmed with marvel were he not somewhat concerned, but she recovered in a moment or two, and taking his hand gently, she explained everything without uttering a single word.

They lay in the semidarkness while their pulse returned to normal. At last, Shiva spoke.

"Tonight, you will know all of my secrets, Zack Robertts."

"Like the name of your employer in Washington?"

She sat and crossed her legs Indian style. "How did you know?"

"You're the only one who acts like your job is in danger."

"It's more than that," she said, lying back again. "Kama is a stronger master."

"You killed Hanumappa, didn't you?"

This time she shot up in a rage. "How could you have made love to me, if you believe that?"

"Kama is a stronger master."

"It happened exactly as I told you. Suicide. I shall always be convinced of that. He often said he would kill himself, and he tried to more than once." She paused for a while, holding tears at bay; then she continued. "He *was* my guru, and I loved him with all the humility that was due to him. But he was mad, Zack, absolutely mad, and in his madness he thought I, and all the world, had betrayed him. He began working with Jean-Marie. I knew what was going on. I was approached by the CIA. But in spite of everything, I wanted no part of it. I was threatened, by a loathsome creature . . . I . . . Krishna had compromised herself in her life, in a selfish, personal way. I . . . I accepted. Now I'm not sorry."

She finished speaking on a narrow edge of strength, which suddenly gave way, however, and she wept pouring the sorrow from her eyes. Zack Robertts had no wish to pry further. She wiped her tears away and told him how her mission would end.

"We shall be intercepted. That is all that I know for certain. I assume it shall come when all the evidence against O.N.A.N. is gathered or easily seized. Aboard the ship, I should guess."

"One more question?"

She nodded.

"Why ziggurat?"

"I don't know what you mean."

Zack Robertts sat up now. "You're not Abraham?" he asked watching her with the polygraph of his eyes.

Her voice rose indignantly. "Who in God's name is this Abraham you keep harping on?"

He stared at her with pain on the ridge of his brow. "I don't know," he said weakly.

Shiva left shortly afterward. Vicky looked into the room at six. Zack Robertts was asleep, but his head cocked at the sound of the door and he opened one eye.

"Oh," Vicky said. "I didn't mean to . . ."

"What time is it?"

"Very early. Go back to sleep . . . I've been up all night working with Jean-Marie. I thought . . ."

His eyes closed. "Are you Abraham?" he mumbled.

"You're dreaming, Zack."

"I guess so."

"I'm Vicky, remember? The one who's dying to fuck?"

"Later, Vicky, later."

"I don't mean now, you clod. I'm drained. But I can see I'm going to have to try harder."

He was asleep again. His personal security system was a functionless tangle. If the good witch were not watching over him, Zack Robertts would never find the way home.

The O.N.A.N. group met that afternoon at Tommy Kaneoka's request. He wore a freshly laundered black turtleneck tucked into jeans. He stood in front of a blackboard, on which he had sketched the main features of Gustafsson's blueprint. He explained how they would break into the Svenska Nuklear plant. They were all present, Zack Robertts, too, and their silent attention was witness to their eagerness to learn how.

"Most of this stuff," Tommy began, pointing to the blackboard with his green felt pen, "is just window dressing, which doesn't concern us at all. Whoever designed this junkpile was robbing Svenska Nuklear blind. Ninety percent of the hardware is useless, since the only thing that needs this kind of sophisticated protection is the plutonium strongroom. It's got it, all right, but the weaknesses are glaring and sometimes just dumb."

Zack Robertts, like everyone else, studied the blackboard. The flaws were less than apparent. But Tommy spoke with the derisive surety of an old plumber called in to redress the sins of a cost-cutting contractor, and one knew from the start that Tommy was the man for the job.

"Look at the ventilation system," he went on with unyielding scorn. "You could send a tank through it, right into the strongroom, if you knew how to beat the alarm, which I do. The reason they made it so wide was to make less work and sell more alarms. If it'd been built right, the pipes'd be thick as my thumb, and they wouldn't have needed any alarm."

He indicated a small outbuilding along the inside perimeter of the fence. "And look at the generators. They spend millions on a jungle of wires for the plant and leave the generators up for grabs. If we had some hard data on them, we could probably walk into the plant through the front door, wearing squeaky shoes."

"But we do not have this data," Jean-Marie blurted with his insufferable captiousness.

Zack Robertts hoped to one day have an opportunity to give Jean-Marie a brief demonstration on his knowledge of Okinawan karate. One quick chop, in the name of good manners. Until the interruption, he had been enjoying himself immensely, and he had found Tommy's remark about squeaky shoes a quaint eyeopener, an insight into the occult discipline of the cat burglar, who, he suddenly knew, must pass a month of semesters mastering the differential properties of shoes.

"Okay," Tommy said, "we don't, and I'll save you the bother, Jean-Marie, of adding that even if we could get it, there's no time. Now should I go on?"

"Please," he said humorlessly, lighting a Romeo y Julieta.

"Okay. We can't go in the front door. We can't go over the fence, only because we'd have to kill all the dogs. That'd be the surest sign of a break-in, unnecessarily limiting our getaway time to Malmö. Besides, I like dogs . . . So, we go in from the top."

He tapped his pen on a chimney connecting to the ventilation system and leading through a maze in the walls to the interior of the strongroom.

"That means a helicopter. A four-hundred horsepower, French-built Le Fort–17 would be perfect. It's almost as light as an eagle and makes hardly more noise than a fan. I don't know where you're going to get one, Jean-Marie, but that's the kind we need."

"It should not be impossible," Jean-Marie said starting a shopping list.

"Good. Now, the roof is wired for weight, but we don't touch it. The chopper comes in low, hitting zero air speed at twenty-five or thirty feet. One of us goes down the tow line right into the shaft to a bend in the duct, where he settles in. A second man sends down the equipment and then follows him in. Two good men are all we need."

"And the equipment?" Jean-Marie asked.

"No problem. All supermarket stuff."

"Very well," said Jean-Marie. "You have two 'good men' — one of them yourself, I hope — inside the duct that opens on the strongroom. I presume you have made provision for the helicopter, which cannot simply hover above you until it runs out of fuel, or is seen by a passing plane, or who knows what else. But what then? You have not forgotten the safeguards inside, I am sure. The vault, for example."

"Safecracking is the easiest part; alarms are the thing to beat." Tommy looked directly at Zack Robertts, who understood now that what he was repeating was tried-and-true dogma from an underworld catechism. He knew, on faith alone, that Tommy had the whole system on its knees, and was only biting back at Jean-Marie.

"There are only two alarms that matter at this point," Tommy continued. "One, the closed-circuit television cameras. Four of them. My hunch is that what they transmit has a lower audience interest than a test pattern ..." He paused waiting for Jean-Marie to criticize, and when he opened his mouth to do so, Tommy put up his hand like a traffic policeman, and went on, "... *but*, naturally we have to assume that it's being watched by the whole Swedish Army."

His words gained velocity as he spoke, and his enthusiasm swelled. He was full of smiles and energetic gestures. When his hair fell on his eyes, he was too busy to brush it away. He looked like Toscanini.

"Okay. What happens when you project a strong light

source, say, from a flashbulb, into a TV camera? It drives electrons crazy. The picture goes black, for a minute, maybe — that's something I still have to figure out — but for as long as you want if you keep firing bulbs. Now, say, a cop is watching the screen. Remember, no alarm has gone off. He scratches his head, slaps the monitor around, and after a while the picture clears. Everything returns to normal. But by then the two of us are in the strongroom."

"That sounds a little magical," said Jean-Marie.

"It is. It is. I do it with mirrors. Or, at least with lenses and cameras. Polaroids. Get it?"

No one seemed to quite understand, but by now he had won everyone over, and even Jean-Marie did not question him further.

"Two. The pressure-sensitive floor. It's set to trip the alarm at fifteen grams per square centimeter. Remember that number: fifteen . . . I don't know if I'm the lightest one here — ladies excluded — but I may be, and my weight, one hundred and thirty-three pounds, stripped, reads out to plus or minus one hundred and four grams per square centimeter. That means I'm seven times over the maximum. But it looks like our alarm designer never heard of a snowshoe-effect, or if he did, he kept it to himself . . ."

Shoes again! Zack Robertts thought. He perceived immediately where Tommy was headed.

"If an Eskimo in trapping gear and snowshoes can walk on ten feet of wet, freshly laid snow, there ought to be a way to walk on the strongroom floor. There is: inflatable rafts. And I'm going to fill them with helium to give them lift, just like those guys who sell kids balloons. They'll float like balloons, too, until we get on them. And when that happens, I calculate that on every square meter of helium-filled raft, my weight is redistributed on an average of one point eight grams per square centimeter — eight times *under* the maximum . . . I could ride a horse in that strongroom — and so can the man who comes with me!"

If Ibrahim were not such a rock; if Shiva were not with the CIA; if Muhammed were not so enamored of his beard; Vicky so adoring of Jean-Marie; Phil E. Stein so stuff-nosed; Olle so monolingual; Zack Robertts so alone; and if Jean-Marie had not broken the mood with an asinine question, there would have been cheers for Tommy-*san*. Instead, Jean-Marie brought up the vault, as if Tommy would have neglected it.

"This is how the safe works," Tommy said in a rapid-fire reply. "An eight-digit combination that changes every ten seconds — apparently randomly, but probably according to a complex mathematical equation with a string of factorials. Which means, even if you knew the equation, it would take more than ten seconds to solve it, and you'd have to start over again. But what happens when you know the *combination*?"

He held up his calculator and lighted an eight-digit number.

"You press buttons like these, installed on the face of the safe. Each button hits a wire behind it, and a specific electrical circuit begins to be formed.

"Okay. An eight-digit number can be arranged in ten to the power of eight different ways. That's one with eight zeros, or a hundred million. If I walked up to the safe and punched out eight digits, I'd have one chance in a hundred million of hitting the jackpot. But if I could punch it a hundred million times in ten seconds, the door to the safe would swing open. I can't do that — not with my fingers, at any rate.

"But suppose we bring in a small computer, say, a third-generation Massey-Nicholson, which weighs under seventy pounds, stripped down — a beautiful machine. She does a million operations a second. We hook her up to hit all the wires behind the buttons on the safe — it's done with a microwave stimulator and a cold tank — and we give her an idiot program: count Massey-Nicholson, just count. She counts to a hundred million, beginning with eight zeros. It takes her a hundred seconds. But in the meantime, the right combination has changed ten times. So, in any ten-second period, the computer has one chance in ten — that's nine to one odds — of hitting the winning number. Well, those odds are better than one in a hundred million, and if you play a nine-to-one shot long enough, it ought to come in."

"How long is enough?" Jean-Marie asked.

"There's no way of knowing. The odds never change, though the probabilities say you should score once every ten tries. You get three hundred and sixty tries in an hour . . . It all depends on luck."

Again Tommy looked at Zack Robertts. He was finished, exhausted. He seemed almost disappointed with himself, as if, in the end, in spite of science and genius, the whole world was ruled by the spin of a wheel.

"Well," said Jean-Marie rubbing his palms together, "it sounds reasonable to me." He scanned the faces around him. "Are we all agreed?"

No one dissented, but Phil E. Stein had something to say.

"I think we ought to congratulate Tommy for a brilliant piece of work."

There was a general rumble of approval, although Jean-Marie leered at Stein, and of course Ibrahim was still.

Tommy grinned boyishly. "This is the fun part. The work comes out there."

"Agreed," said Jean-Marie. "And since we are not here to promote personality cults, Dr. Stein, I suggest we continue . . . Looking around the room, I fail to see anyone as physically prepared as Kaneoka for this assignment."

He was not in fact "looking around the room"; rather he was confronting with sneering aversion Phil E. Stein's more prominent obesities and his habitual snorting. Jean-Marie knew how to carry a grudge, and Stein squirmed underneath it.

Jean-Marie went on. "We shall have to bring in someone from the outside, so to speak. This has been foreseen. I think ——"

"I get to pick my man," Tommy interjected with a peremptory quality in his voice.

"You have more important ——."

"Or, I don't go."

"Naturally, the final decision is yours, but ——."

"I've already picked him."

"And whom, may I ask without interruption, have you already 'picked'?"

One quick chop, Zack Robertts thought.

Tommy replied. "Zack Robertts."

"You are foolish, Kaneoka!"

Tommy seemed not to hear Jean-Marie. He was staring at his man.

"Will you do it, Zack?" he asked.

Zack Robertts felt like someone who had just walked into a glass door. But, as almost always, his face did not betray him. He returned Tommy's stare, and doing his best to fascinate Vicky, he said, "If I get to blow up the balloons."

In his Langley, Virginia, cubicle, Huntz Merriwether was thumbing through the latest issue of *Intercourse in Colours*. Published from time to time in Copenhagen, it had been bought there by an employee of the Central Intelligence Agency and sent to him from the CIA Stockholm Station, making the entire journey in a Department of State diplomatic pouch.

Like most periodicals, *Intercourse in Colours*, edited by a certain P. Kristiansen, had a rather strict format. The editor apparently favored the principle that a color photograph, no matter how ineptly exposed or reproduced, had more value than words, since there was an effusion of the former and absolutely none of the latter. Issue after issue, the first few pages invariably introduced two men, who looked like what Danish seamen look like when they are unemployed. They call on the sparsely furnished apartment of a young woman with blond hair. She always wears black stockings and blue mascara. For reasons never made clear, she takes an immediate fancy to both of them, and as a consequence, everyone decides to undress. For the next sixteen pages or so, they try, not always successfully, to fulfill the promise of the magazine's implied editorial policy, often in collaboration with one another. Finally, the last part of the magazine shows the threesome at rest, featuring a gleaming efflux on the young woman's face.

The only elements that changed from number to number were the actors, their apparel, and the configurations of their anatomical possessions, but one had to be a faithful and careful reader to detect them. Huntz Merriwether was such a reader. He had even discovered, with the aid of his illuminated magnifying glass, that though the furnishings were continually moved around and redecorated in a cursory way, the apartment was always the same. Sometimes he wondered just where in Denmark it might be.

He was not yet half way into the newly arrived issue, when he reminded himself that he had to send a message to the Stockholm Station. This was to be in reply to a brief report that had arrived in the same pouch that had carried *Intercourse in Colours*, which had temporarily distracted him.

Not that Huntz Merriwether was slack; on the contrary, he was a disciplined man with a vigorous initiative. His handling of the Ziggurat affair, which until now had gone precisely to plan, was an exemplar of what up-and-comers in the agency were beginning to call "innovative intelligence."

Years ago, other up-and-comers had called the same thing "preventive intelligence." But they had belonged to a faction that, Huntz Merriwether believed, had been wrong. Many of the contingencies they had sought to prevent had actually been brought on or worsened by their innovations. This had been a mistake. They had caused public embarrassment for the director — not to speak of the dead and the injured — and those up-and-comers went. The new faction, in which Huntz Merriwether hoped to come up, was not wrong. Their concept was not a mistake. It was Right.

"Sister," Huntz Merriwether said ringing for his secretary, Mary Clapperton, "please step inside for a moment."

"Dictation?"

"Dic — tation."

Mary Clapperton entered. She was wearing a black skirt with pleats all around and a white blouse that was made to fit like a shirt. They hung on her almost exactly as they had hung that morning on a hanger in her closet. She sat beside his desk and crossed her legs so that her right heel touched her left ankle.

"You're looking exquisite today, sister."

Mary Clapperton winced. She jiggled her pencil, as if to prod him to business.

Huntz Merriwether picked up his copy of *Intercourse in Colours.* He was flagrant in his leafing through the pages before her eyes. Mary Clapperton jiggled her pencil.

"Telex, Greenland code, to the Stockholm Station," Huntz Merriwether finally began, using his nifty magnifying glass on the middle sixteen pages. "OPERATION ZIGGURAT RE YOUR blah, blah, blah, OF THE blah, blah, blah. FOR ABRAHAM. EYES ONLY."

Huntz Merriwether cleared his throat and wiped his lens with a crumpled, grayish handkerchief, which he left lying on his desk near Mary Clapperton. She jiggled her pencil.

"Where was I? . . . Oh, yes: LEAK — no, kill that — SO-CALLED LEAK IN STOCKHOLM STATION PLUGGED IN YOUR FAVOR. STOP. WOP SHIP . . ."

Mary Clapperton looked at him questioningly.

"You're right, sister. Make it 'destruct after reading.' "

Mary Clapperton winced and made a wiggly line at the top of her steno-book page.

"WOP SHIP," Huntz Merriwether repeated, "ON MALMO COURSE WITH GOOD O."

Huntz Merriwether went back to *Intercourse in Colours*.

"Will that be all?" Mary Clapperton asked.

Huntz Merriwether turned the magazine around and showed her a picture on the last page.

"Don't you think that's shaving cream, sister?"

Mary Clapperton winced. He handed her his lens, insisting on an answer.

"I wouldn't know," she said getting up and leaving the magnifier in his extended hand. "I don't shave."

Mary Clapperton went out. She could feel Huntz Merriwether's eyes on her skinny ass. A job is a job, she thought, but one could always retain one's dignity.

The Uppsala Castle had watched over the city for three hundred years. It remembered a small country town on the plain where peasant boys came to learn holy orders. It remembered Descartes and the hunchback queen, Kristina, who rode out of the castle in black velvet and white lace to go to Rome as a Catholic. It heard the Gunilla bell ring every hour.

Lilac bushes bloomed on its slopes in June. Swifts whistled shrilly. In June, a woman pushed a man in a wheelchair to the terrace on Castle Hill. It was not an easy climb; she had strong hands. He sat bundled in a blanket, smoking cigarettes, staring at the lighted ends. She gathered lilacs from the slopes, and talked to the castle, the flowers, and the birds.

"Miklos is coming," she said to swifts shifting their line of flight.

"Where is he?" von Schwarzwald cried impatiently. "He was to be here now!"

Miklos Brody appeared from behind the Wennerberg statue. He approached them smiling. They greeted one another, though Kerstin scarcely looked up, continuing to pick her flowers. Miklos sat on a mora stone beside von Schwarzwald.

"I have good news, Miklosh ... Ze SS is preparing to shtrike!"

"This is good," said Miklos.

"Ze double agent in ze Shtockholm Station has proved very useful. Herr Robertts is theoretically alive! He is in ze O.N.A.N. hideout, wherever that is. They are all going to Malmö to join ze ship ... You have heard from ze girl, this Deborah?"

Miklos nodded. "She was able to call me from Bremen. After Malmö they go to the Savlbard islands in the Arctic. Why, she does not know; but she has heard to speak of a bomb."

"Why? To do a *Schweinerei*, that is why! But ... it does not matter now. At Malmö they vill all be arrested — for kidnaping Herr Robertts and whatever else they are finding out, including this bomb ... Excellent, Miklosh, excellent! How did you know that ze ship was at Porto Ercole?"

Kerstin looked at Miklos. Her eyes seemed to unnerve him.

"What?" he asked.

"I said, how did you know where ze Italian ship was?"

"This was not me. It was her."

"But how is this possible?"

"We must ask her when we see her."

Kerstin spoke to her lilacs. "Is she beautiful, Miklos?"

"Extremely."

"Does she love Zack Robertts?"

"She risks her life. Is that not love?"

"Vat is this sentimental schidt-talk" von Schwarzwald interjected.

"Yes," Kerstin went on, "that is love. Do you love Zack Robertts, Miklos?"

"He is dear to me."

"I am pleased . . . Because we are all double agents, are we not, Miklos?"

Both Miklos and von Schwarzwald were taken aback.

"In life, I mean," she said. "Therefore, it is good that we love someone, Miklos." Suddenly, Kerstin screamed at Miklos in unbridled thunder. "Why don't you say you love him?"

"Shot op, you idiot! This is not a homosexual confessional society!"

Miklos responded nevertheless. "You are right, Kerstin. I understand you. I tell you that I love him."

"I am pleased. Love is the only thing Zack Robertts has now. It is his only chance."

Kerstin gave Miklos her flowers. Von Schwarzwald gazed at the lighted end of his cigarette.

CHAPTER ELEVEN

THE SKY was green and pink and brown and bursting gold at midnight. It was furrowed like a fleshy brow. A helicopter came out of the folds, silently for a moment, then trailed by its chucking sound. The rotors pitched slowly in a sharp attack. They spun caught light into threads of brilliance. The skeleton tail rose, pointing to invisible stars, and the helicopter descended and hung on currents of air like a paralyzing wasp in the scent of caterpillar meat.

Dogs began to bark. The stadium lights flooded the helicopter, casting and blanching its trembling shadow in a crossfire of light. A cable was dropped. It twanged and rattled and slithered for a while, then dangled limply directly over the ventilation chimney. Tommy Kaneoka moved out of the aircraft crouched like an ogre. He wore heavy boots, gloves, and tight-fitting ski clothes with a hood. A belt of leather pockets girded his waist. The pockets bulged.

He was strapped in a harness with a steel ring protrusion that gripped the rough surface of the tow line to help brake his descent. He squeezed the line between his knees, lowered his body to a sitting position, and slid, repeating these motions until he disappeared in the maze of ducts.

The harness was lifted, empty. A cage was used now. It shuttled up and down for twelve minutes delivering Tommy's tools. The dogs wearied. They stared, leaning forward.

Zack Robertts, dressed exactly like Tommy, came next, feeling moist air on his face. The dogs howled at the smell of new blood, louder as he came down. As a boy, Zack Robertts had climbed trees, fences, and ropes, and occasionally had fallen from all of them. Since then, he had climbed nothing but stairs. He could see the eyes of the dogs. They were not like Beatrice Cenci's. Saliva dripped on the ground. He went into the ducts.

The pilot, raising the gear, landed on the field within the confines of the fence. He cut his engine and waited for a radio call from Tommy to collect them. When the rotors stopped spinning and stirring dust, the straining dogs attacked the helicopter.

They flung themselves against the perspex, scratching the plexiglass with their nails and smearing it with their soapy mouths. They came within inches of the pilot, who was jolted violently at every assault. He could see the muscles in their shoulders and haunches flatten as they slammed against him, whining in frustration. He sat in fear that they might somehow break in or turn the entire helicopter on its side. They were living weapons, each of them more destructive — to human beings at least — than a mortar shell.

One of the dogs sunk his teeth into the metallic skin, cracking his jaw. He fell to the ground and whimpered. The others grew silent and huddled around him under the helicopter, obscured from the pilot's view. The pilot breathed deeply and lit a cigarette. Liquid began to drip from the puncture in the belly of the aircraft. The dogs sniffed it, watching a puddle form.

Tommy Kaneoka and Zack Robertts crouched in the ventilation duct that led to the strongroom. The passage seemed to sag under their weight and the still heavier load they had brought with them. A chorus of humming from electrically driven equipment inside the plant struck tinny vibrations around them. They could feel the upward draft of air that blew through the system. It was hot nonetheless and both of them sweated profusely.

Light filtered through from the strongroom. The duct narrowed as it went into the wall; it was barely wide enough for one man to crawl and was covered at the end by a plastic grillwork, which seemed readily removable, however.

Tommy had already explained the precise details of their entry, and no words were exchanged between them now, each man performing his preassigned task. This was the most difficult moment, Tommy had said, when an error in timing would trap them. The aim was to neutralize the television cameras, of course, blacking them out for as short a period as possible. Ninety seconds was the target; it could not be done in less.

During the blackout the grill had to be lifted and one of the rafts inflated inside the room to allow Tommy to enter and stand on the pressure-sensitive floor. Four exposures had to be made with a Polaroid camera from angles that matched the TV views. Closeup lenses had to be attached to the television cameras, by which they would be refocused on the Polaroid photographs of the strongroom. When the blackout would fade, the television system would then be transmitting full screen images of the strongroom, no longer "live," but as it had been photographed seconds before.

Tommy withdrew a small screwdriver from his belt. He had painted it matte black. Zack Robertts handed him a photographic strobotron that could flash every ten seconds. Tommy wore two Polaroids around his neck. Zack Robertts linked a length of rubber tubing from the nozzle of a cylinder of compressed helium to one of the deflated rafts.

Tommy watched him like a teacher, checking the attachment lenses strapped to his body. When Zack Robertts was ready, he nodded sharply to Tommy, who smiled.

"If you ever need a stake, Zack, I still have friends in Tokyo."

"Think I got a talent?"

Tommy poked his gloved fingers through the grill very slowly and began to work the screwdriver with equal caution. He looked back at Zack Robertts.

"You look like you were born with a silver crowbar in your mitt."

Zack Robertts felt good; a man could go through a dozen lifetimes and not once receive a compliment like that.

Tommy Kaneoka's fingers could actually be seen on one of the TV monitors in each of the three cooperating police units guarding the Uppsala plant. Tommy knew this; hence his deliberate manner. But he was counting more on the low resolution of television reception, particularly of something so small on the screen. In fact, what appeared was a barely perceptible fluttering, like a moth on a distant wall, well below the threshold of definition, and at that moment, none of the monitors was even being watched.

By mutual agreement, it had been decided months back, after two full years of tiresome, uneventful viewing, that threefold monitoring was an unnecessary duplication of effort. Each police unit took a turn at the chore instead, and the man on duty tonight was in the toilet reading the Swedish edition of *Mad* magazine.

His name was Lars Jönköping and by the time he returned to his post, Tommy had the grill unscrewed from its moorings, although he had not yet removed it.

Jönköping, a muscular man with a gun hanging in a shoulder holster, glanced at the four screens as he took his seat. He returned to his magazine, which he had already read more than once. It goes without saying, that he disliked this part of his job, known to whoever had to suffer it as the worst detail. There was something morally unsavory about working at no extra pay for private enterprise, and the feeling was shared by all. Lars Jönköping wished he were home watching television.

In the thirty months or so since the closed-circuit system had been installed, he, like everyone else not in command, had stood watch for a total of about ninety hours. Once he had seen a blurred shadow moving aimlessly across one of the screens. He had done nothing about it. Experience had taught him and his colleagues to recognize a fly on a lens when they saw one. Now, however, all of the screens went black.

Lars Jönköping looked up. The black began to wash away. But the four screens went white in a flowery burst and then black again. He blinked, laying his reading material on the console. He looked at the row of alarm lights. They were green. The monitors flashed white, then black once more. His eyes shifted to the dim spotlighting in the room and he stared at a bulb to see if it would flicker. It did not. When he turned back to the console, he saw only the lingering retinal impression of the bulb on the black screens.

He blinked again to wipe the image away. He rubbed and pinched his lips and grew suspicious. In the toilet, a helicopter had passed directly overhead. Unusual, for this hour. And now that he thought about it, had he or had he not heard dogs barking faintly on the wind? He listened. Nothing now, but still very unusual.

He turned back to the monitors. White fireworks. Black nothingness. He began to time the frequency of this pattern on the second-hand of his watch. He worried.

There was a telephone on the console. There was a contingency plan for suspect phenomena in which the alarm lights remained green. An armored vehicle and a preliminary investigation squad would be dispatched to the plant. It took only a phone call to arrange it. That was how the fly on the lens had been discovered. It was better to act and be covered than to worry.

Lars Jönköping, looking at his watch, calculated. The white fireworks and black nothingness had recurred five times in one minute at more or less equal intervals. He stood up. He lifted the phone. He dialed the first of a three-digit emergency number. The black screen faded. He dialed the second. The picture cleared. All four screens appeared normal. He looked at each of them carefully. Yes, normal. He hung up. He relaxed. He hoisted his shoulder holster and sat. He went back to *Svenska Mad*. What, me worry? he thought.

The appearance of the strongroom had in fact been totally transformed. It resembled the interior of a space craft. Weightless rafts floated in mid-air. They were pulled by currents created by the ventilation system. Zack Robertts, moving unsteadily on the cushion of helium of one of the rafts, painted the bottoms of the others with mucilage so that they could be made to stick to the floor. There was a danger that they might collide with the four music-stand supports that held up the Polaroid photographs being televised at close range by the TV cameras. He had no way of knowing, of course, whether their entry had been successful but he had none of the fears of an ordinary burglar, and Tommy Kaneoka seemed almost serene.

Tommy was preparing the microwave stimulator equipment for hookup with the digit-selector panel on the face of the vault. He stood on one of the rafts, rocked gently by his own movements as if he were working on the moon. He taped ten, threadlike platinum wires to the number buttons on the panel. The free ends of the wires were attached to a master generator fed by a tank of liquid helium under a pressure of twenty-five atmospheres. The temperature inside the tank was minus 270 degrees centigrade. The device amplified emitted energy projecting a narrow beam of electrons that passed through the digit selector and excited specific circuits according to the computer's programmed instructions.

The computer began to count. Tommy looked at his watch. Zack Robertts, who had anchored all of the rafts, bounced across the floor and came up to Tommy.

"It's one-twelve," Tommy said, removing a one hundred crown banknote from his pocket. "How long till we hit the lucky number?"

Zack Robertts matched his bet. "An hour on the nose."

"I'll say, seventy-seven minutes. Close man takes the pot."

They sat on one raft, put the money between them, and waited.

Outside, the pilot dozed. The dogs had lost interest in the motionless object in their midst and had gone elsewhere. Sunlight began to pour through the trees throwing snowflake shadow pictures on the pilot's eyelids. He awoke with a start. He checked his watch and shook his head. He felt nakedly exposed in the daylight, though it was less bright than the floodlamps. He lit a cigarette. He thought he smelled kerosene. He sniffed around the cockpit. But the sensation disappeared in the odor of burning tobacco.

Below him, the puncture continued to drip. The puddle had grown to its largest size and was running off the rainwater slope of the pavement, cascading into a sewer.

The cockpit was smoky. The pilot opened an air vent. He could hear the liquid flowing into the sewer. The aroma of kerosene returned. The pilot stiffened and crushed his cigarette. He strained in his seat to see the ground below him, but he dared not open the door for fear of the dogs. He saw nothing, but the kerosene smell was unmistakable now.

He switched on his instrument panel. He had lost sixty gallons of fuel. He had less than half of what he needed to recover the men inside as planned and return. He began to estimate the rate at which he had been losing fuel and the diminishing possibilities of escape.

Zack Robertts and Tommy Kaneoka had stared at the vault for a full thirty minutes without speaking. Their eyes were fixed on the thin black line between the door and the jamb, waiting for the safe to spring open as one might watch for a shooting star or the approach of a comet.

"Did I hear you say the odds never change?" Zack Robertts asked, breaking the long silence.

"Never."

"It could take forever."

"It won't. We had three hours of power in the batteries. Two and a half now."

Zack Robertts looked at him. He had not envisaged having to return empty-handed.

"You getting jumpy?" Tommy asked.

"Bored . . . What do you talk about when you rob a bank?"

"Money . . . Women."

Zack Robertts thought of Deborah. He wished she could see him now.

"You ever been in love, Tommy?" He was sorry he asked; the question would surely be returned.

"I had a wife in the States," Tommy said. "It didn't work out . . . You?"

He remembered the first time he had met her, how, after they had sat up until dawn, their hands had clasped and had remained together, learning about each other from skin heat and the infinitely variable pressures of touch; receiving power, discharging weakness, absorbing through knuckles and fingers and the sweat of the palm love rushing into empty spaces. Their hands had made love, and everything after that had seemed anticlimactic.

"I don't know," Zack Robertts told Tommy.

The two-way radio link to the helicopter began to beep softly. Tommy picked up the telephone-type receiver and listened. Zack Robertts watched his face lose its apricot color. Tommy continually looked at his watch and grunted into the receiver. Finally, he slammed it down in a fury.

"Goddamn!" he shouted.

He hurled some loose wire against the vault, striking it forcefully. It fell on a part of the floor unprotected by the rafts. Zack Robertts recoiled, though he realized it was not heavy enough to trip the alarm.

"It was all perfect, *per-fect*!" Tommy raged. "And — You need luck, Zack. I told you, didn't I?"

"Why don't you just start from the beginning?"

"Beginning? You mean the end ... Those fucking dogs chewed up the fuel line. And I'm the one who didn't want to kill them! ... We have ten minutes to clear out of here, with or without the plutonium, and definitely without our gear." Tommy looked around the room. "What a fucking mess!"

"It could still take days before it's discovered." Zack Robertts felt childlike compassion for Tommy and self-pity for himself; he felt that someone mean was breaking up their game.

"How do we know? They can find it all in the morning. Anyway, it's all over, Zack. All over."

"There's still some time, Tommy."

"There's no luck."

The safe opened, just a few inches, but awesomely open.

Forty-two minutes had gone by since they had made their bet, but neither of them thought of that now. Tommy pulled the heavy door wheeling it on its hinges and they peered into the vault in utter marvel. Hundreds of plutonium ingots gleamed like diamonds in the sun and the hot breath of subatomic particles blew against their skin.

Tommy slapped his sides in sheer glee and began to laugh hysterically. Zack Robertts grinned, shaking his head in admiration.

"Who's a genius, Zack Robertts? Who?"

"Tommy-*san*." He shook his hand.

"I told you. Sonofabitch, I told you!"

He fussed like a circus clown as he lifted the radio and signaled the pilot.

"Come and get us, chopper!" he cried. "We're going home!"

He leaped from raft to raft into the vault. He grabbed two ingots, then a third.

"One for good measure," he said tossing them to Zack Robertts, who put them in a lead box.

"They're warm," Zack Robertts said feeling the smooth metal tingling in his hands. They were stamped, "Pu240."

"Of course, they're warm. They can't be anything else but warm! Energy transfer. Alpha particle emission. Radiation. *Rad-i-ation*! But you can hold those in your hands for a month without a care. I know *everything*! Got to get the safe closed, though. There're thousands of them, and that's death, *de-eath*!"

He resealed the vault and ripped away the wires from the digit-selector panel.

"At least they won't know we got inside until they count every bar," he said. He opened the liquid helium tank to let it boil and escape. "I sure would have liked to clean up, though."

Zack Robertts, holding the box of plutonium, climbed into the duct on a ladder of storage batteries. He could hear the helicopter overhead and the dogs barking again.

Tommy surveyed the room before leaving. He was still in the flush of exultation.

"Shit," he said, "they got the better deal. The computer alone is worth more than three lousy ingots . . . I sure would have liked to clean up, though."

He went into the duct, following Zack Robertts's slow crawl to the top.

The tow line hung over the chimney. Zack Robertts tried several times to grab it. He felt rain, but he suddenly knew that he was being pelted by drops of aviation fuel. At last he took hold of the line. He sent up the box and waited for the line to return with the harness.

Tommy poked him from underneath. "I'll be right back. I forgot the most important thing, Zack."

Zack Roberrts asked what it was, but he was already gone.

The harness and the tow line came down. Zack Robertts strapped himself in, looking back repeatedly for Tommy, of whom there was no sign. He felt concern and hesitated. He was drenched in kerosene, his hair matted on his brow — a human Molotov cocktail. The pilot shrieked at him.

"C'mon! This bird is pissing!"

The rate of loss had in fact accelerated considerably with the activation of the fuel injection system.

Zack Robertts clung to the tow line, as the pilot reeled him in. In a matter of moments he was inside the cockpit tearing himself free of the harness, watching all the while for Tommy.

"If he doesn't come in a few seconds, I'm going," the pilot said nervously, sending down the line and harness again. "We're ten minutes from landing and we've got ten minutes of flight — if we're lucky."

Luck, Zack Robertts thought. "We'll land somewhere else."

"Like hell, we will! This ——."

"Tommy!"

Tommy was below, seizing the line. He smiled broadly, waving something at Zack Robertts, shouting up at him as his face, hair, and clothes soaked up the raining kerosene.

"Your money, Zack! You won the bet!"

"Hurry!"

Tommy slipped his arms into the harness. He spit fuel and rubbed his eyes to see. He tied the thongs around his waist. The pilot began to lift him. Zack Robertts leaned from the helicopter, extending his hand to Tommy, who hung over the barking dogs. His whole body was saturated with kerosene.

"No smoking!" Tommy cried. He seemed almost to be laughing.

Suddenly the thongs came apart. The harness slipped over his back, whipping and winding around his neck and pinning his arms to his sides. He dropped a few feet. He lost his grip on the tow line. The steel ring around it skidded. Tommy slid down to the end of the line, where the ring was blocked by a metal knob.

"Get him up!" Zack Robertts screamed. "Get him up!"

Tommy gasped as the harness pulled tighter and tighter around his throat by the weight of his own body. The leather squeaked.

The line was hauled in as far as it could go. But Tommy still swung helplessly from the knob, an arm's length away from Zack Robertts, if he could only free his arms.

"Got to . . . cut . . . the line," Tommy grunted.

Zack Robertts shook no. Tommy might survive the fall to the ground, which was twenty feet or so, but not the waiting dogs.

Tommy's eyes were like billiard balls. He looked up at Zack Robertts in ultimate appeal. Zack Robertts anchored his leg and leaned still further — to no avail. Tommy tried to speak; no sound emerged anymore, only the wheeze of a dying man.

Zack Robertts spun on his knees to go down the last length of line. He came out of the aircraft looking at Tommy between his legs. He pulled the line toward him burning away his gloves and the skin of his palms. Tommy stared. His eyes seemed to soften.

The weight of the two men made the line unreel. They plunged about ten feet, Tommy swinging barely out of reach of the dogs, who leaped into the air to get at his legs. The pilot lifted the helicopter. Tommy's harness slipped again. It moved over his shoulders, catching under his chin. It drew closed in a leather noose, jerking his head violently to one side. Tommy's spinal column snapped at the neck in a sharp, audible crack. The money he had been holding in his hand fell to the dogs.

Zack Robertts gave a final look at Tommy's gaping eyes. They were crying tears of kerosene. He returned to the cockpit.

Tommy hung limply from the sky. His arms were free now. They spread like wings as the helicopter soared. Beyond the fence, his body hit a power line. Tommy-*san* exploded.

CHAPTER TWELVE

THE *Colomba Bianca* sailed due north, fifteen nautical miles off the western coast of Sweden. It was headed not for Malmö but for Göteberg, the country's largest port. Fabrizio Bentivoglio had heard of the change in plans in a radio message from Jean-Marie received with dire urgency. It had been abstruse and worriesomely brief, but further word had been said to be on its way, which gave him all the more reason to be apprehensive.

He was taking a light supper with Deborah Colt. The sea was calm. They sat by candlelight. She wore her Mexican dress; he wore a navy blue, double-breasted jacket with gold stripes on his sleeves. They ate prosciutto from Parma and Sicilian melon. They drank Barolo, 1967, which was a superior wine but a poor companion for the dish being served. Fabrizio, however, never settled for less than the best — not anymore.

They had little to say to one another. The language barrier was formidable, though Deborah knew far more Italian than she let on. Fabrizio, apart from all other preoccupations, was suffering, and the cause was Deborah. He had grown to care for her self-sufficient, unfrenetic manner, which was a change from the women of Rome. But she was creating an insupportable problem. They had been nine days at sea, all of them abstinent. Deborah "just didn't feel it." Fabrizio could be gentle and understanding, even for nine days, but in the eyes of his crew of twelve he was cutting a poor figure: Fabrizio and Deborah, everyone knew, had been sleeping in separate staterooms. He would leave her at Göteberg and pay for her transportation to wherever in the world she might wish to go. He would send her first class; he would give her spending money, more than she could spend, because he really liked her, and because he really liked her he would not even tell her that if she had not been so mortifyingly obstinate he would have given her a BMW.

Deborah stared out of the starboard window. She could see the coastal lights. A waiter came along and poured wine. He was half Fabrizio's age, a blond Sicilian, but he seemed to be mocking the *comandante's* failures. Fabrizio shooed him away, taking Deborah's hand.

"Shouldn't we be turning south for Malmö?" Deborah asked withdrawing her hand for the wine glass, then realizing this had caused him a further embarrassment.

Fabrizio glanced back at the boy. This was all going to get back to Palermo. Unseemly excuses would have to be made.

"I *non* understand," Fabrizio said sullenly.

"Malmö . . . *andare a Malmö, no?*"

"*No. Abbiamo cambiato idea.* We go to Göteberg. Is near."

Deborah felt concern. She would have to get another message to Miklos. At the port in Bremen, Frabrizio had caught her making a call, frightening her profoundly. Later, he had questioned her as to whom she had spoken. She had told him that she had a friend in Hamburg. He had grown jealous and subsequently amorous, which seemed in his case to be the other side of the coin; but Deborah "just didn't feel it" — a phrase whose meaning he had come to know well.

"What happens at Göteberg?" she asked, trying not to sound over-inquisitive.

"I buy you a ticket. You go home. First class."

Fabrizio pouted. Deborah knew why.

"I don't dislike you, Frabrizio."

It was true. He had a certain tenderness that appealed to her, and he glowed virility, which she had seen and appreciated in his indomitable efforts to become her lover, at least until now. He had learned a good part of his spoken English in the past week, and she liked the way he fought and conquered alien words, reshaping the unused and recalcitrant muscles of his mouth. It was more than she could do. She found him to be an open man, and if this were not as others knew him, so much to Deborah's credit as a woman nice to know. He had told her of his low origins, of his struggles "to make a name," and of his weaknesses. The details were blatant lies, and she could only sense how unsavory his life had to be, but the picture drawn was basically honest. He had something less than a well developed ego, and, though he stood six feet two, in the world he had so forcibly entered, he often felt two feet six.

"Ma che mi frega, if you like me, or not like me," he said, with bravura. "I can have all the womens. I know all important personages. *Li conosco tutti. Nel cinema, i dottori, professori, attrici . . . tutti!* I am . . . how do you say, *'ricco'*?"

"Rich."

"Sì. But also rich in *amici."*

"And handsome."

He looked at her for translation.

"Bello," she said hitting the double-*l* hard.

He turned his head at a modest angle, but could not contain a smile, and he called for the waiter to pour more wine.

"Ma non sono tanto bello quanto dici tu," he said to her, but for the Sicilian's ears alone.

"I find you very attractive . . . *attraente,"* Deborah said to benefit the same cause.

More modesty, but when the boy was out of hearing range again, Fabrizio replied, "But . . . you just don't feel it, yes? . . . *Mah*, what is it, this 'it'?"

Now Deborah took his hand. Her voice was mellow, throaty, moistened by the wine. "There's such a thing as spirit, Fabrizio. It has to flow between two people. It doesn't come out of a tap that you can turn on and off. It's mystical, vibrant, magnetic, beyond control."

"*Nun capisco 'n cazzo.*"

Deborah smiled warmly at the ghetto dialect of the Trastevere poor. Perhaps it was the Barolo or Fabrizio's incorrigible transparentness, but she was suddenly beginning "to feel it."

She held his hand a little more tightly and the spirit flowed. Fabrizio leaned forward. Her eyes closed. He kissed her. Her lips melted. Why not, she thought, why not? And if it would help her gain more information, to assist poor Zack Robertts (whom she imagined, not without feelings of guilt, in chains, hunger and stubble), so much the better.

"*Signor comandante . . . mi scusi.*"

They looked up. It was another member of the crew. He held a sheet of paper. Fabrizio made a display of annoyance, but he was delighted at having been caught in a kiss.

"*C'è un messaggio radiofonico. Urgentissimo,*" said the sailor eyeing Deborah.

"*Dammelo!*" Fabrizio snapped.

"*Sissignore!*"

He handed him the radio message. Fabrizio read it. His face dropped. Deborah felt a thrust of fear. Fabrizio gave the note back to the sailor.

"*Fallo veder al capitano! Subito!*"

"*Sissignore!*"

"*Corri!*"

The sailor ran off as ordered to show the message to the ship's captain. Deborah dared not ask what it was, but she knew it somehow concerned her. Fabrizio was staring at her.

"We *non* go to Göteberg, Deborah. The port is just here, but we *non* go in. These people, my . . . *amici* . . ."

"Friends."

"*Sì*. My friends, they come here. Eight of them. Six mens. Two womens. By helicopter. There was to be nine. One is dead. Killed."

Deborah had no way of knowing if Zack Robertts were one of the eight, but she was struck by the thought that he might be. Or, was he the one counted dead? She shuddered.

"I am worry for you, Deborah. This is not for your eyes. You were not to be here with me. I did not want it. It is a brutal thing."

"These 'friends' of yours, what are they going to do?"

"Better not to know, *cara mia*. I try to get you off the ship as soon as is possible. At Svalbard, for certain." He was not at all certain. He looked at his watch. "They will be here soon . . . I am sorry, Deborah. *Mi dispiace assai*. Do you understand?"

They had been using each other, recklessly, perhaps. She could not fault him anymore than herself.

"I understand Fabrizio."

"I am a weak man, Deborah. And for that, I am too . . ." He searched in vain for the English word. *"Impegnato."*

"Committed."

"*Sì*. Committed."

"To what, Fabrizio, to what?"

He lowered his head like a sinner.

The captain of the *Colomba Bianca*, an obedient man from Palermo, eased his ship into a position thirty-nine minutes north of the fifty-seventh parallel and eleven degrees and forty-four minutes east of Greenwich. This was a point due west of Göteberg lying just beyond the territorial waters of Sweden. He cut his starboard engines, set his rudder to the waves, and the *Colomba Bianca* held steady, standing on the sea.

Fabrizio and Deborah had gone up to the stern deck, which

was large enough for the helicopter to land on. There was no wind. It was as dark as it possibly could be, but the sky was still red, purple looking to the east. Gulls screamed and scattered as the helicopter crept up. It settled near them, slowly. Deborah closed her eyes and held her long hair behind her head.

Jean-Marie, carrying the plutonium box, got out, followed by Vicky and Ibrahim. The crew unloaded cargo, mostly suitcases. The helicopter returned to shore to bring more cargo and another three passengers.

Jean-Marie spoke to Fabrizio in Italian. He asked him first who Deborah was. Fabrizio said she was his secretary. Jean-Marie called him "foolish" and asked to be shown to his quarters. Fabrizio fawned. Deborah looked away sadly.

"*Dobbiamo montare la bomba,*" Jean-Marie said, taking his overstuffed briefcase from Vicky.

"*Qui?*" Fabrizio was fearstruck. They were going to assemble the nuclear bomb on his ship. Was it dangerous? "*C'è pericolo?*"

"*Beaucoup,*" Jean-Marie replied, switching to French.

The risk had been great all along, he said, but now that Tommy Kaneoka was dead, the only one who could do the job was Shiva, who had none of Kaneoka's professional skill.

Fabrizio looked up at God and led Jean-Marie to his room. Jean-Marie, waving to Ibrahim to come with him, shoved his briefcase into Fabrizio's hands and followed, holding the plutonium box. Deborah had understood everything but the box.

"He's rather tall for an Italian," Vicky said to Deborah when they were alone.

"What?"

"I'm Vicky Walsh, Jean-Marie's secretary. You work for Signor Bentivoglio?"

"Yes."

They shook hands and Deborah told Vicky her name.

"Lovely . . . Handsome, isn't he? Signor B, I mean."

"How many more are coming?"

"Let's see. There's Dr. Stein. I don't like him very much. Get's on your wick, y'know. Then there's Dr. Rahmani. The quiet type. Shiva, she's Indian. Wears a bloody jewel in her nose. And Olle, who's quite nice when you get to know him. And . . ." Vicky hesitated. She felt cameraderie in the presence of a "colleague," but she wondered if she was saying things she ought not to, especially concerning Zack Robertts. But she could see no reason for secrecy and went on. "And then there's this American chap. Zack Robertts. With two Ts. He's a writer . . . Have you met any of them?"

"No." Deborah could barely form the word.

"Good. I shouldn't've been sounding off my cloddish opinions. You'll like Zack Robertts, though. He's super."

The helicopter returned. Instinctively, Deborah fixed her hair.

Zack Robertts, however, was at that moment sitting in the Volvo beside Olle waiting for the last airlift. The car was parked in a wood outside Göteberg.

He had been very subdued since Tommy died and had scarcely taken note of the events since then, which had been precipitous: the rapid dismantling of the hotel basement workshop, the cross-country flight from Uppsala, Jean-Marie hurling lightning bolts of bad temper. It had been a sleepless twenty-four hours, except for a few neck-creaking nods in the back of the Volvo.

He had tried to find meaning in Tommy's death, though he knew all along that there was none. Tommy had seemed almost obsessed about the need for luck, but if one thought about it, Tommy had had an incredible run of luck to survive his thirty years. The equation had to be balanced, like one of those algebraic formulas where everything cancels each other. Tommy must have known that better than anyone else. Why else had he gone back for the money if not to tie the thongs wrong and ask to be eaten by dogs? He liked dogs, violence, and gambling. There was a sense to the senselessness of his death, the internal logic of chaos. Was Tommy Kaneoka Abraham? He had worked for the Pentagon and was known to the CIA. Had he killed Abraham for his "kids," or had Abraham killed him for his? Was Zack Robertts Abraham, who had somehow misplaced an episode in his life; was Vicky Abraham, the wiliest woman who had ever lived . . .

"Are you Abraham?" he suddenly asked Olle.

Olle bared his rotten mouth in what passed in the twilight for a grin. He knew as much English as Zack Robertts knew Swedish, and both could set it to paper in full with one pen on its last drop of ink.

Olle looked at Zack Robertts contemplatively for a while, then nudged him like a pal with his elbow. He reached into his inside pocket and withdrew a flask of aquavit. It was pint-sized and could not do much damage, and Olle knew Zack Robertts would never turn him in for shirking his job. He offered Zack Roberrts first slug.

He drank long. Olle drank longer, returning the flask and watching with country boy eyes as to what the writer would do. Zack Robertts was inclined to wipe, if not sterilize, the effluent of Olle's dental decay from the drinking end of the bottle, but Olle had wiped nothing, so he drank from the wet opening anyway, trusting the antiseptic qualities of alcohol. Olle appreciated the gesture. He nodded affirmatively to Zack Robertts as if they had just become blood brothers.

He elbowed Zack Robertts again. It was not painless. This time he extracted a photograph and handed it over proudly. It was a snapshot of Olle and the plump widow they had met at Gustafsson's home. It showed them standing outside her pottery shop, arm in arm, beaming with love or something close to it.

"That's wonderful," Zack Robertts said, happy to have had a role in the match, although, given Olle's occupation, he was a little concerned for the widow. "She's a handsome woman."

Olle concurred, motioning to him to look at the other side. There was something written on the back of the photograph in Swedish. Zack Robertts could not make it out, but he recognized the word *stor*, meaning "big," and *blomma* — "flower," and by the look of the boldly struck exclamation mark at the end of the feminine scrawl, he had the impression that the plump widow thought Olle to be a "big flower" — which in a sense was true.

"*Stor blomma*," Zack Robertts said.

Olle nodded. He smiled a little lecherously, made a fist, and drove it home. Zack Robertts knew what that meant.

When the helicopter came, they had already drained the flask and had flung it into the woods.

The flight to the *Colomba Bianca* was a mere hop of a few minutes. As the helicopter came over the deck, a strong northerly wind began to blow and the pilot had difficulty landing the craft. He flew in a circle, making a second pass in an attempt to set it down between gusts.

Zack Robertts looked out from the cockpit. The group that had arrived before him was still on deck — Phil E. Stein, Muhammed, and Shiva. He saw Vicky speaking to a third woman, whose face was turned skyward following the arc of flight. Deborah!

His mind reeled confusedly. He paled and his heart beat fast. He was physically dizzy, nauseated, and his legs were like string. The aircraft banked hard. He lost his sense of orientation, feeling that he was down and the ship was up.

Vicky waved to him. She seemed to be beckoning him to pass over a fault, beyond which boats flew and oceans filled the sky and men were not pasted to the ground. He felt himself rising toward Deborah, and a powerful eagle perched on his hand, digging its talons into his skull: he knew that there was more than one reality; there were many, and one was as real as another.

The helicopter came down routinely. He jumped from the cockpit with his eyes cast on Deborah, as hers were on him. He had an urge to run to her, but she turned away and moved off to one side, and he took that as a signal not to show recognition. Vicky pulled him by the arm.

"I want you to meet my friend Debby," she said, introducing him to her by his name.

"Hello, Debby," he said, knowing helplessly how much she disliked being called by that girlish version of her name.

They shook hands; hers were icy and tremulous.

"She works for Signor Bentivoglio," Vicky said. "He's Italian."

"Signor Bentivoglio?" Zack Robertts asked.

"Yes," said Deborah. "He owns the *Colomba Bianca* . . . I'm his secretary."

"How fortunate for him," he said.

"Funny, isn't it?" Vicky remarked. "I mean, you two, both Americans, both in Italy, and you don't know each other."

"But we do," he said, stunning both of them, "as of now."

Jean-Marie appeared on deck, glancing at them suspiciously. He summoned Vicky, who excused herself and left them alone.

"How did you get here?" Zack Robertts said urgently, while trying to maintain a deceptive smile.

"Never mind that. I have a message from Miklos."

Vicky returned.

"Jean-Marie wants to hold a meeting straightaway," she said. "We're all supposed to go inside."

"Where 'inside'?" Zack Robertts asked deliberately.

Deborah was quick. "I'll show you, Mr. Robertts. Come with me."

Vicky went around informing the others. Zack Robertts followed Deborah and they spoke at safe intervals.

"Miklos says . . ."

They went through a gangway, moving in single file down a hall. Zack Robertts ran his fingers along the wood paneling. Deborah spoke again.

". . . the only one you can trust ——"

"*Swietenia* mahogany," Zack Robertts interrupted as they passed some of the crew. "I doubt that this ship was built in Italy. The wood is West Indian . . . Who, Deborah, who?"

"Nkele. Ibrahim Nk ——"

"Is he Abraham?"

She started to look back at him.

"Don't turn . . . Is he Abraham?"

"Miklos said Ibrahim. I'm sure he said the only one you can trust is ——."

"My guess would be the Bahamas," he broke in again as they entered a large salon where Fabrizio stood waiting. Zack Robertts took note of the gold braiding on his sleeves and he continued speaking, directing himself now to Fabrizio. "Am I correct, sir? I believe your magnificent ship was built in the Bahamas."

Fabrizio looked at him without sign of comprehension. Deborah introduced the two men, while the others filed in from behind them.

They all took seats around a Siena-built billiard table with tiny net pockets and chess pawns lined up on white dots in the cloth. Fabrizio whispered something to Deborah, who seemed awkward and flushed. Zack Robertts had never seen her that way, and it hurt. She got up and started to leave.

"Where are you going, miss?" Jean-Marie shot at her with a cobra's quickness.

"Fab — Signor Bentivoglio feels it would be better if I ——"

"Stay," he commanded. "We we have no secrets."

Fabrizio opened his mouth in protest; Jean-Marie stitched it shut with a needlelike leer. Fabrizio slumped in his chair. He was unable to look at Deborah but he made a digging gesture with one hand, which meant sit.

Jean-Marie told her in his imperious style that he had a secretarial job for her to perform. She was to cut a sheet of paper in strips and then squares, and following the seating order around the table, she was to assign everyone a stateroom, doubling up if need be. When she had done that, he said, she should pass out the little squares with the room numbers written on them to everyone at the table. He asked her if he had been clear. He spoke to her as to a child. Deborah had a Master's degree in sociology from Berkeley, and she wore it on the outside. She was nobody's secretary; Jean-Marie knew it. He was torturing her.

Two quick chops, Zack Robertts thought. He watched her tear strips of paper, and Jean-Marie unwrapped and fiddled with a cigar and told everyone else to rest for a day while they made for the open sea. Deborah wrote on the squares. Zack Robertts hoped she would not attempt to send him a message. Jean-Marie would think of that; perhaps that was his purpose. Her hands were shriveled, blotchy, and shaky. She had none of the conspiratorial graces that Zack Robertts had picked up in the last few weeks like a dance school beginner with rhythm. He knew what Deborah was thinking: I am going to die. He trained his thoughts on her trying to reach her: I will save you, Deborah. And he felt fatuous, idiotic — as if anyone could know and much less control what the next breath might bring. He was angry at Miklos; yet Miklos had given him Deborah . . . and Ibrahim Nkele.

He looked at the black man, who sat stiffly in his Polish suit waiting with waxworks patience for life to enter his body.

Jean-Marie said they would follow a route to the Arctic

through the Norwegian and Greenland seas, with a supply stop at Svalbard, an island territory belonging to Norway, which lay far north of the Circle stretching across the eightieth parallel. Their port would be Vest Spitsbergen harbor, where the ice in the fjords had melted early this year, toward the end of May. On last reports, the temperature there was well above freezing and the sun was already shining twenty-four hours a day. He wished everyone a pleasant time off tomorrow. He sounded like a tour director until he said that they would assemble the bomb on the following day.

Deborah had completed her task, and she began to hand out the squares. Jean-Marie stopped her and asked to see them first.

"It is always a Proustian pleasure," he said in a laugh-extorting way, "to know who is sleeping with whom."

Zack Robertts knew it had been a ploy after all. Jean-Marie went over the scraps of paper with care. Zack Robertts tensed for a moment, but when he saw that Deborah had calmed, he did too; she had avoided the teeth of his trap. Jean-Marie made a change in two of the squares, saying nothing. He gave them back to her, bidding a rampant good night, and went out, Vicky tagging along. Zack Robertts knew what the changes were.

It was intuited, to be sure, but his paper square confirmed it. Deborah with some courage had put him in a room alone with Ibrahim, which was a risk but hardly greater than that which prevailed. Jean-Marie had annulled this, moving Zack Robertts to a room by himself and shifting someone else in with Ibrahim. Obviously, Zack Robertts's comfort had not been the decisive factor. Ibrahim might already be under suspicion. Jean-Marie had wanted him at his side in the helicopter and now he had apparently designated a trustee to take up the watch. Zack Robertts decided to escalate the risk a notch higher. The crossed-out version of his square was still ambiguous enough to allow a claim of mistake.

Fabrizio had opened a bottle of cognac, which attracted some of the group around him. Zack Robertts took silent leave in search of Ibrahim's room. On the way out, he passed Shiva, who whispered that they had to find time to talk. He agreed.

Ibrahim was in bed when Zack Robertts entered the stateroom. He had occupied the upper berth. His Polish suit hung neatly on a wall rack. He wore prison-striped pajamas, made in Poland, but they were concealed by his blanket. Only his head protruded lying face up and motionless on a white pillow. He looked like a coconut. He said nothing.

Zack Robertts undressed down to his Italian briefs. He tried to remember if he had ever heard Ibrahim speak. He had not. Perhaps he knew only Swahili.

"Well, Ibrahim, I guess I'll take the lower."

He watched for some sign of comprehension. There was none. He slipped in beneath Ibrahim and shut the light, expecting Jean-Marie's envoy at any moment. He would have to get through to the black man at once.

"Mr. Robertts," Ibrahim suddenly said, "we are in grave circumstances." He had a basso, East African voice, which rose, then seemed to fall to the floor of the sea.

Zack Robertts clutched the sides of his bed.

"Mr. Robertts, my mission has failed."

"Are you Abraham?"

"This nightmare was to have ended at Malmö, Mr. Robertts. The authorities were prepared to intervene. The death of the Japanese and the passage through Göteberg could not be anticipated, you understand. To say that I regret this, would be insufficient."

"You *are* Abraham."

"No. But Abraham's effectiveness has also been undermined, Mr. Robertts . . . Very seriously."

"Who is he?"

"We can only hope for the best."

Zack Robertts raised his voice. "Who is he, Nkele?"

Ibrahim had fallen silent. The door opened. It was Phil E. Stein, who came into the room full of one-liners.

"Who's who? How do you do? I made *Who's Who* in 'seventy-two . . . Either one of us is in the wrong room or two of us is in the wrong room. Or vice versa, if you can figure that out."

Zack Robertts went through the required pretense, without much aplomb however, and he ceded his place with a shrug. He dressed to his waist and went down the hall with his shirt over his shoulder hooked to his thumb. Ibrahim had slept through it all. Or, he had kept his eyelids as closed as a stone.

The room he was in now was several times larger than the one he had left, and he felt that the seclusion and the space would help him put the new fragments in some sort of order. Learning the identity of Abraham seemed paramount, although he had to accept that he or she was as likely as not someone he did not know and that even if he were successful he would be as powerless as ever.

He began with the premise that he would hold no one above suspicion, and while he was able to tentatively eliminate Jean-Marie and Phil E. Stein by virtue of the events of this evening, he was left with any of the others on and off the ship. Taken one by one — with the exception of Muhammed Rahmani — each of their candidacies was either absurd or unthinkable, or both. Muhammed's was thinkable but only a shade beyond the ridiculous. The Iranian ecologist had worked in the United States for years in a field of some interest to, and infiltrated by, the CIA; it seemed a useless extravagance, however, that the CIA would have *three* agents on the ship, none of whom in a position to act decisively.

At least Abraham had not been Tommy. Abraham was

alive, though weakened, which made no sense whatsoever. Why the CIA interception had to take place only at Malmö, was unfathomable. It could still come by sea or at Svalbard. Yet Ibrahim had conveyed the impression that that was in difficulty. The CIA Zack Robertts once knew could mount an invasion. Those were old days. He had been away.

He lay the problem aside, throwing himself on the satin spread that covered the bed to the floor. He was doing something wrong. He would have to return to the beginning, to the man in the tower, to the ziggurat of Shinar, and the wrath of God. But not now. He was waiting for a wind from the sea to blow freshness through his pores like linen on a line in the sun. He was also waiting for Vicky.

CHAPTER THIRTEEN

HE SLEPT for a quarter of an hour, and when he awoke to soft knocking, the sun shone obliquely through the portholes casting elliptical lights that looked like thin sheets of ice, harbingers from the inhospitable Arctic. Never in his life had his bedroom door been under such continual strain as lately, and opening it this time, Vicky said, "Hi," and ran her fingernails like a comb through the hairs on his naked chest. He glanced down the corridor before closing her inside. Phil E. Stein had left his shoes outside his door as if the *Colomba Bianca* were just another wayside hotel.

"Alone at last," Vicky said, dropping her gold-colored robe and crawling nude into his bed. "No headaches?"

Zack Robertts, standing ten feet away, shook no.

"Lovely. 'Cause there's no Bibles. I double-checked every drawer. But I've got aspirin, Dramamine, and the pill. So both of us are covered."

He moved to the bed and sat on the edge. He was still in his trousers. He had known she was coming the moment he saw that Jean-Marie had given him a room to himself. A part of his vanity had been hoping that he was mistaken, that her interest in his being had been moved by the sum that was greater than his parts and not by commands from above, but now, in her confirming presence, he was pleased with himself. A thought line had straggled on the wool in his head. He began to sense where he may have gone wrong. It was a line that had to be pulled, unraveling the whole obstruction.

"Hey," Vicky cried softly. "Look at me, not the bloody wall."

He turned to her.

"Warm me up, Zack," she said, extending her English-white arm like the neck of a swan. "I won't take but a bit. Not with you, I mean."

A bit, he thought. One of Jean-Marie's favorite words. The plutonium bar had been a bit. With bits one could bridle a horse, drill a hole in a wall, and blow the world. Words; his life was a tower of words. He undressed and lay beside her under the satin spread, and he watched the man die.

"Is Debby your lover, Zack?" Her hands sought warmth.

He ran it backwards, and the puddle of blood went back into the man's head and the crowd became happy again as the man rose from the gray mass of stone to the top of the Qutb Minar.

"What makes you ask that, Vicky?" His voice was cold.

"Your eyes. I mean, *your* eyes, Zack. They're bottomless, so full of thoughts you're not ever going to say. But they speak to me ... Besides, women can tell those things." She was not warming.

"They can?"

The man backed down the spiral staircase, his breath returning.

Vicky nodded like a priest. "Is she?"

"Is that your turn-on, Vicky?"

"Sometimes."

When she lied, he noticed, her body lost all motion, holding as still as an iguana taking readings of the sun.

He saw the man retreating from the entrance, passing the guard, and he read the sign by the ticket seller and the words were clear.

"Hearing all the intimate details about how we do it? *Son et lumière.* The inside story, you might say."

Vicky giggled. "Horses for courses, Zack."

The man returned his ticket; then, there was another man

with him throwing him from the top of the Qutb Minar, and Zack Robertts knew who he was because of words that made his face clear.

"That's an American expression, Vicky," he said making the men fade away. "You ever been to America?" He could feel her grow tense, dissipating heat.

"I've got lots of American friends."

It was less than an answer, or more, but he said nothing.

"Aren't we going to fuck, Zack? You're always changing the subject. I'm getting a bit suspicious, you know."

She smiled at him, but his face hardened in the Arctic-sent light, and an arm's width divided their bodies.

"I didn't mean that, Zack. I promise you ... You're not cross, are you?"

"How about India? Got lots of Indian friends?"

She looked at him oddly, almost frightened. "I've never been to India ... Is this *your* turn-on, Zack? Chattering like we was drinking our tea?"

"You told me you'd been there. The first time I met you."

"You've got it wrong, Zack. You really do." She rose and leaned on one elbow, suddenly sure of herself. "I said I was *going* to India with this boy I know — who happens to be an American, by the way."

He barely waited for her last word. "But you said you were in India in April with Jean-Marie."

"He didn't take me on that tr ——" She threw her head back on the pillow and lay flat, staring at the ceiling. "You tricked me, Zack Robertts!"

His bottomless eyes gloated. "Twice, Vicky, twice ... I never saw this Debby character in my life. She is kind of beautiful, though, isn't she?" He felt cruel.

"It's not fair. You know I'm not supposed to tell you Jean-Marie's business. A good secretary is a sacred trust. Like doctor and patient. The first half of the word 'secretary' is 'secret,' in case you didn't know."

"That's three times, Vicky."

She was horrified. He chose his words with surgical care. He was opening her but he would have to close her as well.

"Your loyalty is to be admired, Vicky, but now I know that the only reason you keep slipping in and out of my room like Santa Claus concerns Jean-Marie's 'business,' as you put it — like finding out if this woman is my secret weapon."

Vicky gasped indignantly and sat tucking the satin under her body as if to prevent all access to it.

"So I do my job and tell him things I hear, but I ain't no bloody tart, Zack Robertts! Not Vicky Walsh! I really went for you, Zack, I really did. And Jean-Marie didn't tell me to either! But now . . . now I . . . hate you!"

She rolled over and sobbed. He let her cry for a while, thinking of the half-century of turmoil life was yet to unleash on this woman and that he was as much a tail on that whip as Jean-Marie. Then he whispered in her ear.

"That was four, Vicky," he said as she burrowed into the pillow, her hair spreading like fire. It was time to fascinate her. "I just wanted to hear you say you went for me."

Her body stopped quivering. She looked up at him, her nose runny and milky, her cheeks aflame. They made love to the throb of the sea.

That was five.

During the luminous night, while the *Colomba Bianca* sailed west for the mile-deep waters of the North Atlantic, Vicky kissed him on both eyes with lips lighter still than her breath on his brow and she left him. He had been feigning sleep. His mind in fact rattled like a press flapping out the morning news. The moment she had gone and he could hear a second door close in the hall, he rose and dressed in his track suit. It was half past five, Saturday, the sixteenth of June.

For nineteen days following form alone he had been living

in the narrow confines of logic and reason and all the other sober arts that spoke of what ought to be, but not always of what was; now he wished to run in the cosmic space between them. He went topside. Someone with dust thick on his soles had stomped on Phil E. Stein's shoes, and it cheered him. When he had boarded the *Colomba Bianca*, he had heard the crew speaking Sicilian, which was about as far from Italian as English was from German. Proud people these Sicilians: their sailors sailed; their bootblacks shined shoes.

When he reached the deck, he took a bearing on the sun, which leaned on a hazy sky. The *Colomba Bianca* had turned north again. It was climbing the fifth meridian to the baldness on the top of the world. He ran clockwise to celebrate his break with his nineteen days. The sewn planks of wood underfoot were wet with sea spray. He ran slowly, throwing his elbows toward each other now and then to free his lungs from the curtain of muscle on his back. His half-clenched hands were cold. Steam poured from his mouth as if caldrons boiled inside him. He ran for forty minutes, gaining speed, dripping hot sweat that cooled on his face in lines. A Sicilian seaman shouted, *"Ué!"* When he stopped running he felt salted and peppered.

He swathed his neck in a towel and he bounced on the balls of his feet in a short forward shuffle, dancing to the drums he had set beating inside him. At this pace, he went to the prow to look at the north, a bleak mantle of gray on the horizon. Shiva was there, packed in a coat of Kashmiri rabbits. With their backs to the ship, she took his cold hand in her furs. There were lines around her eyes and no gem in her nose, only a little hole. But her beauty was not alterable; it was melancholy.

"I've been up all night, Zack," she said when they had decided that they were safely alone. "Half of it in conference with Jean-Marie. I have come to the unhappy conclusion that he is a beast."

"He killed Hanumappa, you know."

"A beast, yes. A killer, obviously. But not my guru, Zack
... My goodness, be reasonable."

"Have you ever been to the top of the Qutb Minar, Shiva?"

She smiled wistfully, the forward motion of the boat flattening the rabbit hairs, which were damp with tiny bubbles
of foam.

"I lived two years in Delhi as a child, and I longed — oh,
how I longed — to go to the Qutb and stand at the top and see
the sacred river, just like the little princess for whom it was
built and who spoke to me in books. But my father was a type
— Oxbridge, the London School of Economics, the Indian
Civil Service, and all that — who detested mingling with
crowds, meaning even one person who was of the lower
castes. And once, when my class went to the Qutb on an
outing, Father forbade me to go. I finally climbed the tower
only a year or so ago, but by then it just seemed like the inside
of a cannon, and the river was obscured by high-rise buildings and smog."

"You went alone?"

"No. With Shri Hanumappa, as a matter of fact. He would
go often, always dragging one of us with him, or some visitor,
exhausting everyone. He had become quite Islamophile and
would go on for hours how if it hadn't been for the sultans and
Mughals, India would be nothing but a land of cows. This
was all during his illness, of course. He sometimes claimed to
have converted to Manichaeism, if you can imagine that . . .
But what are you driving at, Zack?"

"That he didn't commit suicide. That he was thrown from
the top. By Jean-Marie . . . Because you can't go inside the
Qutb Minar alone, Shiva. There's a little sign at the door, by
the ticket seller. It's written in Hindi and English, and the
English says something like — 'No one admitted unless accompanied . . .' It's to prevent suicides. And there's a guard."

She stared at him with a look of recall on her face. "But

there have been suicides at the Qutb. One reads about them every so often."

"Not because they got in alone. If Hanumappa had killed himself there would have been someone with him to tell the story. There was. Only he hasn't told. Because the story is murder."

"And why Jean-Marie?"

"He was in India in April."

She smiled. "That is not what I would call an open-and-shut case, Monsieur Poirot. So were five hundred and fifty million others, including you."

"We didn't have a motive . . . Hanumappa had something to tell me, Shiva. About the CIA. Maybe who Abraham was. Definitely about what ziggurat meant. Things he had already revealed to a friend of mine. He, too, was murdered. Hanumappa told me to meet him at the Qutb. Jean-Marie got there first. Somehow he got him to climb to the top."

Shiva shook her head. "Zack, if Pandit Hanumappa had learned of CIA infiltration, although I confess that I cannot imagine how, he would have gone directly to Jean-Marie, not to you or your friend. They were working together, very closely. The entire O.N.A.N. adventure revolved around them. Of that much, I am absolutely sure."

"He would have . . . unless Jean-Marie was the CIA."

"You are not being realistic, Zack."

Zack Robertts was silent for a long while. He was not being "realistic." On this day, he had purged *the* reality, gouging its Cyclopean eye and turning it on end. He had kicked it. There was another reality, in which he had supposed that the CIA had *not* infiltrated O.N.A.N.; he had supposed that the CIA *was* O.N.A.N. He had supposed that Abraham was not working for the CIA but *against* the CIA. He had supposed that ziggurat was *not* a plan to intercept the O.N.A.N. "adventure," as she had called it. He had supposed that ziggurat *was* the adventure!

But he could not expect Shiva to understand *this* reality. It lay across a Rubicon, to where his whole life had been pushing him, urging him, easing him gently, until it had finally grabbed him by the neck and ran him over the divide. There, he was alone, and, like Abraham, he felt his position weakening.

"Shiva," he said at last. "You've got to build the bomb wrong. So that it doesn't work."

She shook her head. "I shall have enough trouble putting it together correctly. You are speaking of another impossibility. Jean-Marie knows as much about the assembly as I do. And worse, we are dealing with plutonium-two-forty, not the more stable isotope we had been hoping for. It is potentially a spontaneously fissionable material. If it is not constructed with utmost precision, well I don't have to tell you what might happen to us . . . We must wait for the interception."

He stared at her at length. She was being realistic. She took his hand again.

"Krishna thinks of you often, Zack. Alone, at night, in her bed."

The sea had been showering them with droplets of moisture. Crystals of salt sprinkled their faces. They sparkled. He knew all that had to be known now. He wished he could call to Shiva from beyond their divide, but Krishna would surely betray him.

Joachim von Schwarzwald had summoned Miklos Brody to his office, and the moment he arrived and Kerstin had closed the door, he blurted the latest news.

"Miklosh, ze SS have washed their hands of ze entire affair!"

"This is not good."

"It is tragic," Kerstin said, still facing the door.

"It is worse than tragic! It is scandalous! They say that ze Italian ship is not in Shvedish territory, but, ze truth is that they refuse to act because they are covering up ze robbery of ze plutonium at ze Svenska Nuklear. And ve know who is ze robbers and ze *Schweinerei* they are up to. They say that ze O.N.A.N. did not get enough plutonium to do serious damage ... But, this is lies! They are embarrassed and are covering up. Here, in Shveden!" He looked up at Miklos appealingly. "Miklosh, you know what you must do?"

Miklos regarded him questioningly.

"You must go to Oslo."

Kerstin turned to assess Miklos's reaction. He seemed torn, but agreed.

"This is true," he said. "I understand."

"Ve have no contacts there. But you are a United Nations official. They vill listen to you. They have nothing to cover up, like these shpineless Shvedes! ... You must get to ze Minister of Interior. They must be shtopped at Norvay. There vill be no more chances after that! ... You vill go at once?"

"Yes, at once." Miklos could feel Kerstin's gravid eyes.

Von Schwarzwald handed him an airline ticket. He looked at his watch. "There is a flight in two hours. You have time to pack. Ze foundation is paying. To protect ze name of Pär Sjögren. But I vill have much to explain. Ve have no funds for such things."

"This ticket, I am not needing. I can ——"

"No. There is no time to debate. You must get to ze airport. Ze driver is waiting."

Von Schwarzwald rolled his chair around his desk and ushered Miklos to the door. He told him to call from Oslo as soon as there was something to report. He wished Miklos well. Kerstin kissed him. She stroked his face and his forehead and his eyes with both hands until Miklos became uncomfortable with so much love, and she kissed him saying nothing. She spoke when he was gone, watching from the window as his car drove away.

"Poor Miklos is slipping away," she said.

"What are you talking about, voman?"

"I can feel his presence slipping away."

"He is going to ze airport, to Arlanda, to Oslo." His tone grew flaccid and timorous.

"Slipping away. Like the lilacs on Castle Hill. The sun is burning the grass. The lilacs are wilting, *älskling*."

"In Oslo, they vill listen. They vill listen in Oslo." Von Schwarzwald began to tremble. He tightened his fists on the wheels of his chair until his fingers whitened.

"They need help, *älskling*. They need help. Real help. Or they will die."

"Ve have no funds," he said faintly, rolling himself so that his back was to Kerstin. His whole body shook in violent paroxysms. "I have no funds ... I have no funds ..." His voice sank to a broken whisper.

On Sunday, the seventeenth, the *Colomba Bianca* spewed its anal foam on the Arctic Circle, and north of it, Shiva began to build Menes-II, the plutonium implosion bomb.

She worked on the Italian-made billiard table. It had been covered with joinable oak panels, which gave a level, uniform surface and legroom below the perimeter. Everyone watched, including Deborah Colt, the captain, and most of the crew. Jean-Marie had no secrets.

The weapon, with its ventral cavity sprung open, was anchored at one end of the table by means of wires sunk into the wood. The sea heaved like a giant's chest. The boat pitched. It was raining and the windows looked like translucent parchment. Shiva had suggested waiting for a calmer day, but Jean-Marie, who had consulted the captain, said the weather was expected to worsen.

The table seemed like an altar, on which Menes-II, standing tall in its silver skin, was a totem, and the objects around it, if one could abstract them from their function, were like fetishes within the circle formed by the congregation. In actuality, the objects were these: one Smithfield electric furnace, which was about the size of a television set; one tubular glass distilling apparatus attached to the exhaust tube of the furnace at one end, and at the other, to a Landau laboratory bottle; two ceramic crucibles, each of them hemispheres sixty-five millimeters in diameter; one Victoreen Geiger counter, connected to a high voltage battery; and the plutonium box. A large array of other equipment and materials, to be used at a later stage, lay strewn on the carpeted floor.

Shiva wore white, asbestos gloves. She lacked only a few touches of greasepaint to evoke Al Jolson in blackface. But there was nothing facetious about her demeanor. She was fidgety. She dropped things, which slid across the table when the ship inclined. Jean-Marie glowered at her. Zack Robertts marveled at her imperishable beauty, immutable in any circumstance. She was dressed in black leotards, and when she stood against the even light flattened on the windows, she seemed a naked shadow on a screen.

The electric furnace was on, drawing power from the ship's generators, which had raised the temperature to 600 degrees centigrade. Plutonium melts at 639.5 degrees centigrade. The temperature went up. It activated a thermostat holding the heat inside at a preselected constant: 700 degrees.

Shiva opened the plutonium box. She removed two of the feverish bars and closed it again. The Geiger counter began a slow tattoo announcing the presence of the twin ingots encircled by their alpha warriors — an army of mindless killers.

Plutonium of itself was among the most lethal substances in the universe, Shiva told the others in a voice that seemed restrained by viscous glue. An invisible speck of plutonium dust, a thousandth of a gram breathed in would bring on a fatal paralysis of the lungs in a matter of hours; a thousandth of a thousandth of a gram — a microgram — would stream through the blood and settle in one's bones causing death slowly by its everlasting rays.

The tubes rising from the furnace, however, would serve to trap and condense the gaseous impurities escaping from the melting metal, and she attested that there was therefore no cause for concern. But when the bars were in the crucibles inside the furnace and the glass began to cloud, then chime with the rocking of the ship, she, as the others, stood watch with fear, and she chose to withhold that the greatest peril lay ahead.

The plutonium bars, leaning on end, melted into a blue liquid, which could be seen through a window in the furnace door, and they dripped slowly into their containers like sweating ice, taking on identical hemispherical forms and overflowing. When at last they were left to resolidify in the cooling Smithfield, there was general relief, and Jean-Marie announced a pause in which a special Sunday lunch would be served.

The ship's cook came out smiling under a sagging chef's hat. The boys from Palermo rolled in steaming carts of Sicilian specialties. Fabrizio, with Deborah at his side, beamed like a headwaiter in the presence of his most discriminating clientele. But almost no one ate. Zack Robertts sat in a lounge chair watching raindrops strike the deck outside. They danced on a wet stage that reflected the heavy clouds passing overhead. He saw ballerinas performing on top of the sky. He felt untithed.

Later in the afternoon they gathered around the billiard table once again. The crew members who had watched the earlier session ceded their places to those who had been below. This had been done at Jean-Marie's request, and Zack Robertts thought he understood why. Jean-Marie, he believed, wanted as many witnesses as possible; hence his repeatedly enunciated no-secrets policy. While this diminished Zack Robertts's fears for Deborah's safety, it heightened those for his own. His importance as a credibility factor was necessarily lessened the more others could vouch in his stead, and he knew that he knew too much.

The weather forecasts were proving accurate. Electrical storms bearing hail were being moved by northerly gale-force winds onto the course of the ship. The *Colomba Bianca* pitched harder than before; it moaned.

Shiva broke the ceramic crucibles with a hammer. She peeled away the excess metal like an orange, and when all the scraps were removed, she placed the two hemispheres together in a perfect plutonium ball.

The Geiger counter began to click at an extremely fast rate. The indicator on the instrument's dial shot from 2 curies per minute on a scale of 150 to 67 per minute. Fabrizio crossed himself, much to the surprise of the captain and the crew.

Shiva explained that the sphere was only slightly subcritical now. Tommy Kaneoka had calculated the critical size — at which a nuclear explosion would occur — at 140 curies per minute. But that had been for plutonium-239. Plutonium-240 would fission at less. Tommy had not lived long enough to work out the lower figure, although Shiva was aware that it was in the range of 25 percent less, which brought the chain reaction point down to 105. She drew the fail-safe line at 100.

The Geiger counter continued to hold at 67 curies per minute. From here on, Shiva said, she would be working under high-risk conditions until the assembly would be complete. She reminded everyone of the problems involved in the shaped-charge, implosion-system nuclear bomb, which the Italians and Deborah were hearing for the first time.

The beryllium container, the C4 waxlike TNT that had to be packed around it, and the high-explosive lenses continually escalated the danger of collision between the atoms in the plutonium core and the free neutrons that were exciting the air chamber of the Geiger counter. They were being reflected back against the minimally subcritical mass by the steady addition of the core's outer components. The bomb could go off in her hands. The Geiger counter was their only safeguard. As long as it read under 100 curies per minute, theoretically there should be no spontaneous explosion.

Fabrizio did his best to translate what Shiva had said. Deborah helped him. Apparently they were successful because at a certain point — Zack Robertts noted that it was on the word "theoretically" — the captain and his crew crossed themselves in unison.

Shiva declared herself ready to begin. She collected the plutonium scraps, put them in the box containing the one bar still intact, and as there was no longer any need for these radioactive remains, and it being wiser to have as few free neutrons around as possible, she instructed that the whole box be dumped in the sea. Accordingly, this was done by a member of the crew and $40,000 worth of plutonium sank to the ocean floor west of the Norwegian northland.

In the meantime, Shiva rearranged the table, which had been cleared except for Menes-II and the Smithfield. She brought out the beryllium sphere, the wickless C4 candles, and the high-explosive lenses, which looked as if they had been molded in plastic on a female breast, nipple and all. The mere presence of these materials on the same surface as the plutonium ball raised the Geiger counter dial to 73.

Shiva put the plutonium core in the wire cage that held it in place at the center of the beryllium reflector. She closed the two halves. The Geiger counter jumped ten points with a distressing accentuation of its clicking that began with an electronic gasp. No one spoke.

She soldered the beryllium sphere together, leaving a tiny

opening on the seam, into which she inserted the nozzle of a vacuum pump, and she exhausted the air inside.

Zack Robertts watched her with a vague feeling of having known at some distant time in the past that she would be doing exactly as she was now. But time came toward him like a launched fist and struck him with a boxer's glove: *he knew Hanumappa's secret and where it had been obtained.* It was all so easy now.

When the interior had been vacuumized the nozzle was withdrawn. It had been fitted with an adhesive rubber membrane that closed the breach on removal long enough for her to seal it with additional solder. She lay the gleaming ball aside.

She had regained her composure since the morning and seemed now in keen command of her task. She removed her gloves and her rings. She heated the C4 TNT in the furnace at a low temperature and began to knead it in her hands. The yellowish substance obeyed the wishes of her fingers, giving off its aromatic smell. She rolled it out like baker's dough taking wads from the warmed candles, and when she had a pancakelike sheet, she smoothed it on the beryllium surface, repeating the process continually. Each time she added more of the explosive, the Geiger counter responded, and when the sphere had been completely covered with an even layer of TNT, the indicator read 85 curies per minute.

In this way, she estimated that if for every layer the count were to rise two points, and if the total number of layers were nine, it would pass one hundred, creating an atomic fireball. She looked at the candles, which represented the precise amount of TNT that had to be packed on the sphere, and she tried to gauge how many layers they might make. It seemed that there would be more than nine in all, but she knew that there was a point of diminishing returns, which would tend to taper off the effects of accretion. She hoped it would come soon. She said nothing of this to the others, nor of the remote possibility that the TNT, under the constant manipulation of her hands, could itself, if imperfect, explode accidentally, splitting the creaking *Colomba Bianca* in two on the lonely sea.

Even without this knowledge the tension in the onlookers grew as the count moved toward 100. This was manifest less in their eyes, faces, and hands — although that, too — than in the air they communally breathed. It was as if there were only so much oxygen in the room, which had to be passed around the table after each labored respiration, the way soldiers in combat share a canteen of water. By now the air had become rubbery and sticky and its effect on the mind was drugging, numbing all sensation but fear, which lashed out like a solar prominence.

At least it seemed that way to Zack Robertts. He feared the vaporizing fireball, the dispersal of the finite self and the ultimate, timeless encounter with the universe. He no longer thought of that as death, however, nor as romantic birth; his was a fear, an apprehension, of a journey of return, of going home with nothing done.

Shiva's work was a painstaking effort in achieving absolute symmetry around the beryllium sphere. This was essential so that after detonation the implosive shock wave would exert a uniform compression on the core, without which the result would be a fizzle yield of scarce effect. If there were a stage at which she could "build the bomb wrong," as Zack Robertts had requested of her, it was now. But, under Jean-Marie's fierce gaze, the thought never occurred to her. Rather, as she began to reach the end of the supply of candles, and the Geiger counter clamored in the low nineties, she repeatedly passed a thin, stiff measuring wire through the layers of TNT to the depth of the reflector to survey the evenness of the outer shell.

Hours had gone by since she had first begun to knead the TNT, and it was all she could do to flatten the remaining mass of the last candle and smooth it into place. Her palms ached as if she had been squeezing a handball for the same length of time, and her fingers were no longer capable of subtle movement. Nevertheless she completed the procedure without mishap, and after a few final probes with the measuring wire, she declared the job done. The sphere resembled a shaved human head, a horribly faceless creature with the sallow skin of jaundice.

The Geiger counter, though it had continued to climb, had remained under 92 for the past thirty minutes or so. This, and the remarkable accommodative faculties of human beings over time, had made for some relief. But when Shiva set the first high-explosive lens on the sphere, the count leaped over the 100 line.

Vicky screamed.

Jean-Marie shot up and leaned forward on his clenched fist in an attitude of protest against an unexpected outrage.

Phil E. Stein covered his eyes with his hands, then peeked through his fingers. His African hat fell from his head.

Muhammed yanked his beard violating the roots.

Ibrahim pursed his lips.

Zack Robertts looked at Deborah as if he desired the image of her face to accompany him to the long forever. She was bluish white.

Nothing happened.

Shiva had lifted the lens instantly, and those who had shown no outward reaction had probably not even noticed that something had gone wrong, although the captain departed from the table saying that he was needed below. When he got to the door, he quickened his pace, muttering something in Sicilian.

There was a busy, multilingual exchange for a minute or

two in which the event was discussed and relived with incoherence. It was left to Shiva to bring order.

"Apparently," she said speaking thickly, "the margin of safety is wider than anticipated — how much so, I cannot imagine. Secondly, the lens may be defective. For my part, I believe it is a question of both." She paused drawing a breath so deep it made her grow. "I am prepared to try another."

Jean-Marie nodded easing himself back into his chair. Fabrizio made the sign of the Cross again, as did the crew. Vicky crossed her fingers on both hands. Olle was lost. He kept his eyes on Zack Robertts, as if he were not his prisoner but his protector. Zack Robertts, avoiding the wrench of Deborah's blue white fear, looked at the mammillary lenses.

There were four of them on the table, two more, as reserves, on the floor. Their shape was identical, each designed to encase a quadrant of the sphere. The offending component lay off to one side. Shiva tried another one, lowering it in the still air gently into position. The Geiger counter registered 97 curies per minute, and everyone sighed, but it could hardly be taken as good news.

"It seems I was correct in both propositions," said Shiva. "However, I expect that the addition of the three other lenses, assuming no further defects, shall bring the count to one hundred and twelve. I cannot say for certain that the plutonium core will withstand that degree of pressure. But it is all too clear that we must either take this grave risk or abandon our plans entirely. I think this is something we shall have to decide among us, after searching our souls."

No one seemed in need of such profound contemplation. There was in the air a feeling of willing unconditional surrender, and if the long momentum could have been struck down in that moment, there would have been a glorious celebration of defeat. Zack Robertts watched Jean-Marie.

"My dear Shiva," Jean-Marie said, "this is not a church

or a house of parliament. The miscalculations were yours. The decision is mine. I shall let you know what it is . . . shortly."

He got up and took leave, ordering Olle, Fabrizio, and the crew members to go with him.

They were gone for a quarter of an hour, time enough for Shiva to remark confidentially to Zack Robertts that she had done all she could and that Jean-Marie was a beast. Zack Robertts looked at Ibrahim, who was as impassive as ever. He wondered if he were secretly armed.

When Jean-Marie returned, the captain and the men who had left the room with him, as well as several other members of the crew, entered with him. Olle stood by the door. Fabrizio's face had the color, his legs the consistency, of Dijon mustard.

Jean-Marie made a prefatory speech about moral principles and how the danger had been known from the start, but it had been plain from the moment he came back what he had done in the interim, and what his decision had been. Some of the crew had taken up strategic positions around the room. Their pockets were as full as Olle's. There would be no mutiny aboard the *Colomba Bianca*.

A black storm had broken overhead like an egg on the edge of a knife. Hail squalls pelted the ship with ice shot, and rain splashed it by the lakeful. Forked lightning plunged into the sea, and with every jagged stroke thunder rattled the windows, and the air the lightning had ionized made the Geiger counter click faster for a while. The jade-colored lamp that hung over the table swung wide displaying the arc at which the ship, not the lamp, was being tossed. The inhumanoid sphere rolled until Shiva picked it up and cradled it in her arms. They could do nothing but grope for and clutch objects fixed to the floor and wait for the worst to blow past. When it did, Shiva resumed.

No one doubted that she could get at least two of the high-explosive lenses in place, and with that done, the count was at 102. Ibrahim rocked back and forth hardly watching at all, but there was sweat on everyone's brow, his, too, as she put the third lens to bed with a motherly touch. The fourth quadrant gaped on the three-breasted monster. Shiva checked the count: 107. The intervals between clicks were almost indistinguishable now, and the sound was like a purr.

Shiva had noted that the instrument reacted proportionately to the distance between the lens and the sphere. Thus in bringing the former closer to the latter, the movement of her hand regulated the rate of increase on the Geiger counter dial. She could raise it point by point until contact was made, and conversely lower it if necessary. She was prepared to allow an increment of five points, although, as she had said, she had no way of knowing if this were above the tolerance of the plutonium core. But at least she would become aware in advance of placement, should the final lens be faulty, as the first one had been. She explained this to the others hoping to offer some consolation. If it did, it was invisibly small.

Taking the lens in hand, she lifted the count one point at a time as she approached the last quadrant like a plane trying to land on a rock. At a reading of 111, the lens was a fraction of an inch above the surface. Her large pupils were beamed on her target, a patch like a baby's buttock. Perspiration ran into the corners of her eyes and burned. Her hands fluttered. She could hear flat, irregular breathing around her that seemed only inhalations drawn deeper and deeper. She set the lens in position. The count was 112. She pulled the Geiger counter wire from its battery. It stopped purring. She leaned back in her seat. It was not until then that everyone exhaled.

There were wires to be connected to the lens nipples. The

CHAPTER FOURTEEN

THE REVEREND AGENT IN RECENT DAYS had grown disenchanted with Abraham's performance. Abraham had failed to warn him that the Swedish police had been poised at Malmö to arrest the entire O.N.A.N. group, as well as everyone aboard the *Colomba Bianca* upon arrival at the port. This was information he had received from the CIA Stockholm Station *after* the mass arrest was to have taken place. Furthermore, the news had come to him via his triple agent — the operative in the station considered by Swedish Security as their double agent.

In other words, it was clear to Huntz Merriwether that Abraham had known, or in the most generous instance, should have known — and of course immediately reported — the SS's intentions, since he was being kept continually informed of its activities in this matter.

Abraham's negligence or ineptness, if indeed not something infinitely worse, had been a first-class "fornication-ascent," which was a term Huntz Merriwether employed, in substitution of a more common vulgarity, to describe a gross error. Had it not been for another fornication-ascent — the "clumsy" getaway from the Svenska Nuklear plant and the consequent passage through Göteberg — Operation Ziggurat would have been "nipped in the bud" — a phrase that in spite of its usual negative connotation, excited Huntz Merriwether with eye splashes of the blossoming effects of the hormonal sap in pubescent girls, every one of whom he saw himself nipping.

Be that as it may, he now regarded the clumsy getaway as a

"Godsend," or a "stroke of luck," in which "two wrongs had made a right." Good O, because the new concept of innovative intelligence gaining ground in the CIA permitted no fornication-ascents, or at least none that could ever become publicly known.

In this vein, there were two questions that were urgent at the moment. First, what to think and do about Abraham, and second, what to think and do about Zack Robertts. Huntz Merriwether, as has been said and implied, was a methodical creature. When he had two matters to review, he excluded one absolutely, and probed the other completely, and upon its resolution, he reversed the very same process.

When reflecting, he stood and paced up and down. He thought with his hands in his pockets, which were almost always otherwise empty since most of his pockets had holes worn through the cloth from frequent, methodical thinking. Such, too, was the usual condition of his undershorts, and the threadbare fabric of all these contraptions, as well as the edges of his loose-fitting T-shirts, were quite often stiff, discolored, and wrinkled. Being an orphan, he had never learned to take care of his clothes.

Rising from his gun-metal desk, Huntz Merriwether began to think in his systematic fashion. Abraham had not only neglected the Malmö situation, but he had neglected to report that he had neglected the Malmö situation. That was Huntz Merriwether's first methodical thought. His second was that this could have but two meanings: a) premeditated neglect, or b) postmeditated neglect. The first was treachery. The second was idiocy. Huntz Merriwether drew back from deciding for one or the other, although his method brought to mind a set of old data in support of Proposition A. To wit: (i) Abraham had been reported months back as having been sighted in Dar es Salaam in the company of Ibrahim, who was a dumb nigger; (ii) Abraham was a defector from behind the Iron Curtain, and it was axiomatic at Langley that once a defector, always a defector. On the other hand, Abraham had been an apparently faithful and obedient servant since his recruitment in India near the start of the ziggurat conception. Huntz Merriwether, however, reserved his judgment. His father, Jack, had always taught him to reserve his judgment. Nevertheless he came to the irreversible conclusion that Abraham had blown his usefulness and would have to be stripped of his mandate. This required action.

By now, Huntz Merriwether had painted the floor of his office with the sole-prints of his Florsheim shoes, and his hands were plunged through the holes in his pockets. He turned now to methodical thoughts of Zack Robertts.

Zack Robertts, who had heard the terms "ziggurat" and "Abraham" used in the cable supplied by the SS's double agent (later to become the CIA's triple), had subsequently been reported as: a) having requested the Holy Bible; b) having asked the specific question, "Are you Abraham?"; and c) according to Radio WOP, he had managed to spend some moments of seclusion with Ibrahim, who was a dumb nigger, where he was overheard inquiring, "Who is he?" This raised two questions: (i) had he made inroads in his apparent attempt to decipher the ziggurat plan?; (ii) had such an effort actually succeeded? These were interrogatives that for Huntz Merriwether required no answers. Their existence alone jeopardized the secrecy of the operation. Zack Robertts had blown his usefulness. There would be no fornication-ascents. This, too, required action.

Huntz Merriwether called Mary Clapperton on the intercom, inviting her into his office. He said he wanted to give her "dic — tation," but it sounded like a cry for help.

Facing the door, he was still on his feet, hands buried in the thinking position, when Mary Clapperton entered, her two-dimensional figure filling his eyes. She perceived at once that he had been engaged in strenuous mental activity, and she could tell that he had been so at length from the knobby salient between his pockets. All too well did she know what the next few minutes would bring.

She had learned about his pockets early in her civil service career, when, seated at the side of his desk for dictation, a florid mushroom had ripened out of one hole, coaxed at the stem through the other. It had been then that she discovered that jiggling her pencil to recall him from distractions — a commodious technique adopted on the very first day of her job — had in this case no value whatsoever. In the way good secretaries acquire mastery over the idiosyncrasies of the indivduals whom they are hired to serve, which was nothing less than a trial by punishment and reward, Mary Clapperton created The Ritual. The Ritual was pencil-jiggling by other means, and whereas the latter serviced all other assaults on her person, only The Ritual could alleviate the pressures elevated by Huntz Merriwether's methodical thinking.

Mary Clapperton locked the door behind her and approached Huntz Merriwether with all the correctness of a physician coming face to face with a helplessly stricken patient. Huntz Merriwether had backed up to his desk and he slouched against it like someone with two trick knees out of place. His arms seemed dead branches stuck into the tent he had made of his trousers. He was immobile. Mary Clapperton walked across the room, her pleated black skirt swaying from side to side around her knees. She sat in his deskside chair. She crossed her legs, closing them as tightly as a book in its slipcase. She and he were virtually back to back, which signaled the start of The Ritual. She looked at her watch. Now, she knew, in one minute and forty-five seconds, or thereabouts, it would all be over.

"Sister," he said.

She winced. "Yes?"

Her voice was as vacant as a lonely plain. She had by draft and redraft authored all of her lines and she played her part by rote. But The Ritual was still undergoing change and experimentation insofar as she was secretly trying to shorten its duration by accelerating her delivery without loss of therapeutic effect.

"Did you ever," he asked accusatorily, "perform an unnatural sexual act?"

"Only once."

"When?"

"When I was very young."

"In the age of puberty?"

"Yes."

"Before or after the onset of menarche?"

"After."

"What was the condition of your pubic symphysis?"

"It was partially covered by a triangular patch of sparse, reddish hair."

"And your breasts?"

"They were budding."

"Ha! They never got very far, did they? ... And your nipples?"

"They were budding."

"Where did you perform this unnatural sexual act?"

"In New York City."

"Can you be more specific?"

"In an alley."

"What was the condition of this alley?"

"It was filthy. Teeming with garbage being eaten by rats. It smelled of urine and vomit."

This was the speech she liked best. Not that it revolted her any less than the entire playlet, but it was her penultimate line. She stood now for the finale.

"What was the nature of this unnatural sexual act, sister?"

Huntz Merriwether's face glowed with imbecilic curiosity. Mary Clapperton paused for one second, which was part of The Ritual. Then she went around to meet his eyes and blurted.

"I sucked a nigger's cock!"

"Oh, my God!" Huntz Merriwether cried out in a soprano.

He bolted from the office, as Mary Clapperton calmly unlocked and opened the door with perfect timing. He ran down the corridor to the men's room. He latched himself in a stall. He returned shortly afterward, the paralytic strain expelled. He was limp. Mary Clapperton stole a glance at her watch. She smiled inwardly. She had broken her record and he had broken his, trimming four seconds from The Ritual.

If this were a pleasure minted small, a larger one was to be enjoyed in the striking change in Huntz Merriwether's behavior that invariably appeared in the wake of The Ritual. For a period never less than twenty-four hours, sometimes more, he would be abjectly mortified. During this interval, which they both called The Penance, though never between them, he would, not without difficulty, keep his hands from his pockets, his eyes to the floor (even when she would walk out of his office), and would refrain from calling her "sister." Not once in this respite had Mary Clapperton ever had to jiggle her pencil.

"Miss Clapperton," he said weakly. He sat bent in his chair, his hands clasped in a ball on his desk, his tie hanging loosely between his legs. "I would like to draft a brief memorandum to be transmitted by NADAR message impulse scatterer to Radio W — that is to say, the gentlemen from Palermo."

He did not look up, but he could see from the corner of his eye that instead of taking up her stenographer's notebook, Mary Clapperton was handing him a sheet of perforated-edged paper from the bank of AMRAD automatic decoding machines on the floor below them.

"When did this co—— I mean, arrive?"

"While you were in the men's room."

Huntz Merriwether reddened. Mary Clapperton let the message fall like a leaf beneath his eyes. He read it, his humiliations departing as anger came rushing in.

"This *is* treachery, sis—— Miss Clapperton! There will be no forni—— I mean, no mistakes! . . . Kill the memorandum. Fill out a pink form. I will need immediate travel authorization to Svalbard, Vest Spitsbergen, with a stop at the Oslo Station." He hesitated for a moment. He seemed to be regaining his old self, an extraordinary recovery. "And on the way back," he added, looking up with an ungainly smile, "a stop in Copenhagen."

He began to reach into his desk drawer for one of his favorite magazines. Mary Clapperton was shocked. She stared at him severely. She thought that she might even have to jiggle her pencil. But Huntz Merriwether, closing his drawer, again grew contrite.

"You're right, Miss Clapperton. Kill Copenhagen."

Ibrahim K. Nkele, flat in his berth on the *Colomba Bianca*, had been awake for hours since retiring some minutes after midnight. He listened to the cacophony of snorts, whistles, grunts, moans, and recurrent flatulence emanating from Phil E. Stein, who slept below him, like an idling old gas engine coming apart.

Ibrahim had found a remnant of gunny outside the ship's kitchen and he had draped it over the curtains on the porthole to help keep out the omnipresent daylight. They were nearing Vest Spitsbergen harbor, and only passing clouds, not the earth's rotation, could darken the sky. But the clouds had been occasional since the storm, and in spite of curtains and burlap, and even eyes tightly shut, the light intruded.

His eyes were not closed. They shifted, counting rivets on the ceiling. He thought in Bantu, the kind spoken by the

Wahadimu aborigines of Zanzibar, of whom he was one. The word *tu'ntu* wound through the interstices of his mind. *Serious trouble.* But it meant more than that. It was its inchoate spirit gathering in the culverts of an underworld, rising on squamous wings whose enormous span could cast a shadow on an entire nation, a darkness that endured and settled in the soul.

He had met Phil E. Stein months back in Dar, at an international congress of transnational corporations, or the newest imperialism. Ibrahim was a professor of anthropology at the university in Dar. He had been a one-man air force in Zanzibar's January Revolution, flying an old C-47 with only one working engine. He had also fought the Portuguese across the border in Mozambique, and in place of the bones crushed by scared men with special tools, he had two plates of Essen steel in his legs. Dr. Stein, the Third World's friend, had recruited him to the Good Cause. Through Abraham, however, he had learned of Operation Ziggurat. He had learned that he was regarded by its agents, including Dr. Stein, as a dumb nigger. Nigger had only dictionary meaning to him, but it was ample enough to make him understand how his outrage against injustice was being used. Trading one outrage for another, he had gone with Abraham. But Abraham had been weakened and *tu'ntu* was beating big wings on the air. Ibrahim thought: *Kidole kirefu kinaonesa — The long finger is pointing.* The long finger was pointing at him.

He listened to Phil E. Stein's combustive sleep. The sounds formed a pattern that repeated, suggesting, notwithstanding all the tumult, a state of deep unconsciousness. He rose from his berth and came down stepping sideways on the rungs of the ladder to gain more surface for his bare feet. On the floor, he paused for a moment and stared at Stein, who lay chugging on his back, his mouth sucking on paps of air.

Ibrahim reached for the jacket of his outsized Polish suit.

He turned it inside out, including the sleeves. In each of the sleeves was a zipper, a ten-inch slot on the heavy lining. It opened on a kind of pouch made of the hide of the pygmy antelope that inhabited the Zanzibar *wanda*, the bush-covered coral lands. Ibrahim's mother had sewn the pouches in his sleeves with the hollow needle of the wambatu palm. One of them contained a packet of several of these needles and two dowellike lengths of wood of slightly different diameters worked from the stem of a papyrus plant. They, too, were hollow. The other pouch held a Webley .455 automatic.

He removed the papyrus stems and the palm needles. One of the lengths of the yellowish wood, which was about as long and as wide as a Romeo y Julieta, was sealed on both ends. It was as smooth and as polished as finished platinum. The other, into which the first piece fit as neatly as a piston, was partially closed on one end, where it had a nib that accepted the wambatu needle. At the other opening was a circumferential lip and two carved indentations for the fore- and middle-fingers.

Ibrahim withdrew one of the needles. It was thinner and longer than an ordinary needle, and thinner than a human hair was the natural channel that ran through it. It was greenish brown, and like the others, it had been treated with palm resin to give it a magnificent stiffness. He inserted it in the nib. The device, of course, was a syringe, far better than the commercial varieties in that it was an esthetic piece of workmanship and was unbreakable, although designed to serve one purpose only. Ibrahim, as had many others who had fought the Portuguese, had made it himself for use on himself. Once, he was prepared to do so and he had learned exactly how from a comrade-physician. His legs had been crushed first.

Ibrahim drew back the piston-rod, filling the inner chamber with air. He moved toward Phil E. Stein and stood over him. He carefully lowered Stein's blanket, exposing his noisy chest. He fixed his eyes on a point about four inches to the left of Stein's right nipple. Then he dropped his gaze about an inch-and-a-half to the flesh-covered space between the sixth and seventh rib below the collar bone. Holding the syringe in his right hand, he palpated the spot with the other, lightly at first to gauge Stein's response, if any. There was none. The skin was carpeted with hair. He brushed it aside and felt the soft, fatty circle that shielded his target: the right ventricle of Phil E. Stein's heart.

Stein groaned. Ibrahim retreated sharply, though his feet remained planted firmly and his eyes pressed to the point. He recalled the instructions of the comrade-physician: Hold it as you would hold the wings of a butterfly; strike like a hammer. The needle would have to pass through a fortress of skin, fat, fiber, layers of muscle, membrane, veins, and nerves, and unless the arc of the thrust was perfect, it could crumble on bone or cartilage.

Ibrahim held it like a butterfly. He waited for Stein's chest to rise, to catch it at the instant of its fullest inflation. This, too, the comrade-physician had taught him. Let it come to you, he had said, in a collision of opposing forces. It is painless. Ibrahim let it come once, let it come twice. Stein opened his eyes.

"Huh?" he asked in a voice fogged with sleep.

Ibrahim let it come and struck like a hammer. Stein simply watched him dumbfoundedly, as Ibrahim plunged an embolus of air through the pericardial wall, driving the piston with all the power in his open left hand.

The embolus was propelled by a muscular contraction of the right ventricle. It lodged, as it had to, in the pulmonary artery, producing a coronary occlusion, and as a consequence, a massive myocardial infarction. Stein's blood could no longer receive the oxygen in his lungs. He gripped his chest. He felt a flash of pain that radiated into his arms, his neck, and his teeth. He looked up at Ibrahim as if he were about to ask him a question. He lost consciousness. A few strange sounds fell from his lips. Then he died of internal asphyxiation, the unspoken question graven on his eyes.

Ibrahim removed the syringe and examined the wound. It was invisible, no apparent puncture, not even a speck of blood. Only an intensive autopsy, including microscopic tissue study, could reveal the cause of death as murder. Ibrahim did not expect Stein's body to undergo such treatment. More likely, it would be weighted and discarded at sea. Not that he would have shied from the task had he thought otherwise. The time had come to act in self-defense, and there was no passion in his crime, no trace of vengeance. Phil E. Stein had been a stone in his path; the path had been cleared. He dressed, tidied, and stole down the hall to Zack Robertts.

When he awoke to a persistent knocking, Zack Robertts was in no mood to receive. He looked at his watch with a squinty eye. It was about three-thirty. He saw Vicky arched behind her knuckles on the other side of the door, but the knuckles seemed wrong. He dragged himself to the door and opened it. He was surprised to see Ibrahim, dressed as if he were on his way downtown, but he said nothing, letting him in.

"Mr. Robertts," Ibrahim said, sitting on a straightbacked chair where Zack Robertts had dropped his clothes, "unfortunately, but conveniently, Dr. Stein has suffered a fatal heart attack, and I am using this interlude before the event becomes known, to brief you regarding my intentions."

"I didn't even know he was sick." Zack Robertts's admiration for Ibrahim was growing as it had been since first they met. There was something majestic about this granitelike man that evoked the respect one reserves for the old and accomplished, although there was little difference in their ages, and if Ibrahim wished to flatten his clothes, Zack Robertts had no mind to complain.

"His sickness was that which we tried to quarantine, Mr. Robertts. As you must know, we are nearing Vest Spitsbergen, and I reckon we shall be there by so-called morning. If Abraham has not arranged for our rescue, we shall have to take matters in our own hands, Mr. Robertts. You and I. I, for one, have scarce hope that Abraham has in fact succeeded."

"I take it you think Miklos has lost the game completely."

"It appeared inevitable after the failure at Malmö." He paid no heed to Zack Robertts's identification of Abraham.

"They're all CIA, aren't they, Ibrahim? Everyone on this rotten boat, from Jean-Marie down."

"Some are. Some are not."

"Vicky?"

"A babe ... Miss Colt, you know better than I. The Swede is a hire-purchase marksman. Dr. Stein? Of course. Dr. Rahmani? I have only my strongest suspicions. Shiva Subrahmayan? A well-intentioned dupe. The Italian is a dupe of quite another sort. In the hands of the Palermo organization, who controls the captain and the crew, and who are in turn controlled through New York, and ultimately — under a quid pro quo contract — by your Central Intelligence Agency ... Have I forgotten anyone?"

"Tommy Kaneoka."

"The Japanese was a terrorist, who protested passionately. Of that, I am reasonably certain. As for his sincerity, Mr. Robertts, life has taught me to stand witness for only the simplest of truths ... But we must move straightaway to the substance of our meeting. Mr. Robertts, we must speak of our escape."

Zack Robertts barely noted this mention of escape. Thinking of Tommy, he had heard only the intonations of Ibrahim's speech, the highs and deep lows that he had brought to his English from the Bantu. He sat on the edge of the bed, and as Tommy faded, he pondered the one question for which he had found no reply.

"I understand the meaning of ziggurat," he said as if he were addressing someone endowed with omniscience. "To strip it of a poetry it doesn't deserve, I would describe it as a hysterical machination to turn men against men, rich against poor, in unspeakable violence. But what I cannot understand, Ibrahim, is why it was necessary to go this far, to jeopardize the world of the plotters themselves, unless the bomb they hope to put into the ice is somehow a dud . . . From what you tell me, I don't know if I will ever see Miklos again. I believe you're the only one who can answer this question, which haunts me."

"Mr. Robertts, you flatter one who does not merit. I, too, was a dupe, although I have no one but myself to blame. When I first heard the scheme explained by Dr. Stein in idealistic terms, I willingly subscribed. You see, I was also a 'terrorist,' call it what you will . . . in comfortable retirement, I dare say. It was not until my clandestine meetings with Mr. Brody, who *himself* had believed in the uncorrupted thesis, that I became convinced of the limits of terror."

Though he made no move, his body seemed to grow taut as if he were going to get up. But he remained in his place, shaking his head remorsefully.

"No, Mr. Robertts. This bomb is not a 'dud,' as you characterize it . . . We, that is, Mr. Brody and presumably the others, have been told that it can be rendered harmless by the very same means by which it can be exploded, by a coded radio signal, a counter-signal, if you will. But I no longer believe that; for aside from being a useless redundancy — the neutralization of something that could more easily have been neutral to start with — even if it were true, it would not alter the possibility that it can indeed be exploded, with all the consequences of which you are aware.

"So, I, too, have sought an answer to this question you pose. Mr. Robertts, I have none . . . I can only look back on my modest studies of anthropology. I can only reflect on the phenomenon of self-mutilation, the abuse of the human body to satisfy mystical needs that are never those that are given — a phenomenon common to *every* culture, in *every* age, Mr. Robertts.

"We Africans purposely raise scars on our flesh, as do Germans who engage in the art of fencing. Some American Indians, and other Mongoloid peoples, permanently remove the hair on their bodies, and what physical grief has been caused by the common corset! Natives of Oceania to this day deform their skulls, but it is often forgotten that this was a practice in France, too, well into the twentieth century. Need I mention the plugged lips of the Sara women of Central Africa, whom your Mr. Barnum in a regrettable error made famous as 'Ubangi'; or the stretched necks of the Padaung women of Burma, who drag their vertebrae up from their spine? The Amazons of legend removed their right breast; the Russian Skopsti severed their nipples in the name of the Christian religion. In parts of the Maghreb, one testicle is often cut out and the Catholic Church used to sanction total castration to gain a crop of high voices for the ecclesiastical chants. Think, Mr. Robertts, of what has been done and what continues to be done to the poor penis: stretched, perforated, incised to retain foreign objects, and throughout the so-called civilized world the questionable practice of circumcision is worshiped by Jews, championed by physicians, and cherished by the victims. In Africa, the abhorrent total clitoridectomy is all too common, and the dilation or the virtual sealing of the vagina, the elongation of the labia, and the suspension of rattling objects therefrom, these I have seen with my own eyes, and more; there is much more, but the rest I only vaguely remember, and I do not care to speak of torture.

"I wish to remind you, Mr. Robertts, of only that which passes with *favor* in this or that culture, in this or that time in a cycle. I reject explanations for such behavior that rest on hypotheses about cosmetic effects, religion, health, and what have you, although they may have validity to a certain superficial extent. But there is a reason infinitely more profound that eludes us. I cannot enter into that Western edifice built in the end on a foundation of Dr. Freud's theories of primal guilt — which lies so close to original sin. I can only accept the self-evident proposition that each culture is its own abuser — again, let us not speak of the abuse it may heap on others — and that the principle of self-mutilation can always and readily be extended to self-immolation, that is, individual or cultural suicide. I must also accept the proposition that, as human genes carry and transmit all of the inheritable traits, each member of a culture carries and transmits the totality of his cultural traits, which he begins to receive at his mother's breast from a light in her eyes that shone down through her mother, and so on, back to the start of time.

"So you see, Mr. Robertts, I have no answer to your question. As I said, my studies have been meager, and you have not tapped any source of wisdom."

They were both silent for many seconds. Then, Ibrahim slapped his thighs lightly, and spoke again.

"Mr. Robertts."

"Yes."

"We must speak of escape."

The escape plan was to overpower Olle to get a second gun (Ibrahim had only five rounds of ammunition in his Webley) and take Jean-Marie as a hostage. They had no illusions about the ransom value of Jean-Marie; the CIA would not blink before bloodshed to protect their investment, hostage and captors included, but they counted on a period of indecision on the part of the ship's crew in which the flight could ensue. It went without saying that Deborah would go with them, but Zack Robertts insisted on inviting Vicky, Shiva, and anyone else who wished to join them, a disarmed Olle, too. Ibrahim considered this a "sentimental encumbrance," but he did not oppose him. The moment in which they would strike would depend on when the opportunity arose, but the exit, of course, would have to take place at the docks of Vest Spitsbergen, which lay to the northeast less than two hours away. They agreed that Ibrahim would "discover" Phil E. Stein's death in the first hour, following which they expected much confusion and a great rush to bury him at sea before landing. Such fluid conditions would favor the attack.

They spoke at length of the details, with an eye on their synchronized watches. They conspired to establish tactical positions, discussing the signs they would wait for and devising signals between them. They shook hands.

But it was all to be aborted. Even before Phil E. Stein's sudden demise could be announced, the *Colomba Bianca* was intercepted.

At a quarter to five that morning, a commotion of hurried footsteps and shouting in Sicilian whipped through the halls of the ship. Ibrahim had been about to leave Zack Robertts, and at first they feared that Stein's body had been found prematurely. Zack Robertts spied from his doorway and saw the crew running topside, passing Ibrahim's closed room without glancing. He dressed quickly and followed, leaving his guest to move when he could.

Jean-Marie was already on deck when Zack Robertts arrived finding him forward on the starboard side. He was peering through high-powered binoculars at a trawler not two hundred yards in his range cutting a line in the sea perpendicular to the *Colomba Bianca's* course. The captain stood in a turret directly above them, he, too, fixed on the approaching craft with his binoculars. Jean-Marie looked at Zack Robertts obliquely without comment. He seemed puzzled by what he saw in his glasses.

With unaided eyes, Zack Robertts saw the horizontal cross common to all the flags of Scandinavia and he took it to be Norwegian. He could make out the figures of two men in topcoats and several sailors around them pressed on the rails near the prow. One of the men in civilian dress wore a peaked cap pulled tightly over his brow. He was tall but hunched over. The cap was familiar, but not the manner in which it was being worn. The other man was hatless and balding. His remaining hair was blowing out in two pointed tufts from the sides of his head. The insular profile of Svalbard was etched cleanly on the horizon.

By now, Ibrahim had reached them, and most everyone else was coming on deck behind him in various stages of attire. Ibrahim took a place near Zack Robertts, who was watching Jean-Marie's expression change from bewilderment, to surprise, and finally, to some sort of comprehension. He handed his glasses to Zack Robertts with an ugly smile and climbed the turret to speak to the captain.

Zack Robertts trained them on the trawler, which had halved the distance it had been at first sight of its approach on the choppy sea. The man in the cap, he could make out now, was Miklos Brody. His chin was down on his chest as if he were being frozen by the headwind.

Zack Robertts's heart thundered. He stared at the hatless man, whom he failed to recognize. He passed the binoculars to Ibrahim, whispering what he had seen without excessive caution, for which there no longer seemed any need. Ibrahim looked through them, allowing some time for the ship to draw nearer. Then he lowered them from his eyes and returned them.

"Mr. Robertts," he said, in his intonated way, "look again."

Magnification was hardly needed anymore, and even as Ibrahim spoke, Zack Robertts saw that something was awfully amiss. He swept the glasses to his eyes. There were two ropes tied under Miklos's arms, bunching his coat around his neck. The ropes led to a steel girder above him. They were being used as supports. Miklos's bowed head rocked with the motion of the sea. He was dead. The hatless man was waving to Jean-Marie. The sailors carried Suomi submachine guns.

Huntz Merriwether boarded the *Colomba Bianca* crossing a narrow bridge that had been extended to the Norwegian fishing trawler when it came alongside. He was greeted by Jean-Marie, who presented the captain, while Fabrizio stood by utterly confounded. The reverend agent cast his eyes on Zack Robertts and Deborah Colt, whom he knew at once from the blowups of the ziggurat film. They stood together lacking only the Nepalese mask and loose summer clothing to complete a perfect reconstruction of the image he had fixed in his mind. The same grisly horror was frozen on their faces. They stared at Miklos Brody, whose suspended corpse buoyed on the tips of its toes like a marionette. She was sobbing and he held her closely, dropping the pretense that no longer had meaning. Huntz Merriwether shifted his eyes to Shiva and he smiled like an open wound; she turned away.

The Norwegian seamen, carrying their short-recoil Finnish weapons, came aboard. They were followed by another hatless man in a topcoat who joined Huntz Merriwether. He was introduced as the chief of the Oslo Station, Franklin Brown. He was brown. Huntz Merriwether asked for Phil E. Stein. Someone was sent to get him. The two agents withdrew with Jean-Marie and the captain to the ship's salon below.

Zack Robertts walked with Deborah around the deck to the portside under Vicky's and Shiva's gaze. Ibrahim watched, too. Muhammed Rahmani paced back and forth, crossing

Fabrizio, who was doing the same. When they were alone, Zack Robertts flared in anger at Miklos's titanic arrogance in having thought that a man alone could stop the CIA. Then he cried. He told her that all was not lost, that Ibrahim was armed, and that they would somehow escape. Deborah was skeptical. So was Zack Robertts, although he took her in his arms and kissed her to hide the lacerating doubt in his eyes. They heard running and shouting again, and he knew that Stein's body had been found. He kept this to himself. They looked out on the swallowing sea and wiped salty tears from each other's eyes.

After a while, one of the crew men came up to Zack Robertts and asked that he follow him inside. He whispered to Deborah to stay close to Ibrahim and he kissed the lobe of her ear. He was led into the salon, where he was left completely alone. He poured himself a whisky. It was not yet 6 A.M. The sun was everywhere. He sat in a soft chair and drank. Huntz Merriwether came into the room and he shook Zack Robertts's hand with the ziggurat hand.

"I imagine," he said, after giving his name and good wishes from the United States, "that you have a thousand questions to ask me."

He shook his head no; he was thinking of Miklos and his head was down, and as he shook it, it swelled with the blood of a charging bull.

Standing over Zack Robertts, Huntz Merriwether put his hands in his pockets and caved his chest. "Let me help you," he said.

"Let me help *you*," Zack Robertts erupted sensing his base intentions and standing siege to the revulsion he felt toward this man. "I think you're the one with the thousand questions. Well, the answer is yes. To all of them . . . I'll cut it short. I know what ziggurat means. The whole affair. From Genesis Eleven to the Mafia. I've got it all down on paper. In a safe in my lawyer's office in New York. And if anything happens to me or the others, the *Times* gets it first."

Zack Robertts could barely believe that that patently impossible wish had emerged from his own mouth. But Huntz Merriwether convulsed in a moment of panic, which made it worthwhile. Then, however, he curled his lip in the poor-sport manner of one who has been the butt of a humiliating joke.

"How did you transmit these sensational papers, Mr. Robertts? By pigeon? A floating bottle?"

He shook his head again as before. "Why did you do that to Miklos? . . . Why did you do that?" It was a senseless appeal, and he knew it; words, as they had always done, were failing him.

"Ah, so you do have questions, after all. Treachery must be punished . . . treacherously. But there are more, I'm sure. For example: What is Huntz Merriwether going to do with Deborah Colt?" He smiled lewdly. "An interesting question, that one. Then there's you, Mr. Robertts. I suspect you may be wondering what I intend to do with you . . . I will speak to you frankly. In a sense, I must consider you a colleague, a fellow student of the Holy Bible. It may interest you to know that I hold a doctorate in divinity; my dissertation was in oriental studies. I am, or used to be, fluent in classical Hebrew and Aramaic. But you must speak frankly with me. I'm curious. What do you think of our modest reenactment of Genesis Eleven?"

"Frankly? Frankly, I'd use the term 'genocide.' But I'm accustomed to understatement." Once more, he regretted having spoken to him. He would surrender no more words.

"But you neglect the teleological dimension, and worse, you underestimate the omnipotence of the Omnipotent. The Almighty does not delegate His powers, which are inalienable. The works of mere men are necessarily His, and the new ziggurat is as much so as the old. It's true that Genesis Eleven comes *after* the Flood, although by one chapter only. But that is irrelevant tradition, and when one examines the Qumran documents, as I have, one observes that that was clearly an editorial convenience. What is important is Genesis *Twelve*, which follows *both* the ziggurat destruction *and* the Flood. I urge you to reread it. There you will find, in the very first verse, mind you, the Lord's call to Abraham — known then, of course, as Abram. And toward what purpose is Abraham called, Mr. Robertts? We are, as you know, told in verse two: '. . . I will make of thee a great nation . . .' "

Huntz Merriwether flung himself into a whirling, blasphemous exegesis of the entire thirteen chapters in which the Harranite nomad is transformed into the eternal monument of God's design of redemption for the world. He strolled like a peripatetic. He gestured with his pocketed hands, sparring with his groin. He genuflected one knee at a time in downward strokes that threw him off balance. He rocked with obscene devotions. He spoke of grandeur and malediction, of blessings and covenants; of Canaanites, Perizzites, Amorites, Zuzimites, and Sodomites; of ramskins and foreskins, of concubines and wickedness, and of the brimstone and fire that rained on the cities of the plains for want of ten righteous men.

Zack Robertts followed his peregrinations around the room, observing him with a pathologist's eye. He thought of O.N.A.N. and Ibrahim's theories of self-abuse. Once, he had talked with a black man afflicted with neurosyphilis in its tertiary, terminal stage. The man had been comely and stately, but his hair had gone white and come out in patches and he looked like a mangy sheep. He had been a presser in a Jewish tailor's shop. When the spirochetes had begun to worm into his brain, he had gone to the police claiming that the Jew was the presser and that the shop was his, and as time went by, he discovered in leaping successions that he was the mayor, the president of the United States, the pope, Jesus Christ, then God. When Zack Robertts had met him, in a hospital run by a state, he had learned to play an upright piano and compose his story in song. He sat on a throne in the sky and sang.

Zack Robertts looked for chancres on the mucous membranes inside Huntz Merriwether's haranguing mouth. He saw none. He looked for skin rashes, inflammation of the eyes, and a moth-eaten loss of hair. There were none. Only a spray of spit shot now and then from his mouth. Zack Robertts wished he knew more about disease, or a lot less.

When, at a certain moment in his discourse, Huntz Merriwether stood with his back to his prisoner spitting on a window on the sea, Zack Robertts rose quietly and walked out.

He went starboard looking for Deborah. Crates of supplies brought aboard from the trawler stood in his path. He stumbled and waded through them. Miklos's body had been unstrung. It lay at one end of the gangway that linked the two vessels, and at the other end, stuffed to the neck in a gunnysack was Phil E. Stein. No one had closed his eyes. Hands on both boats were preparing their disposal.

He saw Deborah being led across the bridge at gunpoint. She was preceded by Vicky and Shiva. He tried to run to her but was stopped at the gangway by two of the armed Norwegian seamen. He struggled with them briefly, then called to her as the other two women were being taken inside. She stopped and turned around. She stared at him with opening hands and shrugged her shoulders helplessly. A seaman on the other end took her arm, and as she continued to look back at Zack Robertts, he escorted her from view.

He attempted again to cross the bridge against the force of

the two men. He threw his full strength against them, burying his body and limbs in their flesh. Jean-Marie came up to them and shouted.

"Stop it, Zack! Or I'll order them to shoot!"

Zack Robertts had not seen Jean-Marie, but when he heard his voice, he froze, leaning against the armed men. He straightened himself and turned around to Jean-Marie.

"You are foolish!" Jean-Marie bellowed.

Zack Robertts stiffened his left hand. He swung it like a scythe against Jean-Marie's stomach. He could feel the wall of muscle collapse and take the shape of the edge of his chop. Jean-Marie made a sound like a paper bag full of air breaking. He doubled up, presenting his spinal column, the vertebrae poking through his jacket in a neat bow of ridges. Zack Robertts raised the blade of his right. He had a choice, depending on where on the curve he struck, of either killing him instantly or rendering him a lifelong paraplegic. But he allowed him instead to keel over and fall in a tormented pile at his feet.

The seamen were unsure of what to do. Jean-Marie lay writhing on the deck, trying to utter the words, "Kill him!" but producing only aspirant heaves. Zack Robertts succumbed to two immensely powerful arms that belonged to someone who lifted and dragged him away. It was Ibrahim. He whispered harshly as he pulled him several yards back behind a tower of crates.

"We are being taken away by the fishing boat. All of us except Jean-Marie, the Swede, and yourself. I will do my best."

Ibrahim relaxed his grip. Muhammed helped Jean-Marie to a deck chair. Huntz Merriwether appeared with the chief of the Oslo Station, Brown, and they huddled around him. When it seemed he would recover shortly, Huntz Merriwether drew Brown aside, and Brown, in turn, passed an order to one of the Norwegians. He motioned with his weapon to Ibrahim, Muhammed, and Fabrizio, who carried a canvas Gucci bag, to board the trawler. They obeyed.

Zack Robertts waved a farewell to Ibrahim Nkele. Huntz Merriwether and Brown crossed the gangway themselves. Huntz Merriwether avoided Zack Robertts's eyes as he passed him, but Zack Robertts did not notice. He did not even notice Huntz Merriwether until he got to the other side and he flicked his ziggurat hand for the dead bodies to be dropped into the strip of water between the trawler and the *Colomba Bianca*. They were. Swathed in iron chains, Miklos Brody and Phil E. Stein sank rapidly two miles to the Arctic Ocean floor blowing bubbles going down.

CHAPTER FIFTEEN

THE PALE ISLAND of Joannøya lay packed in ice between Svalbard and Franz Josef Land on the rim of the North Polar Sea. Willem Barents, Henry Hudson, Fridtjof Nansen, and Captain Peary and his black man, Matthew Henson, had been there, but few others. It was shaped like the Arctic primrose, one of the few flowers that flourished there when summer breathed life on the surface of the permafrost for less than a hundred days. Five major fjords formed the petals of its floral appearance and a nameless, moonish mountain at the center resembled the pistil from which the whorl might have unfolded.

Joannøya was nine square miles of tundra. It was granite and gneiss laded with crustaceous lichens, moss, and white spills from the ivory gulls, the wild geese, the puffins, and phalaropes that passed overhead. It was fossil-rich sediment plundered by the primordial ice and brought back from its several invasions of the southlands. But it had never seen a tree.

Sovereignty over Joannøya was the subject of a lasting, albeit dormant dispute between the kingdom of Norway and the Soviet Union. The Russians in the 1920s became a party to the multinational treaty establishing the Svalbard islands, Joannøya included, under Norwegian rule. The convention, however, stipulated that no part of this territory be used for military purposes, and when during the Second World War, this clause was violated, the Allies destroyed all installations and Stalin laid claim to Joannøya, which, he professed to believe, had strategic value. No one understood why, and the

Russians never told, but Stalin, as the CIA was later to discover, was right.

Joannøya sat on the submarine Lomonosov Ridge, which extended from the New Siberian Islands, in Asia, to northern Greenland, and thus the American continental shelf. The Lomonosov formed part of the system of vast underwater massifs that determined the inflow and outflow of the Arctic Ocean. Joannøya was directly in the path of an ice drift that crossed north of the Nansen ridge — a 4800-foot rise on the ocean floor dividing the Greenland and North Polar seas. It was here that the north polar waters rode out on the East Greenland current chilling the North Atlantic.

What twinkled Stalin's dark eye was unknown, but one effect of this ceaseless dynamic was that an object placed in the ice that bore on the coast of Joannøya would move in the time of one winter to a region near Cape Morris Jesup, the northernmost reach of Greenland. Such an object would lodge there, taken up by the mammoth Humboldt glacier in the compacting process that nourished the immense Greenland ice sheet. This ice sheet, or cap, contained in the valleys it buried to the tops of 10,000-foot mountains, hid hundreds of thousands of square miles, a colossus of solid, crystalline ice in a state of perpetual motion, driven by the force of cumulative pressures so great that all its air is squeezed out and the ice turns blue. Apart from relatively small deposits elsewhere of only local significance, the Greenland cap had all the ice of the northern world.

It was the great Nansen himself, with the cold in his evident bones and ice on his long mustaches, who went adrift on these currents in the memorable ship called the *Fram*. And it was Nansen in 1895 who gave Joannøya its name, remembering the voyage of the Icelandic *Viking*; remembering sailing by the midnight sun with she who would give her name to an island; remembering her in his arms in the first summer of their twenties, 1882.

Nansen had discovered the drift observing the movement of the wreckage of De Long's bid for the Pole. The American commander's ship, the *Jeanette*, had sunk near the New Siberian Islands and its remains had been sighted a year later off the coast of Greenland. Nansen rammed the very ice line that the *Jeanette* had sought vainly to escape, having designed the *Fram* to rise under lateral pressure to avoid being crushed. This innovation proved successful and enduring, and although Nansen was more in pursuit of oceanographic science than an imaginary point on the globe — the drifting vessel being his research base — in 1895 he set out from the *Fram* near Joannøya to sledge for the irresistible pole. Setting a record for his day, he came within three and a half latitudinal degrees of the mark, never to return again.

Since the Pole was nothing, a fancy drawn through ice that was constantly shifting, Nansen showed his wisdom in taking a professor's chair at Christiana, the old name for Oslo. From there, more than a decade later, he watched the toeless Captain Peary gain the polar brass ring, only to have it tarnish in his hands by Cook's claim of having been there the year before. Cook's journals were said to be inadequate and he was given a cold shoulder. Frostbitten Peary was given the coveted distinction, though he died unconvinced that everyone thought so. To this day the Pole cannot be tread on. Nansen, the scientist and statesman, was given the Nobel prize for peace, and with an irony that stung, the attentions of Josef Stalin and later the CIA.

The *Colomba Bianca* stood in shallow waters anchored among the floes off the northwest coast of Joannøya. Two days had gone by since the trawler had taken Deborah and the others away. And as the days had been nightless, they had also been sleepless for Zack Robertts, confined as he was to his room. He had been asked to compose a statement verifying all that he knew of the bomb, and when he refused,

Jean-Marie said never mind, that it was already done, signature and all. Zack Robertts knew that he was going to Joannøya to die. He stopped shaving.

It was a splendid day to die, if one had to, and the weariness in Zack Robertts's bones somehow absorbed all the fear. He had seen and known everything in this world that he could hope to without being blunted by too much repetition, and though he continued to ache for the best life could offer, which he decided was love and beauty and little else, he felt it no more or no less on this day than others.

The temperature in a place where it could drop to 80 degrees fahrenheit below zero in winter was in the low seventies on this the first day of summer. The ice and the snow were melting luxuriously making sounds like a brook on a mountain, and the eye-level sun lay sweat on his brow, which felt good. It was eleven in the morning. Eider ducks waddled on wet rocks that poked through the snow like coal. He could see the low, stumpy rise in the island's interior and he looked across a plain of golden primrose and poppy. There were no other elevations.

The ship had turned around pointing home, and he stood on the portside watching the crew lowering a skida on the cold water. This was a small craft made in Denmark, built on the principle of the *Fram*. It was twenty feet long and powered by an inboard engine that could drive it into the soft, summer ice averting the thundering clashes of floes.

The nuclear bomb, Menes-II, was already aboard the skida. It lay encapsuled in a kind of cradle, or coffin, which when placed in the east-west ice drift would float all the way to Greenland. It was a seaworthy container of clear plastic reinforced with steel bands, which was normally used to protect oceanographic instruments launched to study the sea. Zack Robertts thought of pharaohs and mummies and finally of the infant Moses in his watertight basket of bullrushes being placed among the reeds by the bank of the Nile. He wondered if the bomb in the cradle were yet another impiety out of Huntz Merriwether's bag of sin. Zack Robertts was calm; he was going to Dublin with Swift, where the heart can be torn no more by savage indignation. He was going everywhere.

Four of the Sicilians and one Norwegian who had remained behind boarded the skida and started the engine. It gargled diesel fuel and issued bursts of dirty-cotton smoke, scaring the ducks into flight. Olle went, too. He looked troubled. Jean-Marie turned his head briskly at Zack Robertts, who like the others descended the bars fixed to the side of the *Colomba Bianca*, leaping to the deck of the smaller craft. Jean-Marie, wearing two Nikon cameras around his neck, came last. The captain watched from his turret.

The skida, commanded by the Norwegian seaman, struck for the Joannøya shoreline, cutting thin sheets of ice like a scissors and shoving snow from its path, which bunched and fell away in folded white blankets. They were pursued by inquisitive birds and a long shadow.

In minutes, they were in the pack ice around one of the fjords and they seemed to be riding in an elaborate sled. The ice was hard enough to walk on and the skida slowed, then stopped, its propeller twirling in the water below.

On Jean-Marie's instructions, the four Sicilians lifted the bomb capsule to remove it from the boat. It was not heavy. Two of them could easily have done the job, even one, but when Jean-Marie mentioned that if the seal on the capsule were broken the bomb would automatically be detonated, they all got very busy, treating it like a grand piano coming down on the docks of Palermo. Jean-Marie went ashore, ordering Olle to follow, and he nodded again to Zack Robertts, who knew that applied to him, too. He was ready. He climbed onto the ice. He looked up at the sky, which was so profoundly blue he imagined he might see the stars at noon.

The Norwegian tended the craft. The Sicilians, moving behind Jean-Marie, carried the capsule, one man on each corner in pallbearer fashion, and they walked a mourner's gait. They seemed experienced. Zack Robertts followed them, and Olle dogged the rear of the procession.

Jean-Marie appeared to be looking for a suitable place to set the capsule into the Nansen drift, but in fact they were already in it and any point would do. They had only to lay it on the ice, where it would freeze over with the cover of the first snowfall, probably by mid-August, and be carried on to the Greenland cap.

They walked for a quarter of a mile, stomping boot prints in the ice in a cadence that made the wading phalaropes look up and protest in irreverent catcalls at the intruders. The air was motionless. The skida idled in the distance. Water gushed. The seven men trekked on the sheet-white surface in a formation that looked like a cross, their elongated shadows heightening the effect. Zack Robertts fell back to Olle's position to break the symmetry.

"*Hej, stor blomma*," he said, in his most practiced Swedish.

Olle looked away, plodding forward like a bear, not a flower.

They went on a little further over unchanging terrain, and at last Jean-Marie, muttering *merde*, circled back. He stopped where the red-necked phalaropes were bathing in a break in the ice that resembled curdled milk. The birds flew away. There, by a sugarloaf rock, he had the Sicilians lay the nuclear bomb to rest. The capsule sunk several inches into the ice. Menes-II, which could be seen in repose through the plastic dome, seemed in a state of hibernation, awaiting its God-awful season.

Jean-Marie took several photographs of the capsule by the rock. He shot from various angles and distances with both cameras, and whenever the Sicilians came into frame, they showed a well developed skill of turning their faces from the lens. Olle was not as clever and Jean-Marie had to tell him to look away. Zack Robertts knew that his was the only recognizable face Jean-Marie wanted on film, but he aped the subtle movements of the Sicilians, and when, pretending to give in, he allowed Jean-Marie to catch him ear-to-ear beside the bomb, it was only his ploy to pose with a stiff middle finger raised from a quick fist that covered a grin and his face. Jean-Marie failed to appreciate Zack Robertts's good nature, considering the circumstances, but he, as well as Zack Robertts, was aware that he had a document of sorts nonetheless.

Jean-Marie shoved the capsule with his foot. It slipped into the curdle and floated. It drifted. He took some more photographs. In a while, Menes-II was gone.

Zack Robertts began to feel cold. His turn was riding hard. A shiver galloped through his body. A fog was rolling in from the pole, gathering on the horizon the way sandstorms approach the desert. Jean-Marie shouted *"Alla barca, ragazzi!"* to the Sicilians and they headed for the boat, twenty yards away. He went up to Olle for a moment, passed him, and walked to the skida himself without looking back at Zack Robertts. Olle drew his gun.

Zack Robertts stood still, as Olle came toward him head low. The Magnum hung in his hand down to his knee. The fog swept closer bleaching the color of the sky. Olle turned to the boat. The Sicilians were already on it, helping Jean-Marie aboard. Jean-Marie brushed snow from his jacket and stared at the two figures on the ice. The Sicilians and the Norwegian did, too. Olle looked again at Zack Robertts. He pointed his weapon. Their eyes met.

Mist was arriving on a wind that blew granules of snow on both men. The sun looked like a white porcelain plate on a wall. Zack Robertts tried to think of the date — the month, the day, and the year. But all three escaped him.

"*Hör på!*" Olle said in a low but exclaiming voice.

Zack Robertts searched his eyes. He listened, as Olle had commanded.

"*När Jag skjuter, fall ner.*" Olle spoke softly now.

Fall ner. There was a word in that clause that he knew.

"*När Jag skjuter, fall ner,*" Olle repeated. "*Förstår du?*"

Fall. It was an unmistakable Swedish verb, and the underlying softness in Olle's tone was a mighty confirmation.

"*Förstår du?*"

Zack Robertts understood. "*Jag förstår,*" he replied.

Olle smiled through the night in his mouth. He fired one shot from the Magnum. Ice cracked at the sound. Zack Robertts fell. The mist swirled. Olle glanced at the skida. He could barely see Jean-Marie through the fog, but his hazy outline receded and disappeared. Olle tossed the gun near Zack Robertts sprawled prone on the ice.

"*Lycka till,*" Olle said, and he, too, disappeared.

The fog passed over Zack Robertts's body like a train. He hugged the ice until he thought he would stick to it. He heard the skida depart. When the sun came out, he opened his eyes, but still he did not move. He lay there for an hour, in which the feeling of freezing could no longer be differentiated from burning. In the same hour the *Colomba Bianca* set sail abandoning the skida to the Nansen drift, and when both boats were gone, Zack Robertts got up.

He was brittle, like a slab of frozen meat. His fingers were stiff, and he could only pick up the gun by using his hands like claws. He opened his ski-type jacket and exposed his bare chest to the sun, raising his face to the sky. He thawed, warmed. He stood erect and breathed deeply. He was alone, a supplicating figure on the vast expanse at the mercy of the niggardly gods. But his skin glowed back at the sun of its own force. Zack Robertts was alive; he had a little box of Swedish *tändstickor* matches in his pocket and six bullets in his gun. He slipped the Magnum in his belt and turned for the interior of Joannøya, following the call of the unnamed mountain.

He crossed the tundra, a spectacular bed of flowers that grew in whole rainbows of colors, huddled for self-protection. He imagined he would find shelter at the mountain, a cave, a base of operations. There would be much to do. It was only a mile or two away. He studied the vegetation as he walked on wet ground. He recognized many species of plants besides the prevailing primrose and poppy. There were yellow crocuses, juniper, and the prickly saxifrage with hanging berries fit to eat, and the oily seeds of both the poppy and the juniper were fine for fuel. There were cranberries and the island teemed with the edible black lichen, "rock tripe," swollen and crusty, but Zack Robertts, who had tasted raw monkey brains in Taiwan served from the freshly cracked skull, had none of the usual qualms about exotic foods. He saw packs of lemmings in their seasonal browns, the stunted Arctic hare, and birds by the many flockfuls. He would neither starve nor freeze — in the summer.

He searched for mushrooms at the base of woody shrubs, and he found them in abundance. He could easily identify the choice boletus and the brilliant amanitas, turning over with his boot the deadly "destroying angel" and the slightly less poisonous *muscaria*. In Baja California, where Deborah had bought Mexican dresses, they had watched peasants in the southern territory leach the toxic hallucinogen muscarine, but not entirely, and then eat the brick-red mushroom cap to obtain a pleasant high. He knew how to do this. He also knew the high. Zack Robertts knew a little about everything.

He was hungry. Ignoring the caveats of Aristotle, he drank melting snow that poured over a rock like a fountain, but he denied his appetite, driven by the demanding excitement of discovery. The mountain was shaped like a small volcano. It was black sedimentary rock worn smooth, and the absence of a distinctive peak gave it an appearance of being unimaginably old even by geological time. It was only about a thousand feet high and looked lower, and patches of snow near the top dripped continuously on its steep slopes like rain. There seemed to be no way to climb it unaided, nor any reason to do so.

Zack Robertts found his cave, selecting it from many he inspected. It was shallow and wide and faced the southwest, from where he could look out from the top of the world on a friendlier, more familiar direction. The bones and the antlers of a caribou lay inside. He did not disturb them. He removed his jacket, leaving it behind when he went out, the way people reserve seats in a theater or bring a personal touch to a new home.

He brimmed with brand-new energy. He decided that his first task would be to build an enormous outdoor fire, burning anything combustible to achieve temperatures high enough to ignite green plants. His aim was to create a constant, slowly smoldering bonfire evaporating plant moisture in a column of smoke reaching high in the sky. The frequency of aircraft passing directly overhead could not be very great, but neither was such an event unlikely, and sooner or later, by steady perserverence, someone would read his signal. There were still people who knew he was missing, if not alive — the von Schwarzwalds, for example — and he would never cease to hope that Ibrahim would somehow manage to flee with Deborah. Perhaps Olle would aid their cause. All things were possible in the sun. Ships would surely pass at sea and take note of his steaming pillar of distress, and it was not difficult at all to land a light plane on Joannøya. He had the whole of summer, and though cruelly brief in the Arctic, there would be six or seven weeks before the first flame-quenching snows.

He would be gone long before then, he felt sure. In the
meantime, he had only to keep his fire going and survive.

He gathered poppies and juniper by the root. He amassed
a hillock of grasses tearing them from the soil. The plants
and the ground they stood in were sopping wet, which facili-
tated removal, but he soon realized that with his bare hands
alone, he would have to spend many hours each day collect-
ing grass, and much of it was spiny. There was no real wood
from which to make even the most primitive tool, or for that
matter, to get his fire going the way he had hoped to. The
decay of seasons past was mulch, wettest of all; indeed, nothing was dry, not the highest of leaves, not a stone in the sun.

He worked from one until six, when his palms and fingers
were too bruised from rough blades of grass, and it was too
painful for him to straighten his back one more time. He ate
cranberries all afternoon, and after a while, he tried a black
lichen, plucking it from a rock. He knew it ought to be soaked
long before eating to dilute its acids, but lichens had been the
manna given by God to the wandering Hebrews, or so he had
once read, and he expected it to be palatable all the same, if
not uplifting. It was sour and unpleasantly crunchy, like
chewing eggshell. There were all kinds of manna, he supposed, but the gift in the desert was still a gift and it did not
have to rain down shelled and presoaked, as it does for the
Americans.

At six, he spread his plants on a table of rock hoping they
would dry somewhat during the sunlit "night." He would
build his fire tomorrow. He was exhausted and sluggish,
feeling an honest day's work had been done. He felt released
from anguish, the grip of the CIA, and the boundless malaise
that enveloped the world below him. He retired to his cave
with an armload of grass for a pillow and mattress. He
covered as much of it as he could with his jacket and slept.
He slept happy to be alive.

*

When he awoke, he saw that his watch had stopped and he could not get it started again, perhaps because it had lain too long on the ice. It read eight-fifteen, and while he was almost certain that he had slept more than two hours and less than fourteen, he had not the slightest indication of what time it might be in between. The sky was covered with a skin of dappled ermine, and he had already had a thick stubble on his face before going to his make-do bed. He took off his watch and celebrated its demise by hurling it against the wall of his cave, watching it splinter and fall among the caribou bones.

At the time, he felt that he had overcome yet another hindrance, though it was really the beginning of calamity. He had removed his watch as if it had been a shackle, and now he gave up an idea to construct a calendar of stones to count down the days of summer. Instead, he set out to make his big fire, which seemed the only work worthwhile, and after many incalculable hours, he succeeded in getting it right — a white sequoia of smoke. It rose on a damp pyre of hardly any flames, becoming clouds. He rejoiced and dropped into sleep once again.

During the next day, or rather, return to consciousness, he could no longer establish the exact date, and after three or four such episodes, in which he used the largest part of his wakefulness gathering grass and food beneath erratic skies, he became dull to the passage of time. He labored and slept under a sun that revolved around his head without end like a tilted ring of Saturn. There were still ways to tell time, and he knew them — by the always rakish angle of the solar disc, by a gnomon in the ground, by the rise and southing and phases of the moon. But he gave his attentions to his fire and his fire only, stopping now and then to listen to the cannon shots of distant floes crashing on the sea, or resting when the fogs raced by on express runs to the south.

Worse, he lost his sense of orientation not only in time, but in space. Running on a biological clock that had not been properly used in ten thousand years, and never on Joannøya, he overextended himself. He worked until he could not work and he slept until he could not sleep, and as he consumed the grasses closest to his cave, driven farther and farther afield, he found himself awakening less in his cave than in the field. He thought of moving the fire with him, but his thoughts were fleeting, unfixed to the points of reference he had yielded.

He lived like the first men who came down from trees in the morning, only there was no morning and no trees, and the wet ground drew on his strength as he lay there. His fire began to go out. As the distance increased between the fire and the supply of fuel, by that measure was his column of smoke diminished, and sometimes, returning from afar with an aching armful of grasses, he found only wisps on the pyre, demanding energetic stoking, which only kept him from his rounds on the plain. One day he forgot the fire and never thought of it again.

He had denuded the island of twenty-two acres of plant life, and where he had first unrooted grass from the soil, new grass was growing now. A crescent moon had turned full and had disappeared since his arrival on Joannøya. The weekly roundtrip polar flight between Moscow and Anchorage had passed at 40,000 feet above him eight times back and forth, making silent streams, then rivers in the sky. He had noted none of these events, not the jetstreams, the changes of the moon, or the new shoots of grass by his cave, which he had abandoned in the middle of July.

It seemed he had always been on Joannøya, and ever would be. He no longer contemplated either death or rescue. Like all the other living things that inhabited the island, he dwelled there, too, with only a little more self-consciousness.

He was malnourished, thinning, and fatigued; his new beard was striped with white and he had festering sores on his hands; sometimes, he felt cold, hunger, fever, and arthritic holds on his bones, but never longing or the abysmal darkness of wishes unfulfilled. Roaming the shores and flatlands of Joannøya with a stick from the caribou's frame, Zack Robertts knew peace.

He began to hunt the muscarine mushroom. He made slits in the cap in the hexagrammic pattern he had learned in Mexico and he percolated them on heated rocks. He flushed them in water and put them out to dry. He ate them, nibbling on the edges, and he rode on a phalarope's back who flapped its wings like hoofbeats. He felt love and saw beauty, and little else.

He heard planes overhead between sleeping but he never looked up. He carried the dried mushrooms in his pocket and he walked on the ice forever. It began to snow. He held a little boy by his hand so that he would not fall. The little boy was as thin as a caribou bone and he buried his head in the side of Zack Robertts's leg turning away from the wind. Zack Robertts was taking him home. They had frozen tears on their cheeks. They stopped by a break in the ice. The nuclear bomb was floating, stuck in a pool of black water. He told the little boy that he would have to find his way home by himself, that he was on his own now. He admitted to him that he did not know the way home. The little boy cried for a long time and then he said he understood and went away, skipping. Zack Robertts dragged the capsule onto the ice. He saw a plane landing and the hostess brought out a wheelchair. The hostess was Deborah Colt. He was happy that she had escaped, but he was too busy now. Huntz Merriwether whispered Hanumappa's secret in his ear, and he thought that was sporting of him, but he already knew it. Huntz Merriwether said that a prizefighter doesn't push for a knockout; he punches. Zack Robertts said I know. Billie Burke and Deborah Colt helped Lionel Barrymore into his wheelchair, and he began to roll over the ice, gaining speed. The blanket on his legs was covered with snow. His chest and his eyebrows were covered with snow. Billie Burke was wearing the blue-lace gown of the good witch and she waved her twinkling wand and Ibrahim appeared. They all ran toward Zack Robertts, Deborah, too. Huntz Merriwether handed Zack Robertts the Magnum, releasing the safety catch. Zack Robertts knew that if he eliminated the vacuum in the beryllium sphere, the bomb would produce only a fizzle yield, and the little boy might get home safely. He told Huntz Merriwether that if he touched the little boy, he would kill him. Huntz Merriwether said that he would not make any promises. Zack Robertts shot him twice with the Magnum, but Huntz Merriwether said that he would still not make any promises, and he went away. Lionel Barrymore and the others were coming closer, though there was a tremendous gap between the wheelchair traveling at high speed on the ice and the good witch, Ibrahim, and Deborah. Lionel Barrymore called to Zack Robertts in his falsetto, comic German voice. A cigarette dangled from his lips as his hands pumped the wheels of his chair. The cigarette was covered with snow. There was a plaid scarf around his neck, thrown over his shoulder. It was covered with snow. Zack Robertts pleaded with him to turn back. He said he was going to destroy the bomb. Lionel Barrymore told Zack Robertts not to worry, that if he had to destroy the bomb, then he had to. Zack Robertts said that sometimes people have to do *something* to put an end to human slaughter. But Lionel Barrymore was coughing and could not hear him. Zack Robertts shrugged and put his finger to the trigger. Lionel Barrymore slammed into him with his high-speed wheelchair, throwing them both into the snow. The phalaropes screamed. Zack Robertts still

purchase an airplane, a two-engine Bucher-Jungmann, which had cost 850,000 Swiss francs. Zack Robertts thanked him. Von Schwarzwald wept openly, though only Kerstin knew why, and when she tried to console him, he growled, "Shot op, bitch!"

Zack Robertts, to change the subject, asked if anyone knew what had happened to Vicky and Shiva. Ibrahim said that Vicky had gone off to Palermo with Fabrizio, but probably on orders from Jean-Marie, and that Shiva was in Geneva under medical observation; she was almost three months pregnant. Zack Robertts smiled.

Ibrahim insisted now that everyone try to sleep. They had to depart as quickly as possible, he said, for the worst was far from over. It could easily begin to snow again, closing off with everlasting finality the thin corridor of flying weather that remained. On the other hand, good weather would mean the earlier arrival of the CIA, which, he said, was already on their trail. Zack Robertts said that there was a larger problem still, and when asked what that might be, he replied, "Getting the little boy home." Only the good witch seemed to understand, but everyone pretended he had said nothing at all. Deborah stroked his brow until he closed his eyes. He felt her tender hands and little else.

In the morning the sun shone nakedly, but the temperature was falling. It had rained after it had snowed, and the snow was compacting, beginning to freeze. Ibrahim shoveled mightily, opening the way for the Bucher-Jungmann. He dripped sweat that steamed off his body like marsh gas. Kerstin helped him, her strong hands moving almost as swiftly as his. Deborah scraped frost from the aircraft's windows, and von Schwarzwald sat bundled in his wheelchair dropping smoked cigarettes in the snow like pebbles. Zack Robertts was too weak to assist anyone. He walked with the aid of his caribou bone and he wandered off, looking for Menes-II.

His mind felt as limpid as the Arctic air, and knowing the island better than anyone else in all the world, he returned on an unveering line to the pool of black water and saw the snow-covered capsule lying in sight of the plane. He brushed it clean with his hands, and exerting all of his diminished muscle, he stood it upright against a cluster of stones. He stared at it until light reflected broad on the plexiglass lashed out angrily at his eyes, forcing him to turn away as if the bomb were in communion with the powers of the sun. Indeed, there was a godlike arrogance that flared from the face of Menes-II, and Zack Robertts perceived at once that the weapon could neither be defused nor carried away to wherever their flight might take them. The reasons swam like tadpoles beneath his consciousness, as reason itself had been submerged in these weeks of unreserved surrender to nature's way. At this depth he recalled that the capsule could not be breached without setting off the bomb, and bringing it back on the Bucher-Jungmann, or dropping it someplace at sea, would be an even greater mistake. It could be detonated any place in the world, and God only knew what catastrophic consequence would ensue. Menes-II, he understood at the quick of his soul, had to be destroyed here on Joannøya — today.

He felt a chill. The sun was still whole in the singularly deep blue sky, but a flock of sheeplike clouds was heading its way. It would be colder soon, and they would all be gone. The orbital beam from above no longer struck the capsule sharply and he could look at the naked skin of the bomb, the belly with its dormant sphere. He felt for the Magnum — not that he contemplated sacrifice any more. There were real people on the island now, including himself, and he had begun to think conventionally, feeling a loss. He merely wanted to show the devil in Menes-II the power that could break the vacuum rendering it capable of only a fizzle yield. But Ibrahim had taken the gun from him, and he returned his hand to the caribou bone.

There had to be a way, he thought, to penetrate the sphere *after* they had taken to the skies. Tommy Kaneoka would know, and he wished he were here, believing that if he had not died he would be. What was it Tommy had said? No matter how sophisticated a system might be, it always had its own specific neutralizer, which was usually far simpler in design. Zack Robertts tried to think like Tommy Kaneoka; he tried to *be* Tommy Kaneoka, and he wrinkled up his face and he shook away an imaginary lick of hair and he winked one eye. He felt boyish and he stooped to pick up a handful of watery snow, shaping it to about the size of a tennis ball. He held it in his hands, as Tommy had done when he had built the cage for the plutonium core, and he made believe he was thinking in Japanese.

A cloud blocked the sun. A sheer cloak of warmth on his skin fell away. He put a finger in the pool of black water cracking a tissue of surface ice that had formed while he had been standing there. He looked up at the sky. The cloud had passed, but others were coming on, bringing a familiar drone on the wind: somewhere hidden among the clouds was an airplane. He looked at his snowball and hurled it at the nuclear bomb. It struck with a low thud and fell almost intact. Zack Robertts flushed. He knew how to break the vacuum in the beryllium sphere.

CHAPTER SIXTEEN

HE BEGAN TO BUILD A SNOWMAN. He made a ball for the base, another for the chest, and a third for the head. The snow became harder to work as the temperature continued to descend, but that only adrenalized his efforts, for he knew all the more so that his snowman would serve him faithfully. He shaped two oblongs for the arms.

The airplane humming in the patchy sky was not yet visible, but he saw the others searching for it with their eyes, and Ibrahim taxiing the Bucher-Jungmann to the middle of his runway so that it could not land. That would give Zack Robertts time, and he thanked Ibrahim silently. Deborah waved to Zack Robertts to return, but he continued to mold the snow with cold-bitten fingers, and she shouted his name and the words, "Come back!" as loudly as she could.

He made bulbous, rudimentary hands for his snowman, the right slightly outstretched, and because he wished to see beauty, he gave it a happy face with little stones for the eyes, the nose, and the turned-up line of its mouth. He buttoned the creature's suit. His snowman stood eye-to-eye with Menes-II, no more than a long arm away, smiling.

Suddenly, a four-place Cessna was circling above him like a vulture. It was as high, or as low, as the unnamed mountain, a thousand feet in the sky. Deborah had stopped calling. She was running toward him with Ibrahim, while Kerstin helped von Schwarzwald into the plane. Zack Robertts shot up his arm and urged them on.

"Hurry!" he called.

When they saw what he had done, they thought he was

mad, and Ibrahim stiffened, ready to drag him away. Zack Robertts backed off one step beyond Ibrahim's reach.

"Listen to me!" he implored. "I know how to destroy the bomb. There's no time to explain now. Just give me the gun!" The sweat of his labors was turning to ice on his skin.

Deborah pleaded with Zack Robertts to go back with them. There were tears in her eyes, and they were beginning to gel. Zack Robertts's eyes were on the black man, his hand extended, trembling.

"The gun, Ibrahim! The gun!"

Ibrahim looked at Deborah's tears and at Zack Robertts's skin. He turned his head to the coagulating sky and the carrion plane, and when he lowered his gaze, he saw the outstretched right hand of the snowman. His black eyes glowed.

"Mr. Robertts," he said in his Bantu voice, "I reckon you know more about nuclear weapons than I do. Do you really think it will work?"

Zack Robertts smiled. "Can't miss," he said.

Ibrahim gave him the Magnum. Deborah raised her hands as if to stop him, but Zack Robertts clutched them in his. He told her to hurry to the plane with Ibrahim and he promised he would join her in a minute or two. "I know what I'm doing," he said in the most reasonable way he knew. She looked into his eyes wanting to embrace him, but Ibrahim took her arm. "Good luck, my fellow," he said to Zack Robertts, and they ran to the waiting aircraft, Deborah turning her head whenever she could.

Zack Robertts, holding the gun between his legs, tore strips of cloth from his clothing, which was rapidly becoming brittle with freezing perspiration. He wrapped the Magnum loosely with the fabric and set it in the snowman's outstretched hand. The Cessna made a pass overhead, but he knew it was far too high above him for anyone to detect what he was up to, or even that the capsule stood exposed. He aimed the muzzle of the gun at the belly of the bomb, then, scooping fresh wet snow from the ground, he gave the snowman's right hand one fat finger, which he packed tightly against the trigger, leaving an empty space behind it. He adjusted the cloth around the body of the gun and lay more loose snow above it to conceal the weapon in the snowman's hand. He took one last admiring look at his creation.

"Shoot straight," he told the snowman, and hobbled to the Bucher-Jungmann as fast as his caribou bone would allow.

Ibrahim had his engines turning hard when Zack Robertts climbed aboard the plane fighting a backwash of churned snow. His hands were stiff with the cold, and he held them spread, as if they were webbed, while Deborah fastened him to his seat. The wheels of the Bucher-Jungmann strained against its purchase on the ground, the fuselage leaning forward like a leashed dog. Then the plane rolled down the narrow runway, lifting itself on the decks of rushing air, folding its wheels serenely as it soared. Everyone was silent in the cabin. Zack Robertts watched the thermometer on the navigational instruments panel, the indicator dipping below a ground temperature marked in red for freezing.

Gaining altitude, they could see the Cessna making its approach for a landing, but it changed course abruptly at about 800 feet, and it seemed to be pointing for their starboard side. In a few moments it was less than fifty yards off the tip of the Bucher-Jungmann's right wing, and someone was leaning from the Cessna firing a gun. Ibrahim made for a hole in the sky. The Cessna passed below them, and the Bucher-Jungmann hid above the clouds, flying straight into the sun. Zack Robertts had caught a glimpse of two of the boys from Palermo in the Cessna. He had also seen Huntz Merriwether and Jean-Marie.

After a while, making 200 knots, a mile above the ground and climbing still, they knew they were safely on their way. They settled in their seats. Von Schwarzwald, unusually subdued, smoked a cigarette examining the lighted end, and Kerstin stared straight ahead in her unseeing way. Ibrahim, trimming his turn and bank indicator, slipped into the ample confines of his Polish suit. Deborah sat beside Zack Robertts, and Zack Robertts, in softly spoken words, told them all about the Arctic snowman who was bound in a covenant with nature to undo Menes-II.

"As you all know," he said at one point in his tale, "water expands when it turns to ice . . ."

The snowman smiled at the nuclear bomb. But one stone eye had been expelled from his head, and a crack was forming on his face that ran down to a corner of his mouth, giving him a taunting, sinister look. He was hardening, swelling, turning to ice.

The boys from Palermo were standing beside the Cessna, watching the clouds that were blackening like chimneys darken the sun's domain. Unaccustomed to subfreezing cold, they shivered even inside their Arctic clothes, but fear played its part, too. They smashed their fists against their hands and stamped their feet, lamenting that Sicilians were born with "thin blood." The one who could fly the plane cursed his skill; the one who could not cursed Huntz Merriwether's mother.

Huntz Merriwether and Jean-Marie had set out in opposite directions, scouting, and they were no longer in sight of each other. Having had radio access to the very latest meteorological reports, they were quite aware of the threatening weather and knew that they ought not remain on the island for very long. They did not expect to find anything of significance, but they estimated that they had an hour at least to look around, and though the main tasks lay ahead — those of silencing Zack Robertts and his friends and reconfirming the viability of Menes-II — it seemed prudent to do so.

For his part, Huntz Merriwether found the Arctic divinely inspiring and he had understood from the moment he had set foot on Joannøya the timeless call of the north. There was something entirely sensual in the cold loneliness of it all and the assault of the elements on one's skin, like being massaged by the gods. He had felt gnashingly thwarted by the dumb nigger's ploy that had kept them from landing and the failure of the wop with the gun to knock the Bucher-Jungmann out of the air, but now, being rubbed all over by a race of giants, he had an overwhelming desire to one day stand naked on the Pole. He went behind an outgrowth of rock.

The one-eyed snowman lost four stones from the side of his mouth. He was not smiling anymore. He resembled a man in the grip of a stroke. He was scarred and he seemed vicious, and his turgid finger tightened on the trigger of the Magnum buried in his hand. The trigger moved.

Jean-Marie saw the snowman from the rear. He approached it slowly, curiously. The capsule came into view. He ran to it. When he saw the snowman's fiendishly twisted face, a fright, then rage, rattled his little frame. He was overcome with insult, and he felt a strong compulsion to throw the offensive image to the ground. Yet he had a sense of some sort of diabolical trick, and he stood motionless touching neither the snowman nor Menes-II. His eyes sought out Huntz Merriwether, wanting him to see what he had found. Unable to spot the tall, slouching figure, he called to the boys from Palermo. They hurried toward him.

"Huntz!" Jean-Marie cried on the polar wind.

The fat finger of the snowman pressed harder on the unseen trigger, sending it deeper into the void behind it.

Huntz Merriwether stood behind the large rock formation,

feeling an heroic stimulus. He had heard Jean-Marie shout his name, but had not answered. A curve of the sun had broken through casting a spectacular display of colored lights, heightening every effect, and there was nothing on earth that he would let spoil it.

"Huntz!" Jean-Marie's call went out again with spine-shattering urgency.

The boys from Palermo were terrified.

The snowman's finger twitched.

"Huntz!"

There were rainbows around Huntz Merriwether. "I'M COMING!" he shrieked.

An enormous wet black cloud covered the sun, all but quenching it. The temperature plummeted several degrees. The snowman fired into the capsule. The bullet passed through the beryllium sphere, breaking the vacuum. The entire assembly collapsed on the plutonium core, initiating a chain reaction. There was a blinding flash of light. It could be seen as far south as the Bucher-Jungmann in the sky. Zack Robertts knew he might never find the way home, but in that moment of light he felt love and saw beauty and *nothing* else. Part of the island of Joannøya vanished in an atomic fireball. The boys from Palermo vanished in an atomic fireball. Jean-Marie vanished in an atomic fireball. Huntz Merriwether vanished in a rainbow.

But that was all.